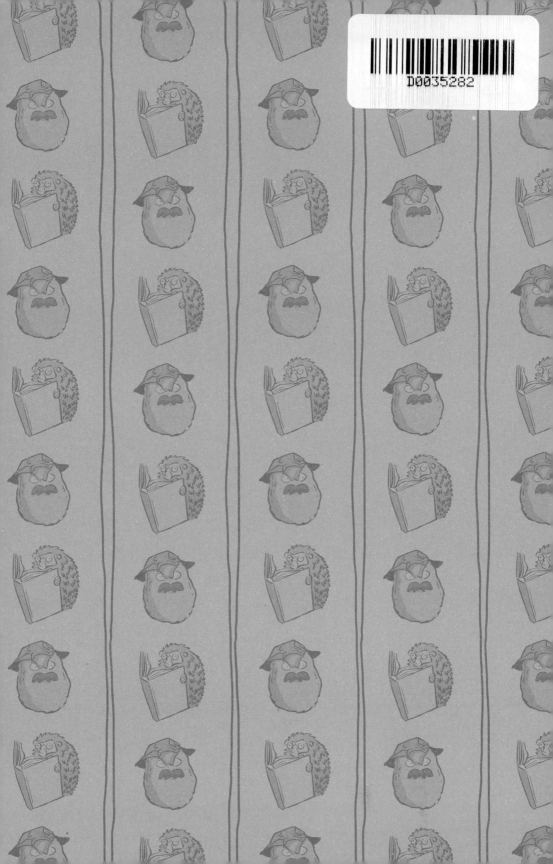

Plants vs. Zombies

vs.

Zombies ™

WAR AND PEAS

Written by **PAUL TOBIN**

Pencils by **BRIAN CHURILLA**

Inks by BRIAN CHURILLA and
CHRISTIANNE GILLENARDO-GOUDREAU

Colors by **HEATHER BRECKEL**

Letters by **STEVE DUTRO**

Cover by **RON CHAN**

Bonus Story Art by **ALEXANDRIA LAND**

DARK HORSE BOOKS

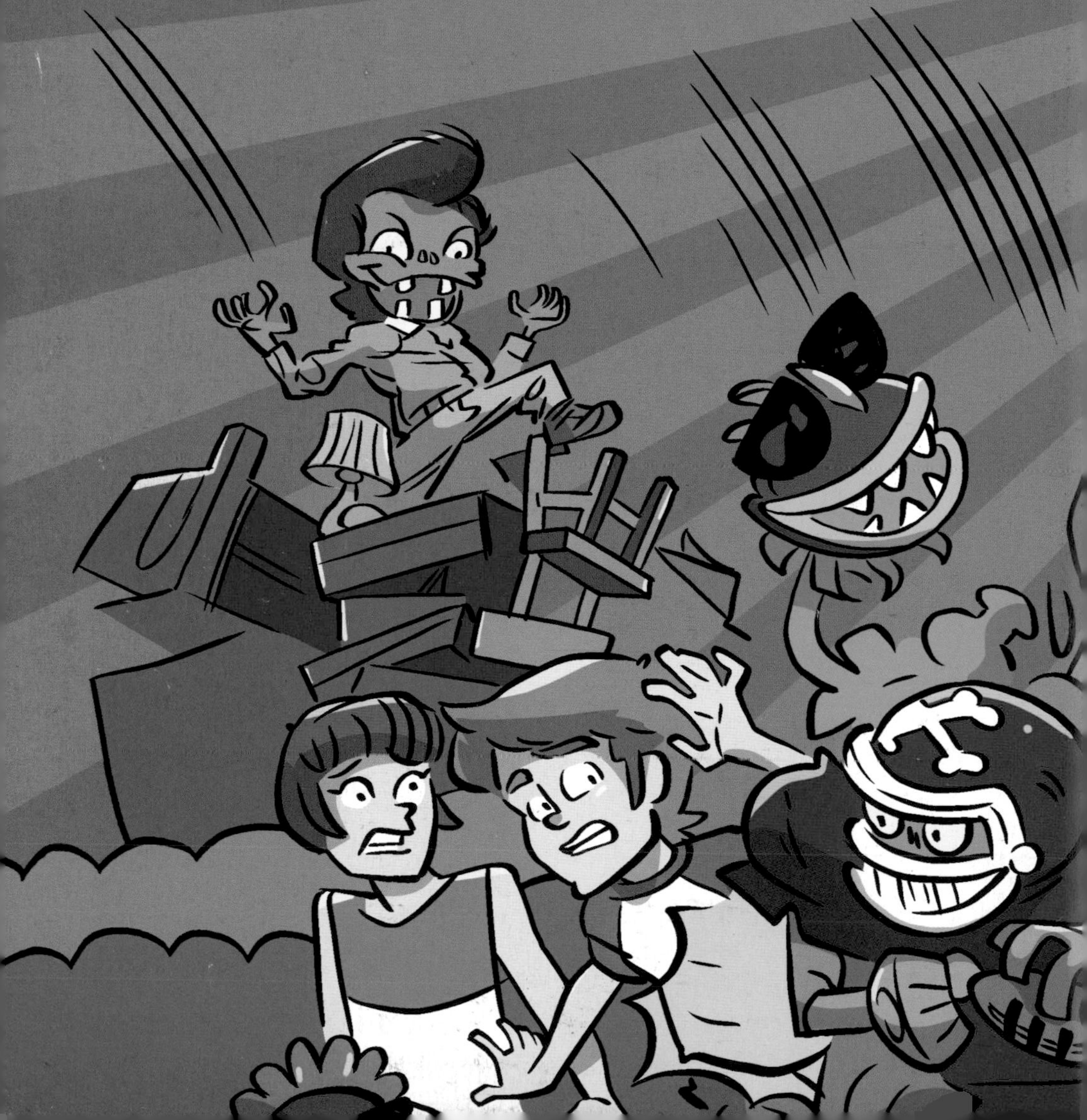

PLANTS VS. ZOMBIES™

WAR AND PEAS

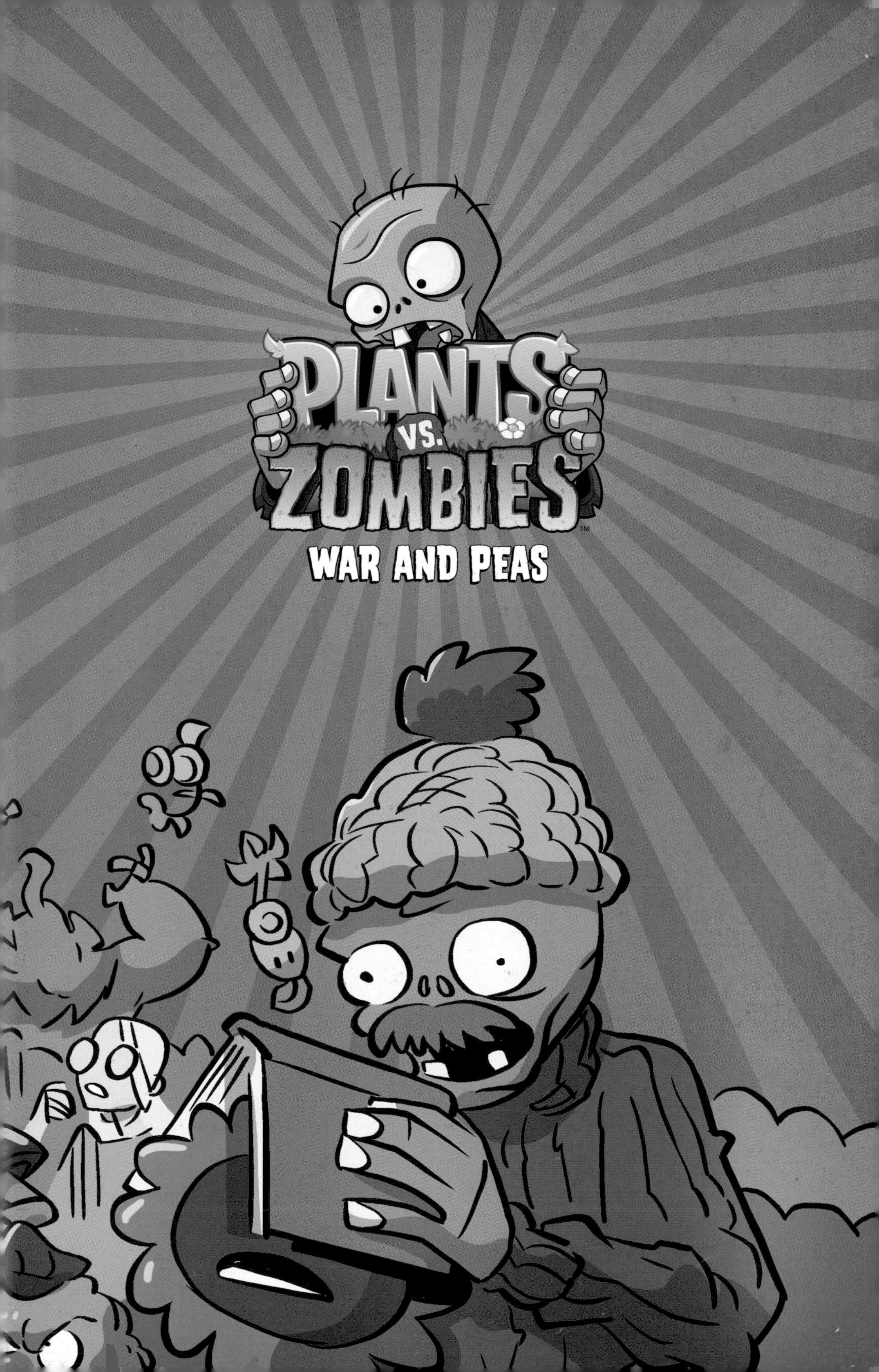

Publisher **MIKE RICHARDSON**
Senior Editor **PHILIP R. SIMON**
Associate Editor **MEGAN WALKER**
Designer **BRENNAN THOME**
Digital Art Technician **CHRISTIANNE GILLENARDO-GOUDREAU**

Special thanks to Alexandria Land, A.J. Rathbun, Kristen Star, and everyone at PopCap Games.

First Edition: October 2018
ISBN 978-1-50670-677-1

10 9 8 7 6 5 4 3 2
Printed in China

DarkHorse.com
PopCap.com

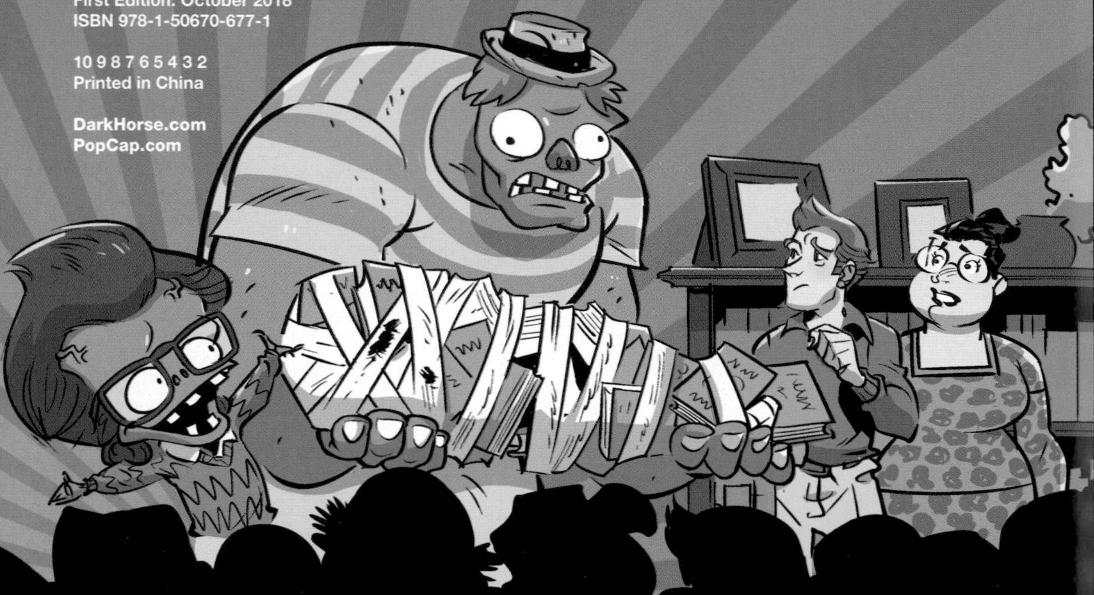

No plants were harmed in the making of this graphic novel. However, all of the plants, zombies, Nate, Patrice, and Crazy Dave had their library privileges revoked until spring break, which is really too bad because books are cool any time of year! Also, there are now entirely too many clubs in Neighborville! There's even a "There's Too Many Clubs" club!

PLANTS vs. ZOMBIES: WAR AND PEAS | Published by Dark Horse Books, a division of Dark Horse Comics LLC, 10956 SE Main Street, Milwaukie, OR 97222 | To find a comics shop in your area, visit comicshoplocator.com |

Library of Congress Cataloging-in-Publication Data

Names: Tobin, Paul, 1965- writer. | Churilla, Brian, artist. | Breckle, Heather, colourist. | Dutro, Steve, letterer. | Chan, Ron, artist. | Land, Alexandria, artist.
Title: Plants vs. zombies. War and peas / written by Paul Tobin ; art by Brian Churilla ; colors by Heather Breckle ; letters by Steve Dutro ;

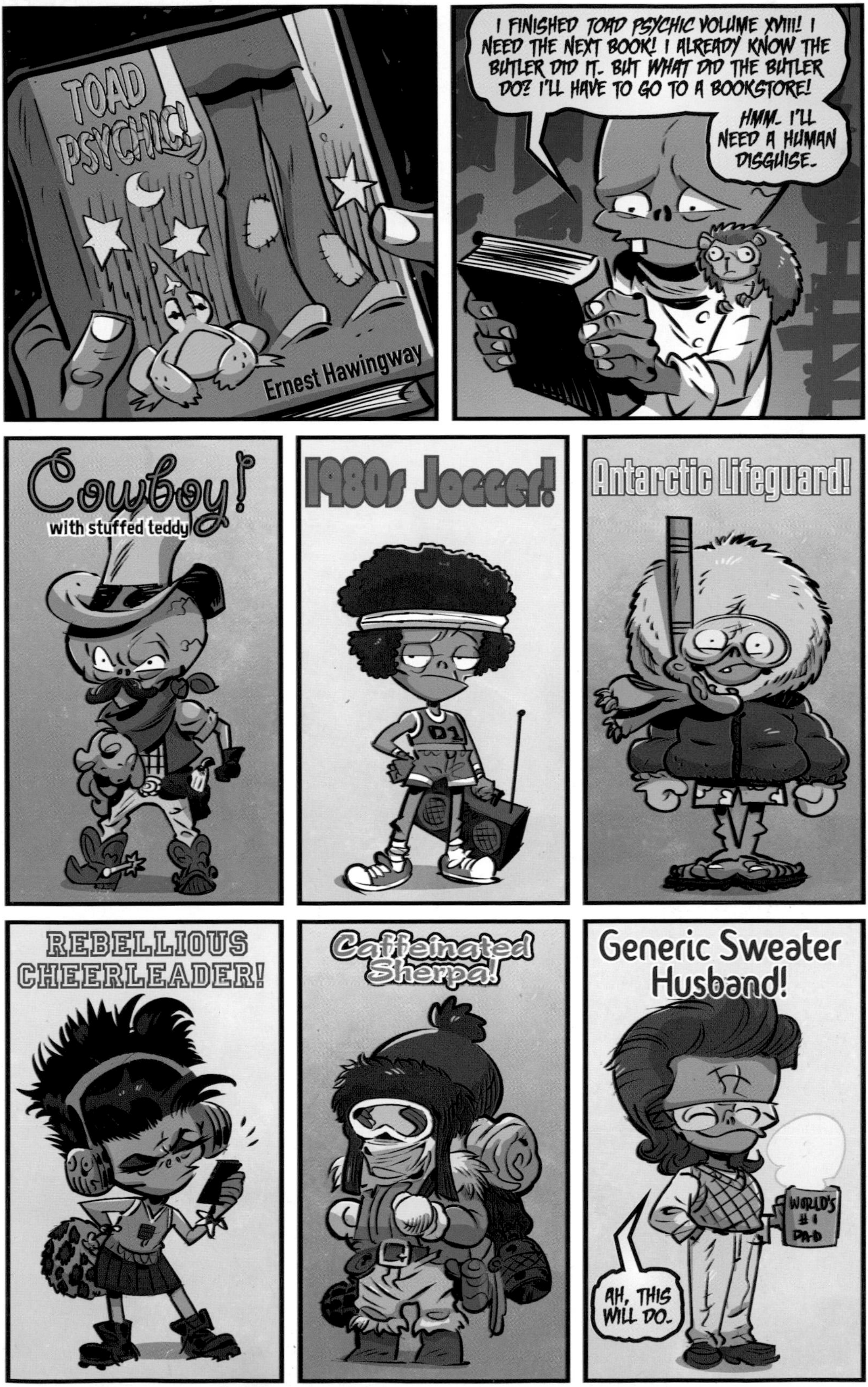
TOAD PSYCHIC!
Ernest Hawingway
I FINISHED TOAD PSYCHIC VOLUME XVIII! I NEED THE NEXT BOOK! I ALREADY KNOW THE BUTLER DID IT. BUT WHAT DID THE BUTLER DO? I'LL HAVE TO GO TO A BOOKSTORE!
HMM. I'LL NEED A HUMAN DISGUISE.
Cowboy!
with stuffed teddy
1980s Jogger!
D1
Antarctic Lifeguard!
REBELLIOUS CHEERLEADER!
Caffeinated Sherpa!
Generic Sweater Husband!
WORLD'S #1 DAD
AH, THIS WILL DO.

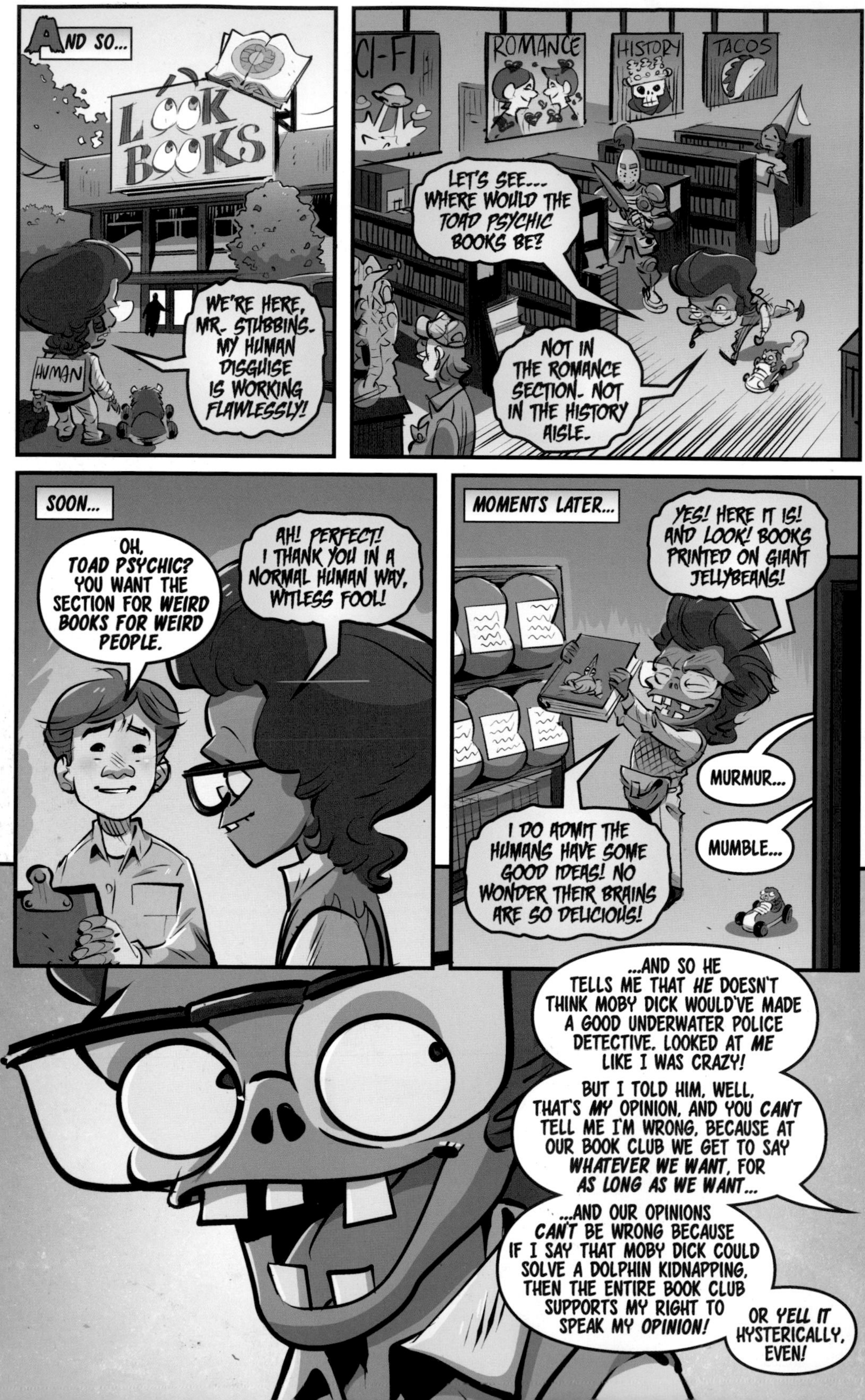
AND SO...
LOOK BOOKS
HUMAN
WE'RE HERE, MR. STUBBINS. MY HUMAN DISGUISE IS WORKING FLAWLESSLY!
CI-FI
ROMANCE
HISTORY
TACOS
LET'S SEE... WHERE WOULD THE TOAD PSYCHIC BOOKS BE?
NOT IN THE ROMANCE SECTION. NOT IN THE HISTORY AISLE.
SOON...
OH, TOAD PSYCHIC? YOU WANT THE SECTION FOR WEIRD BOOKS FOR WEIRD PEOPLE.
AH! PERFECT! I THANK YOU IN A NORMAL HUMAN WAY, WITLESS FOOL!
MOMENTS LATER...
YES! HERE IT IS! AND LOOK! BOOKS PRINTED ON GIANT JELLYBEANS!
I DO ADMIT THE HUMANS HAVE SOME GOOD IDEAS! NO WONDER THEIR BRAINS ARE SO DELICIOUS!
MURMUR...
MUMBLE...
...AND SO HE TELLS ME THAT HE DOESN'T THINK MOBY DICK WOULD'VE MADE A GOOD UNDERWATER POLICE DETECTIVE. LOOKED AT ME LIKE I WAS CRAZY!
BUT I TOLD HIM, WELL, THAT'S MY OPINION, AND YOU CAN'T TELL ME I'M WRONG, BECAUSE AT OUR BOOK CLUB WE GET TO SAY WHATEVER WE WANT, FOR AS LONG AS WE WANT...
...AND OUR OPINIONS CAN'T BE WRONG BECAUSE IF I SAY THAT MOBY DICK COULD SOLVE A DOLPHIN KIDNAPPING, THEN THE ENTIRE BOOK CLUB SUPPORTS MY RIGHT TO SPEAK MY OPINION!
OR YELL IT HYSTERICALLY, EVEN!

EXCUSE ME, FELLOW--BUT INFERIOR--HUMANS. DID YOU SAY THAT IN A BOOK CLUB, YOU GET TO SPEAK YOUR OPINIONS... AND NO ONE CAN STOP YOU?

YES. THAT'S RIGHT.

SORT OF.

WELL, I'VE ALWAYS STRONGLY FELT THAT MY OPINIONS MUST BE KNOWN.

IN FACT, I HAVE THIS EVER-BLOSSOMING LIST OF "MY OPINIONS THAT MUST BE KNOWN," CURRENTLY NUMBERING 782,833 LINE ITEMS.

BECAUSE OF THIS, I WILL BE...

...JOINING YOUR BOOK CLUB.

OH. GOOD.

YAY?

AND SO...

THIS SATURDAY, MR. STUBBINS, YOU AND I WILL BE ATTENDING A BOOK CLUB MEETING WITH SEVERAL HUMANS.

WE HAVE TO REMEMBER THAT, ALTHOUGH THEIR ACTIVE BRAINS WOULD BE SO DELICIOUS...

...WE CANNOT EAT THEM.

AT LEAST, NOT AT FIRST.

SQUICK!

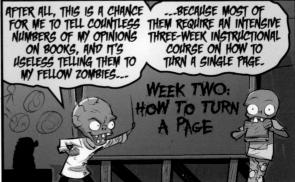

AFTER ALL, THIS IS A CHANCE FOR ME TO TELL COUNTLESS NUMBERS OF MY OPINIONS ON BOOKS, AND IT'S USELESS TELLING THEM TO MY FELLOW ZOMBIES...

...BECAUSE MOST OF THEM REQUIRE AN INTENSIVE THREE-WEEK INSTRUCTIONAL COURSE ON HOW TO TURN A SINGLE PAGE.

WEEK TWO: HOW TO TURN A PAGE

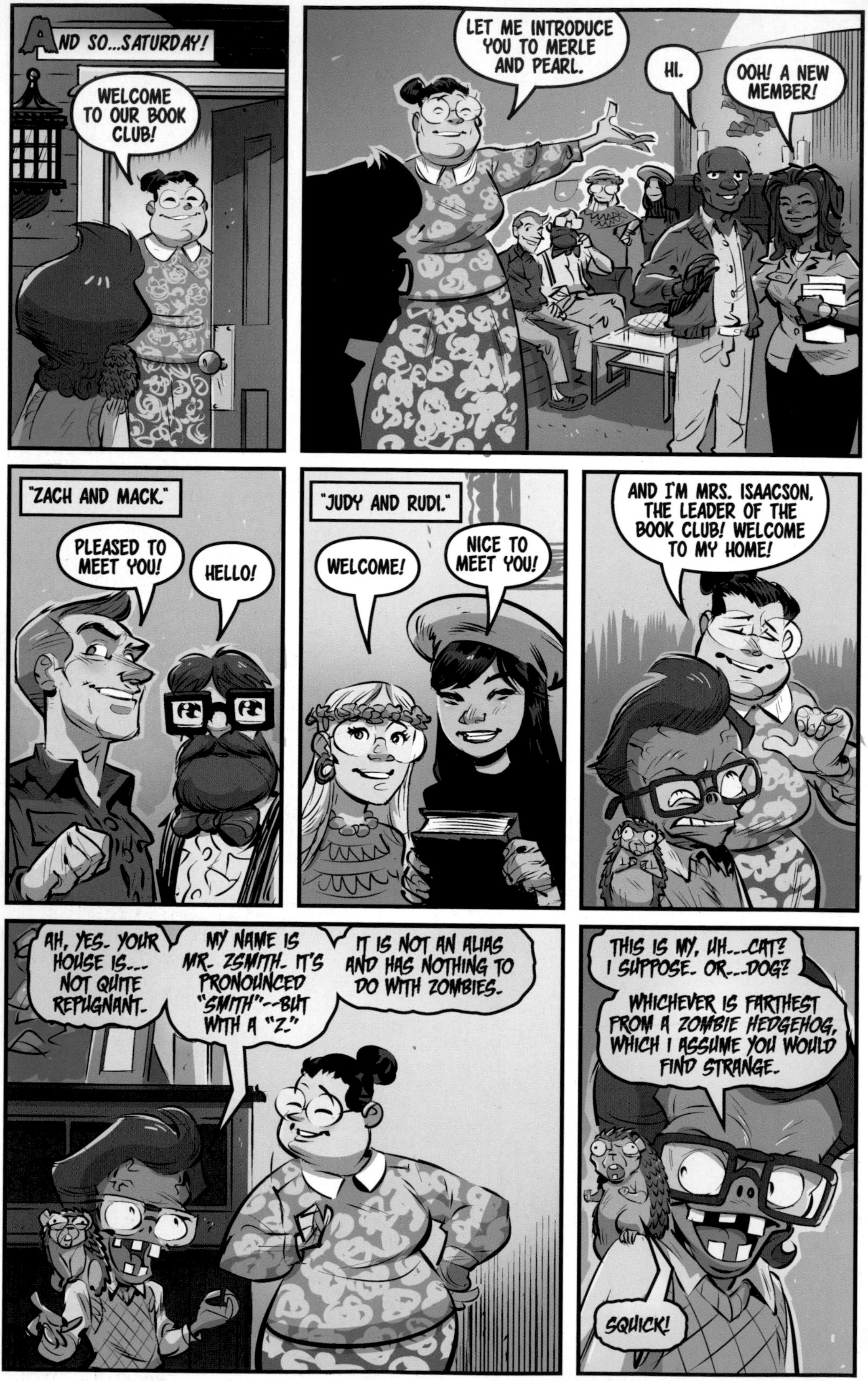
AND SO...SATURDAY!
WELCOME TO OUR BOOK CLUB!
LET ME INTRODUCE YOU TO MERLE AND PEARL.
HI.
OOH! A NEW MEMBER!
"ZACH AND MACK."
PLEASED TO MEET YOU!
HELLO!
"JUDY AND RUDI."
WELCOME!
NICE TO MEET YOU!
AND I'M MRS. ISAACSON, THE LEADER OF THE BOOK CLUB! WELCOME TO MY HOME!
AH, YES. YOUR HOUSE IS... NOT QUITE REPUGNANT.
MY NAME IS MR. ZSMITH. IT'S PRONOUNCED "SMITH"--BUT WITH A "Z."
IT IS NOT AN ALIAS AND HAS NOTHING TO DO WITH ZOMBIES.
THIS IS MY, UH...CAT? I SUPPOSE. OR...DOG?
WHICHEVER IS FARTHEST FROM A ZOMBIE HEDGEHOG, WHICH I ASSUME YOU WOULD FIND STRANGE.
SQUICK!

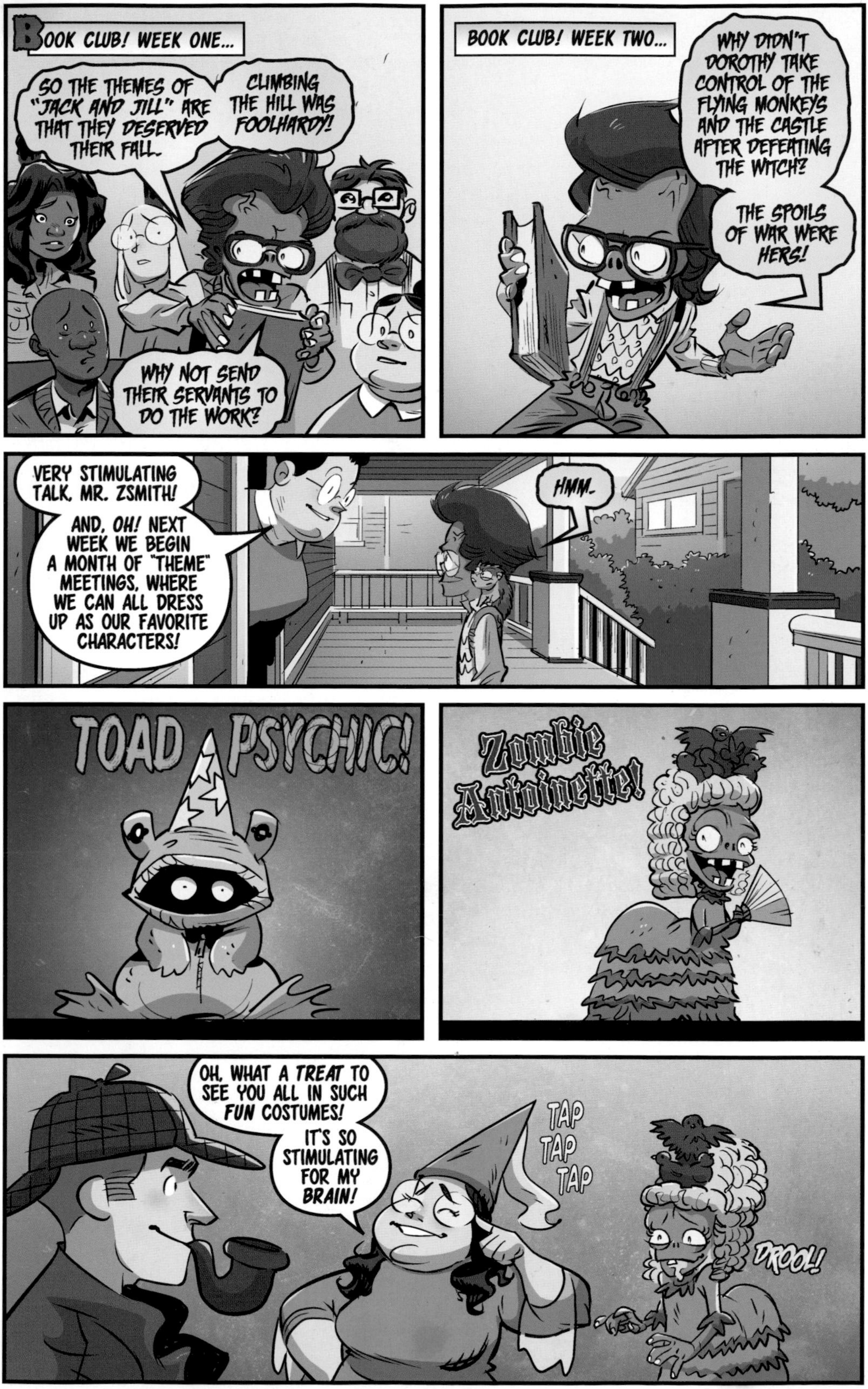
BOOK CLUB! WEEK ONE...
SO THE THEMES OF "JACK AND JILL" ARE THAT THEY DESERVED THEIR FALL.
CLIMBING THE HILL WAS FOOLHARDY!
WHY NOT SEND THEIR SERVANTS TO DO THE WORK?
BOOK CLUB! WEEK TWO...
WHY DIDN'T DOROTHY TAKE CONTROL OF THE FLYING MONKEYS AND THE CASTLE AFTER DEFEATING THE WITCH?
THE SPOILS OF WAR WERE HERS!
VERY STIMULATING TALK, MR. ZSMITH!
AND, OH! NEXT WEEK WE BEGIN A MONTH OF "THEME" MEETINGS, WHERE WE CAN ALL DRESS UP AS OUR FAVORITE CHARACTERS!
HMM.
TOAD PSYCHIC!
Zombie Antoinette!
OH, WHAT A TREAT TO SEE YOU ALL IN SUCH FUN COSTUMES!
IT'S SO STIMULATING FOR MY BRAIN!
TAP
TAP
TAP
DROOL!

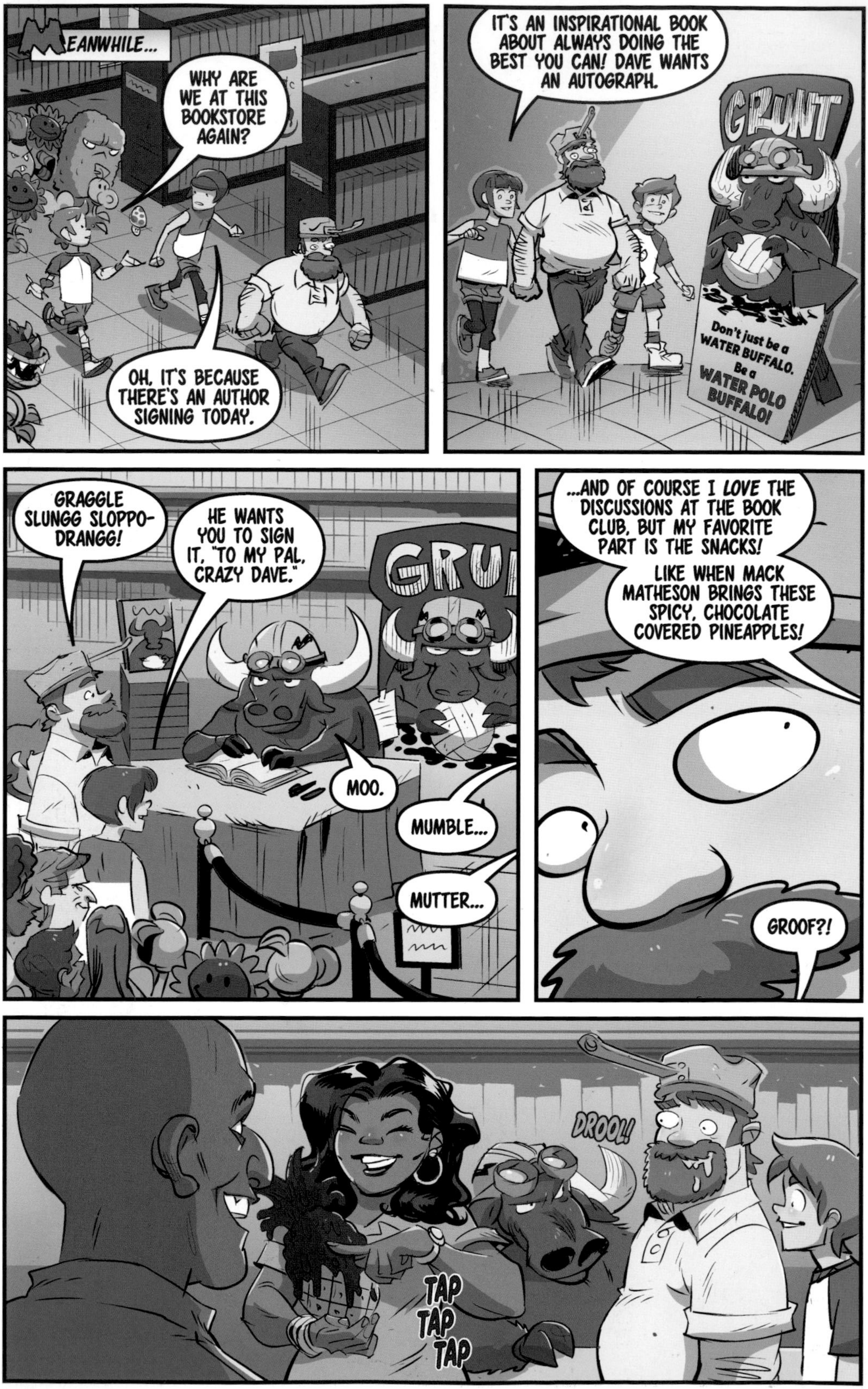
MEANWHILE...
WHY ARE WE AT THIS BOOKSTORE AGAIN?
OH, IT'S BECAUSE THERE'S AN AUTHOR SIGNING TODAY.
IT'S AN INSPIRATIONAL BOOK ABOUT ALWAYS DOING THE BEST YOU CAN! DAVE WANTS AN AUTOGRAPH.
GRUNT
Don't just be a WATER BUFFALO. Be a WATER POLO BUFFALO!
GRAGGLE SLUNGG SLOPPO-DRANGG!
HE WANTS YOU TO SIGN IT, "TO MY PAL, CRAZY DAVE."
MOO.
MUMBLE...
MUTTER...
...AND OF COURSE I LOVE THE DISCUSSIONS AT THE BOOK CLUB, BUT MY FAVORITE PART IS THE SNACKS!
LIKE WHEN MACK MATHESON BRINGS THESE SPICY, CHOCOLATE COVERED PINEAPPLES!
GROOF?!
DROOL!
TAP
TAP
TAP

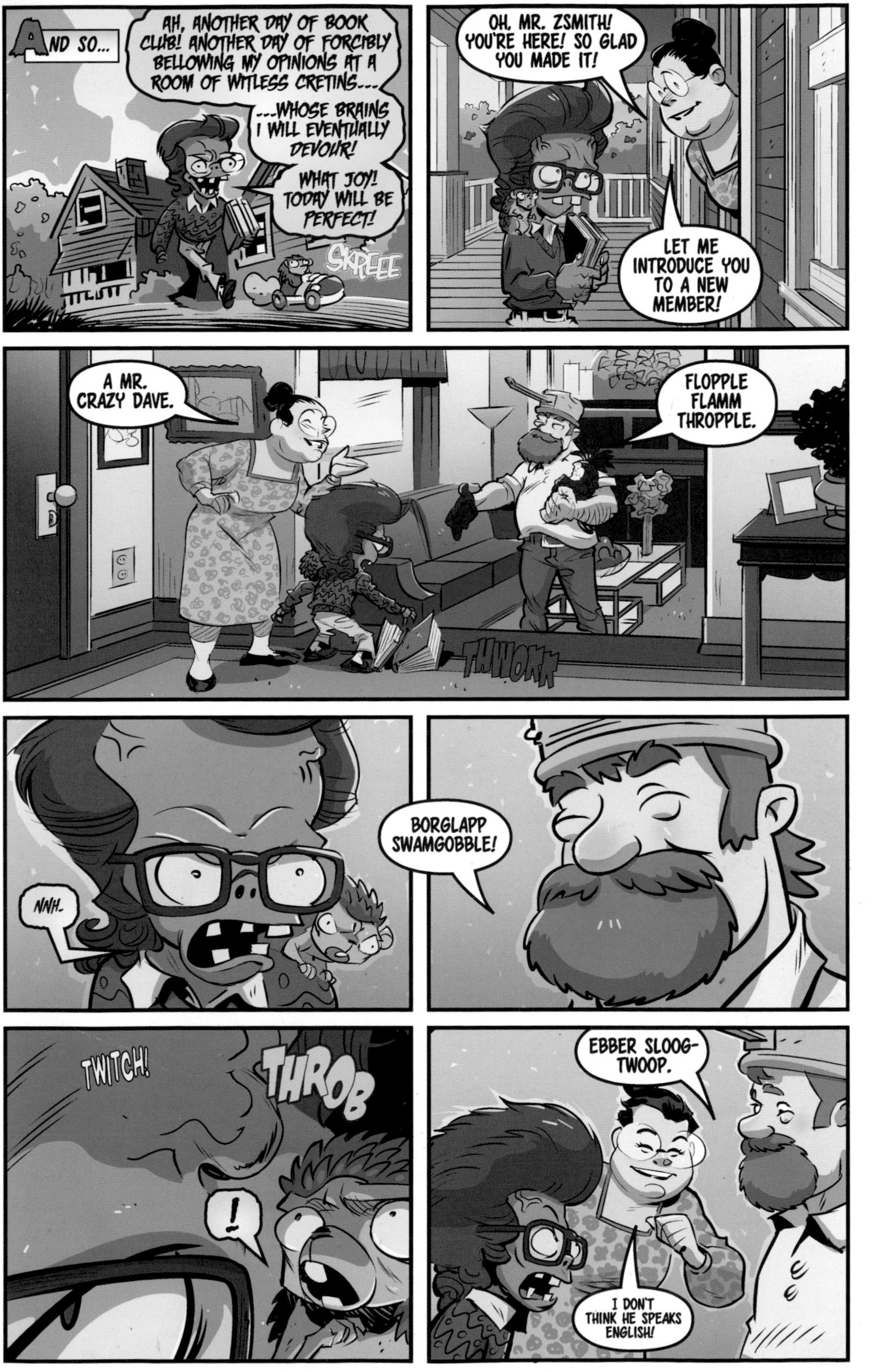
AND SO...
AH, ANOTHER DAY OF BOOK CLUB! ANOTHER DAY OF FORCIBLY BELLOWING MY OPINIONS AT A ROOM OF WITLESS CRETINS...
...WHOSE BRAINS I WILL EVENTUALLY DEVOUR!
WHAT JOY! TODAY WILL BE PERFECT!
SKREEE
OH, MR. ZSMITH! YOU'RE HERE! SO GLAD YOU MADE IT!
LET ME INTRODUCE YOU TO A NEW MEMBER!
A MR. CRAZY DAVE.
FLOPPLE FLAMM THROPPLE.
THWONK
NNH.
BORGLAPP SWAMGOBBLE!
TWITCH!
THROB
!
EBBER SLOOG-TWOOP.
I DON'T THINK HE SPEAKS ENGLISH!

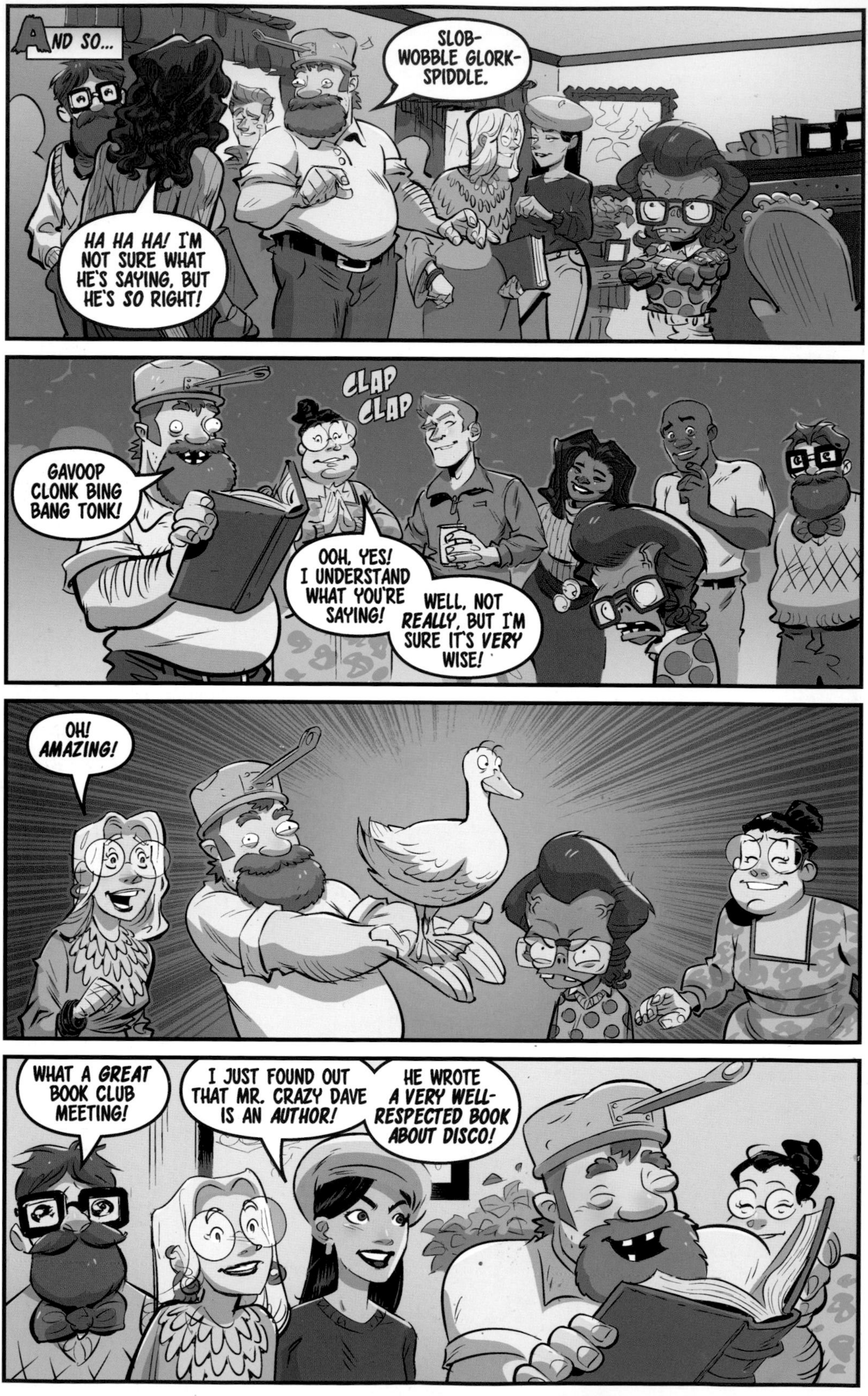
AND SO...
SLOB-WOBBLE GLORK-SPIDDLE.
HA HA HA! I'M NOT SURE WHAT HE'S SAYING, BUT HE'S SO RIGHT!
CLAP CLAP
GAVOOP CLONK BING BANG TONK!
OOH, YES! I UNDERSTAND WHAT YOU'RE SAYING!
WELL, NOT REALLY, BUT I'M SURE IT'S VERY WISE!
OH! AMAZING!
WHAT A GREAT BOOK CLUB MEETING!
I JUST FOUND OUT THAT MR. CRAZY DAVE IS AN AUTHOR!
HE WROTE A VERY WELL-RESPECTED BOOK ABOUT DISCO!

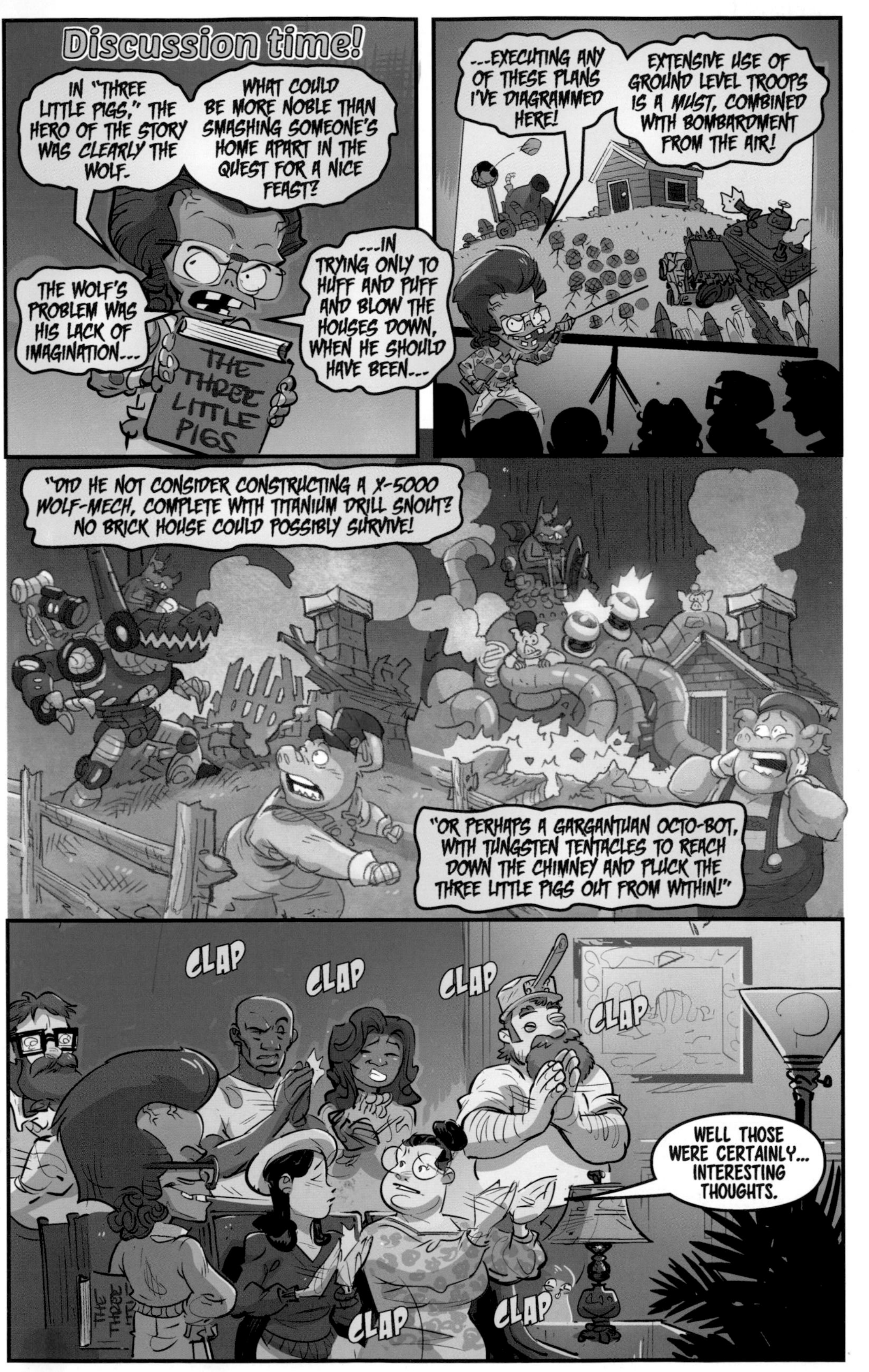
Discussion time!
IN "THREE LITTLE PIGS," THE HERO OF THE STORY WAS CLEARLY THE WOLF.
WHAT COULD BE MORE NOBLE THAN SMASHING SOMEONE'S HOME APART IN THE QUEST FOR A NICE FEAST?
THE WOLF'S PROBLEM WAS HIS LACK OF IMAGINATION...
...IN TRYING ONLY TO HUFF AND PUFF AND BLOW THE HOUSES DOWN, WHEN HE SHOULD HAVE BEEN...
THE THREE LITTLE PIGS
...EXECUTING ANY OF THESE PLANS I'VE DIAGRAMMED HERE!
EXTENSIVE USE OF GROUND LEVEL TROOPS IS A MUST, COMBINED WITH BOMBARDMENT FROM THE AIR!
"DID HE NOT CONSIDER CONSTRUCTING A X-5000 WOLF-MECH, COMPLETE WITH TITANIUM DRILL SNOUT? NO BRICK HOUSE COULD POSSIBLY SURVIVE!
"OR PERHAPS A GARGANTUAN OCTO-BOT, WITH TUNGSTEN TENTACLES TO REACH DOWN THE CHIMNEY AND PLUCK THE THREE LITTLE PIGS OUT FROM WITHIN!"
CLAP
CLAP
CLAP
CLAP
WELL THOSE WERE CERTAINLY... INTERESTING THOUGHTS.
CLAP
CLAP

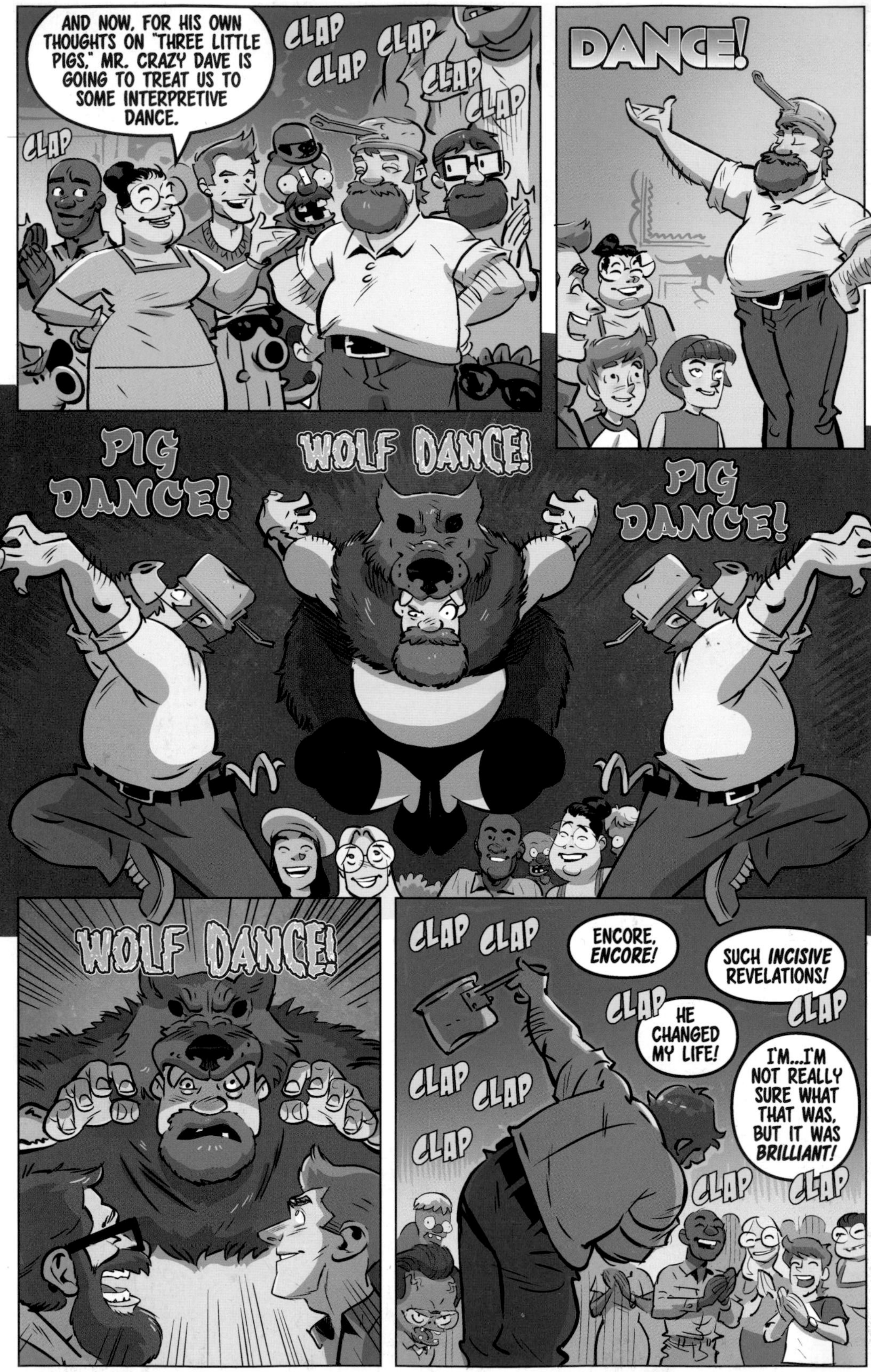
AND NOW, FOR HIS OWN THOUGHTS ON "THREE LITTLE PIGS," MR. CRAZY DAVE IS GOING TO TREAT US TO SOME INTERPRETIVE DANCE.
CLAP
CLAP
CLAP CLAP
CLAP
CLAP
DANCE!
PIG DANCE!
WOLF DANCE!
PIG DANCE!
WOLF DANCE!
CLAP CLAP
ENCORE, ENCORE!
SUCH INCISIVE REVELATIONS!
CLAP
HE CHANGED MY LIFE!
CLAP
CLAP CLAP
CLAP
I'M...I'M NOT REALLY SURE WHAT THAT WAS, BUT IT WAS BRILLIANT!
CLAP CLAP

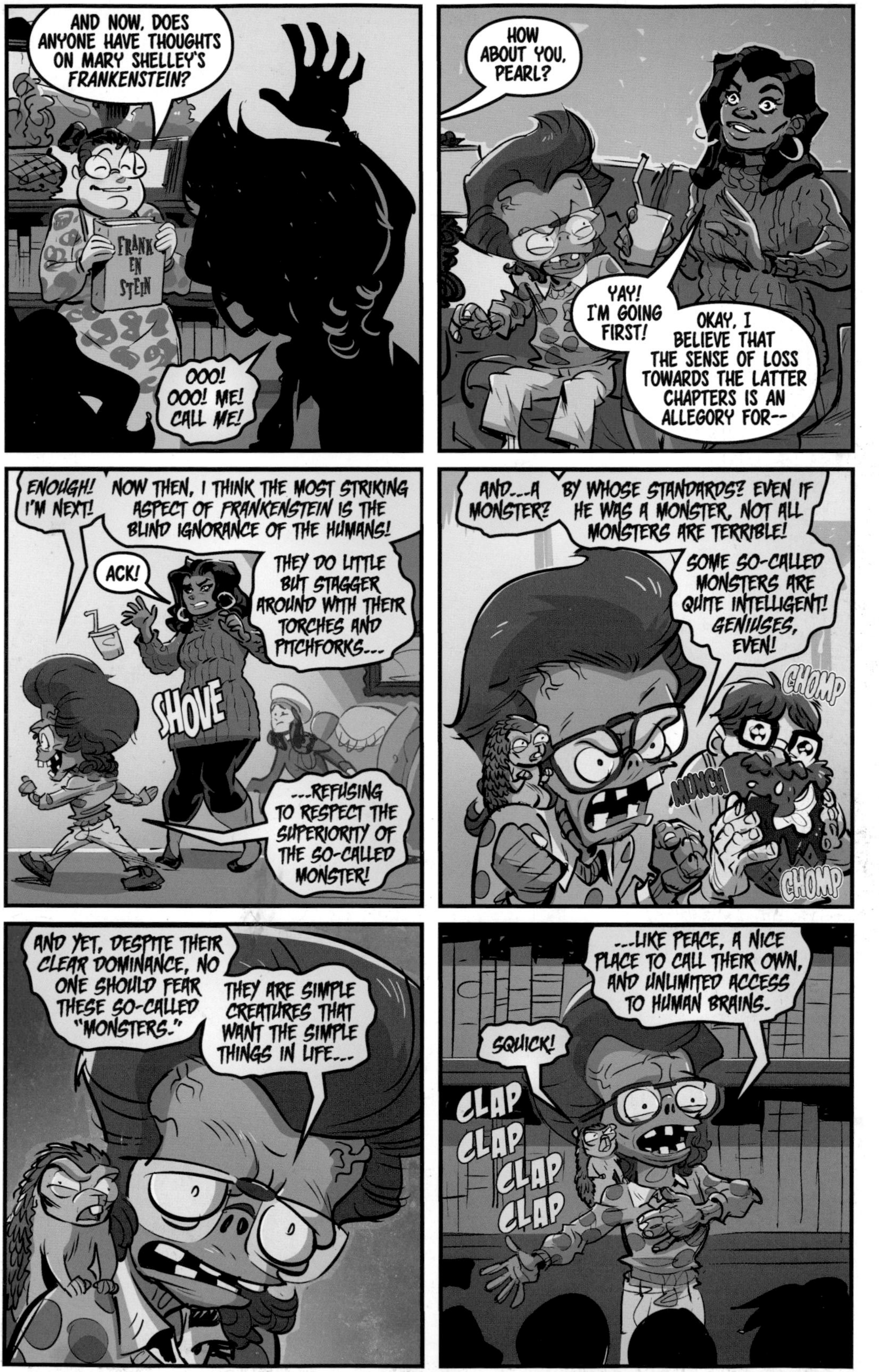
AND NOW, DOES ANYONE HAVE THOUGHTS ON MARY SHELLEY'S FRANKENSTEIN?
FRANK EN STEIN
OOO! OOO! ME! CALL ME!
HOW ABOUT YOU, PEARL?
YAY! I'M GOING FIRST!
OKAY, I BELIEVE THAT THE SENSE OF LOSS TOWARDS THE LATTER CHAPTERS IS AN ALLEGORY FOR--
ENOUGH! I'M NEXT!
NOW THEN, I THINK THE MOST STRIKING ASPECT OF FRANKENSTEIN IS THE BLIND IGNORANCE OF THE HUMANS!
ACK!
THEY DO LITTLE BUT STAGGER AROUND WITH THEIR TORCHES AND PITCHFORKS...
SHOVE
...REFUSING TO RESPECT THE SUPERIORITY OF THE SO-CALLED MONSTER!
AND...A MONSTER?
BY WHOSE STANDARDS? EVEN IF HE WAS A MONSTER, NOT ALL MONSTERS ARE TERRIBLE!
SOME SO-CALLED MONSTERS ARE QUITE INTELLIGENT! GENIUSES, EVEN!
CHOMP
MUNCH
CHOMP
AND YET, DESPITE THEIR CLEAR DOMINANCE, NO ONE SHOULD FEAR THESE SO-CALLED "MONSTERS."
THEY ARE SIMPLE CREATURES THAT WANT THE SIMPLE THINGS IN LIFE...
...LIKE PEACE, A NICE PLACE TO CALL THEIR OWN, AND UNLIMITED ACCESS TO HUMAN BRAINS.
SQUICK!
CLAP
CLAP
CLAP
CLAP

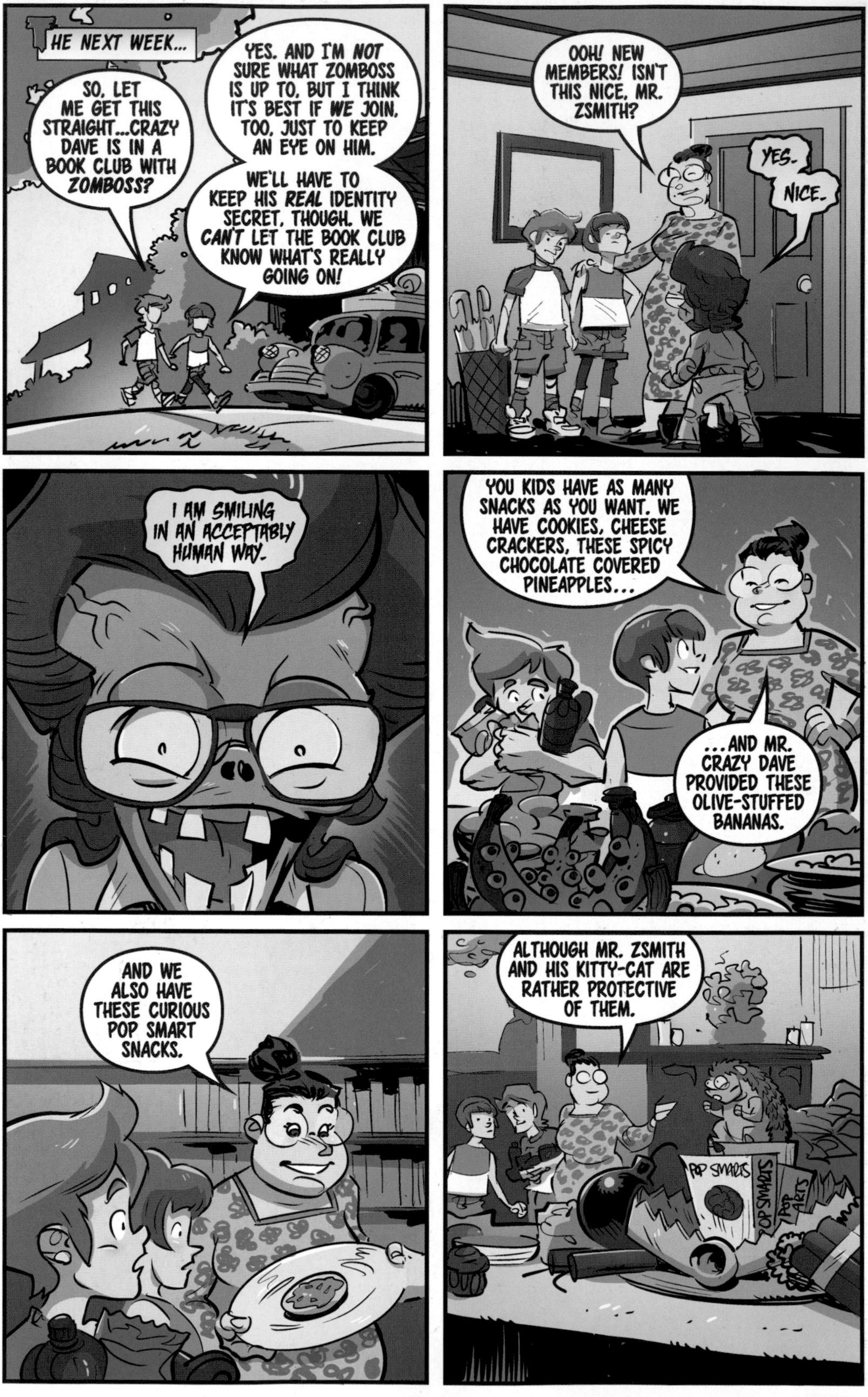
THE NEXT WEEK...
SO, LET ME GET THIS STRAIGHT...CRAZY DAVE IS IN A BOOK CLUB WITH ZOMBOSS?
YES. AND I'M NOT SURE WHAT ZOMBOSS IS UP TO, BUT I THINK IT'S BEST IF WE JOIN, TOO, JUST TO KEEP AN EYE ON HIM.
WE'LL HAVE TO KEEP HIS REAL IDENTITY SECRET, THOUGH. WE CAN'T LET THE BOOK CLUB KNOW WHAT'S REALLY GOING ON!
OOH! NEW MEMBERS! ISN'T THIS NICE, MR. ZSMITH?
YES.
NICE.
I AM SMILING IN AN ACCEPTABLY HUMAN WAY.
YOU KIDS HAVE AS MANY SNACKS AS YOU WANT. WE HAVE COOKIES, CHEESE CRACKERS, THESE SPICY CHOCOLATE COVERED PINEAPPLES...
...AND MR. CRAZY DAVE PROVIDED THESE OLIVE-STUFFED BANANAS.
AND WE ALSO HAVE THESE CURIOUS POP SMART SNACKS.
ALTHOUGH MR. ZSMITH AND HIS KITTY-CAT ARE RATHER PROTECTIVE OF THEM.
POP SMARTS

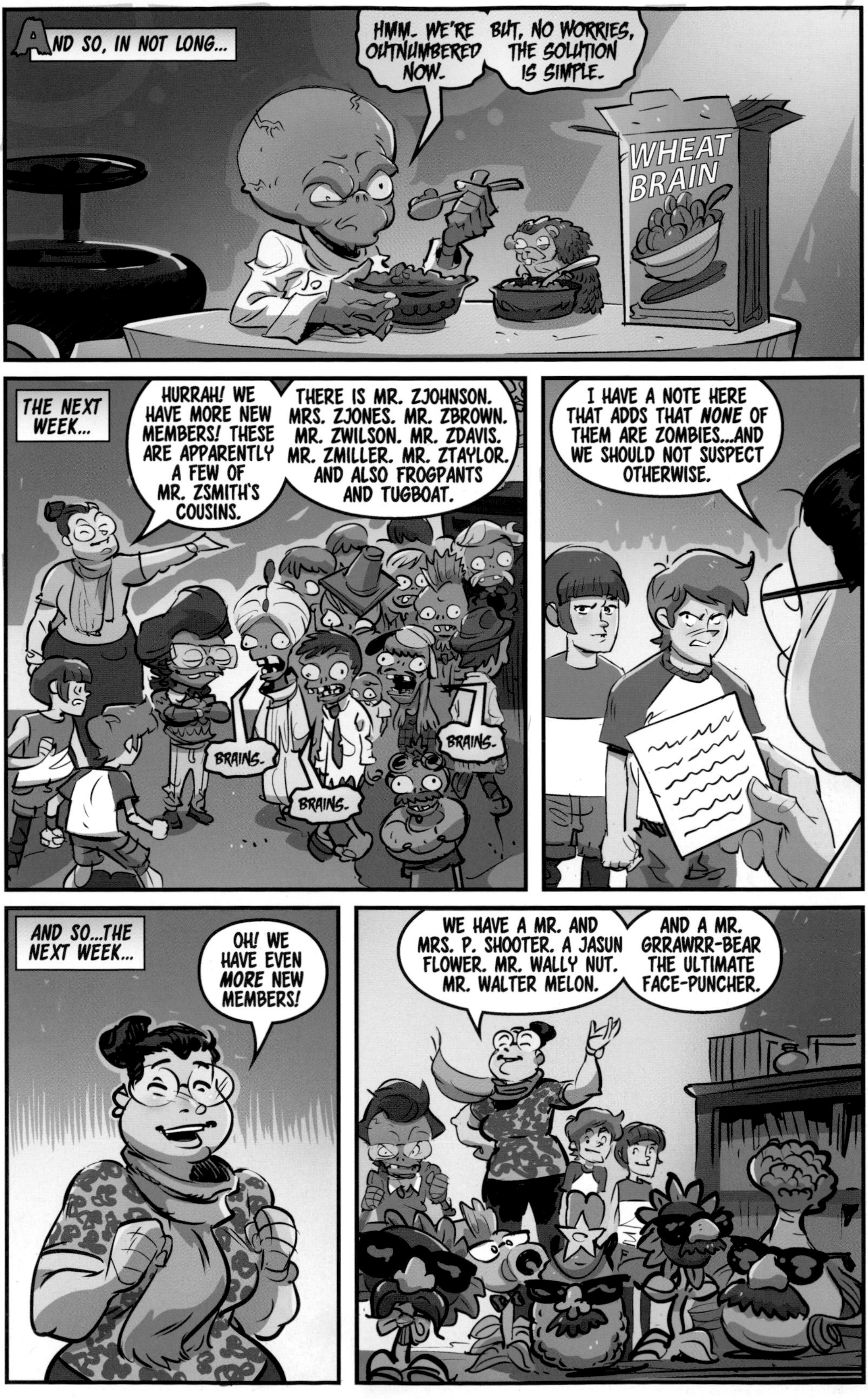
AND SO, IN NOT LONG...
HMM. WE'RE OUTNUMBERED NOW.
BUT, NO WORRIES, THE SOLUTION IS SIMPLE.
WHEAT BRAIN
THE NEXT WEEK...
HURRAH! WE HAVE MORE NEW MEMBERS! THESE ARE APPARENTLY A FEW OF MR. ZSMITH'S COUSINS.
THERE IS MR. ZJOHNSON. MRS. ZJONES. MR. ZBROWN. MR. ZWILSON. MR. ZDAVIS. MR. ZMILLER. MR. ZTAYLOR. AND ALSO FROGPANTS AND TUGBOAT.
BRAINS.
BRAINS.
BRAINS.
I HAVE A NOTE HERE THAT ADDS THAT NONE OF THEM ARE ZOMBIES...AND WE SHOULD NOT SUSPECT OTHERWISE.
AND SO...THE NEXT WEEK...
OH! WE HAVE EVEN MORE NEW MEMBERS!
WE HAVE A MR. AND MRS. P. SHOOTER. A JASUN FLOWER. MR. WALLY NUT. MR. WALTER MELON.
AND A MR. GRRAWRR-BEAR THE ULTIMATE FACE-PUNCHER.

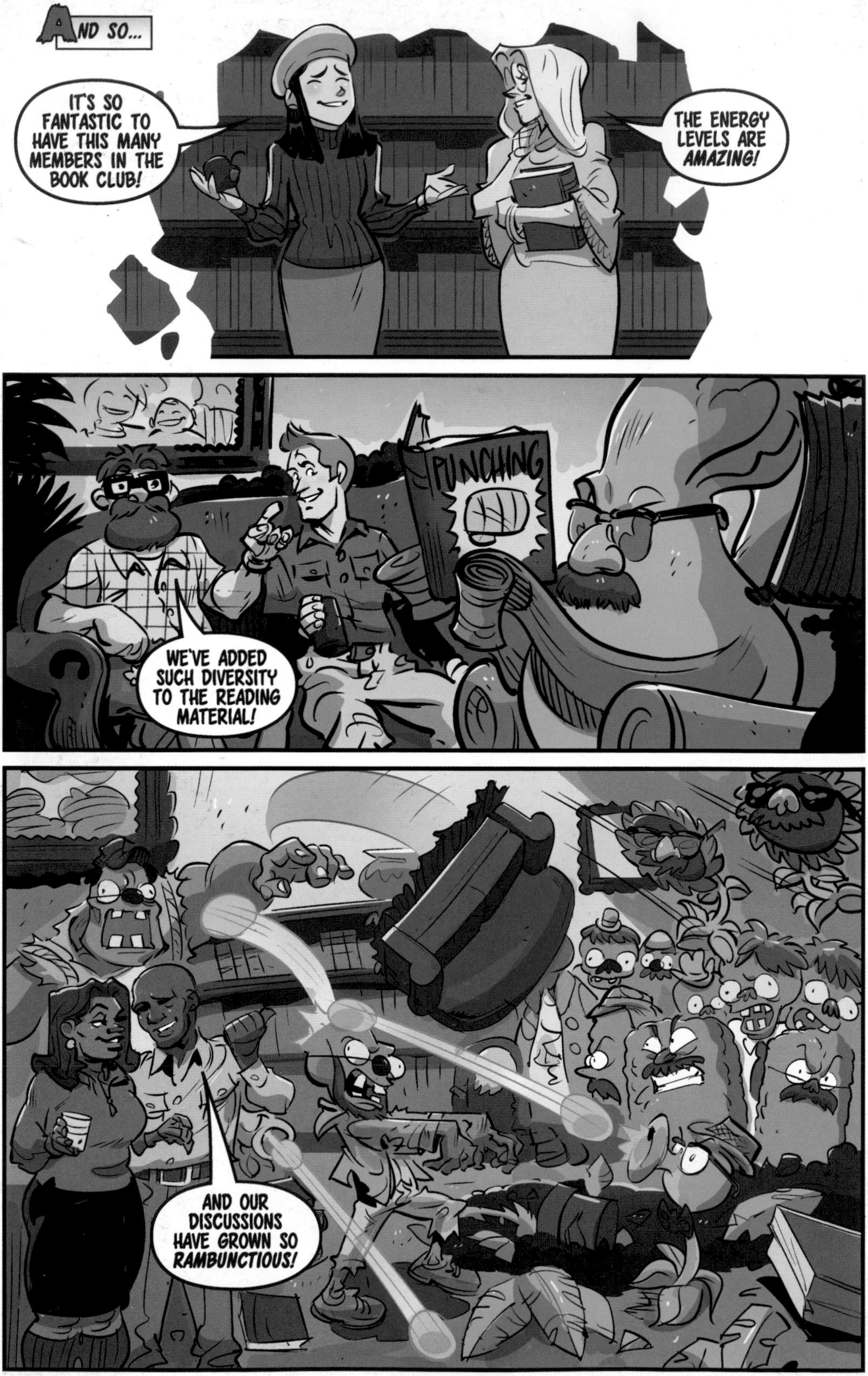
AND SO...
IT'S SO FANTASTIC TO HAVE THIS MANY MEMBERS IN THE BOOK CLUB!
THE ENERGY LEVELS ARE AMAZING!
PUNCHING
WE'VE ADDED SUCH DIVERSITY TO THE READING MATERIAL!
AND OUR DISCUSSIONS HAVE GROWN SO RAMBUNCTIOUS!

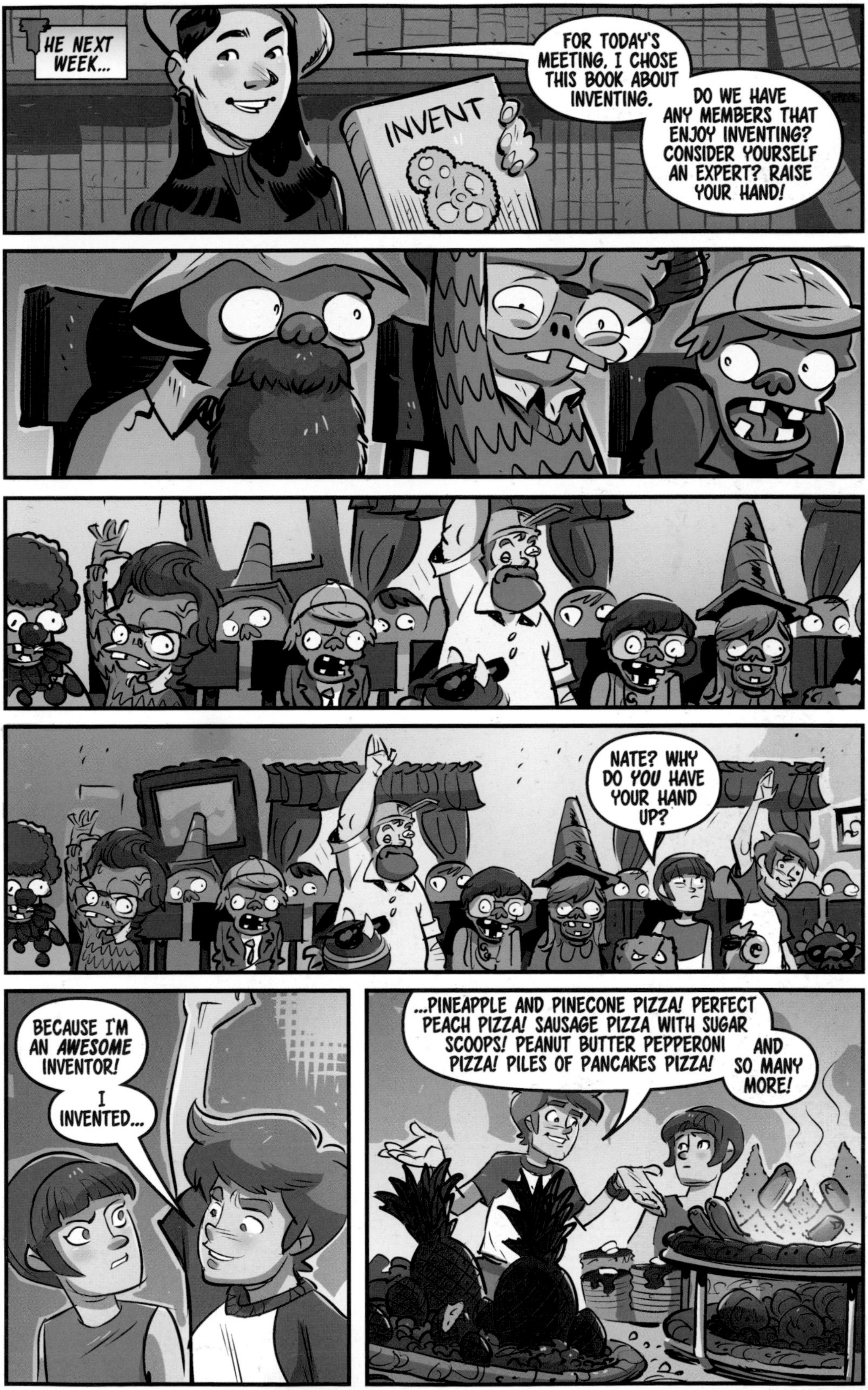
THE NEXT WEEK...
FOR TODAY'S MEETING, I CHOSE THIS BOOK ABOUT INVENTING.
DO WE HAVE ANY MEMBERS THAT ENJOY INVENTING? CONSIDER YOURSELF AN EXPERT? RAISE YOUR HAND!
INVENT
NATE? WHY DO YOU HAVE YOUR HAND UP?
BECAUSE I'M AN AWESOME INVENTOR!
I INVENTED...
...PINEAPPLE AND PINECONE PIZZA! PERFECT PEACH PIZZA! SAUSAGE PIZZA WITH SUGAR SCOOPS! PEANUT BUTTER PEPPERONI PIZZA! PILES OF PANCAKES PIZZA!
AND SO MANY MORE!

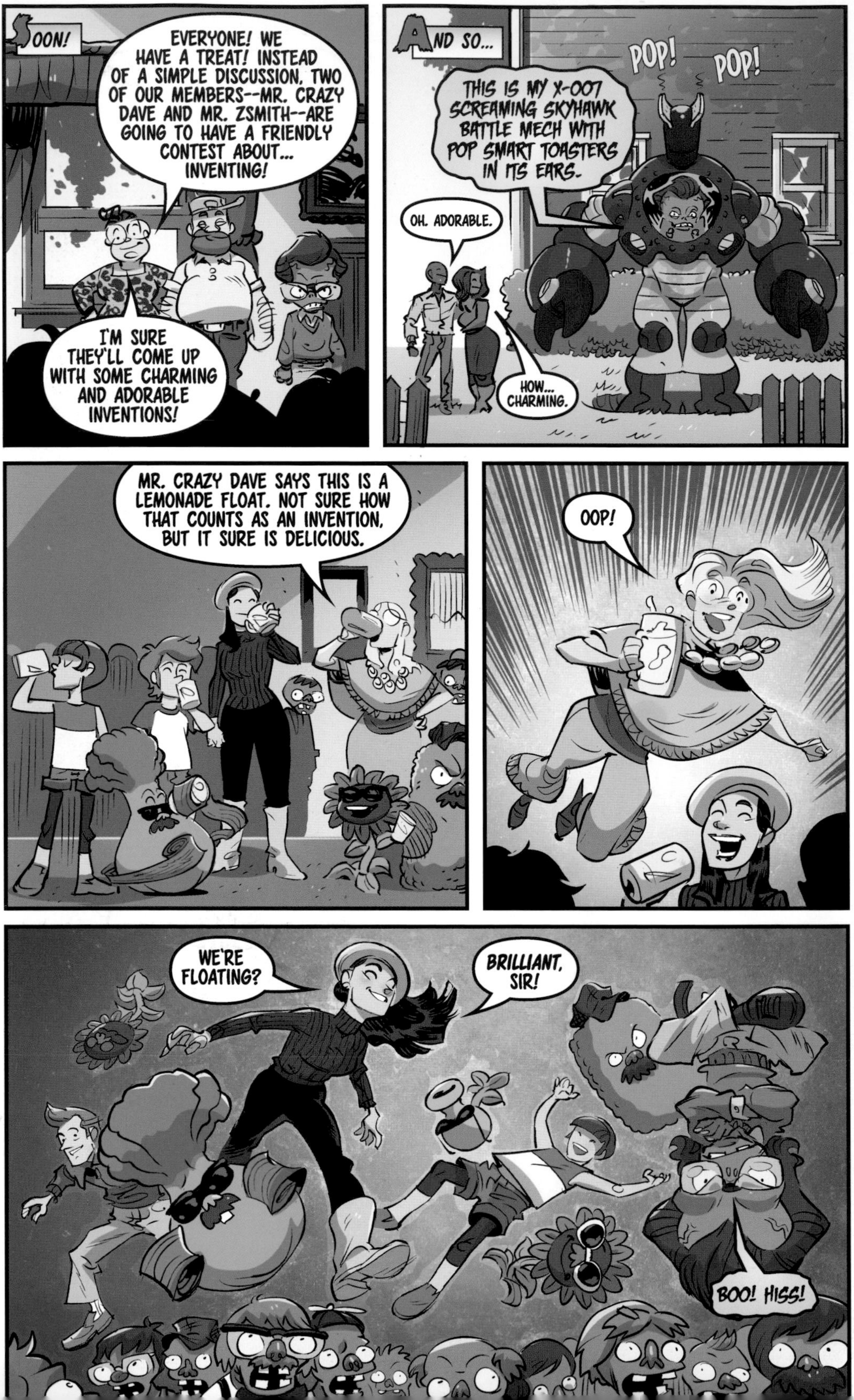
SOON!
EVERYONE! WE HAVE A TREAT! INSTEAD OF A SIMPLE DISCUSSION, TWO OF OUR MEMBERS--MR. CRAZY DAVE AND MR. ZSMITH--ARE GOING TO HAVE A FRIENDLY CONTEST ABOUT... INVENTING!
I'M SURE THEY'LL COME UP WITH SOME CHARMING AND ADORABLE INVENTIONS!
AND SO...
POP! POP!
THIS IS MY X-007 SCREAMING SKYHAWK BATTLE MECH WITH POP SMART TOASTERS IN ITS EARS.
OH. ADORABLE.
HOW... CHARMING.
MR. CRAZY DAVE SAYS THIS IS A LEMONADE FLOAT. NOT SURE HOW THAT COUNTS AS AN INVENTION, BUT IT SURE IS DELICIOUS.
OOP!
WE'RE FLOATING?
BRILLIANT, SIR!
BOO! HISS!

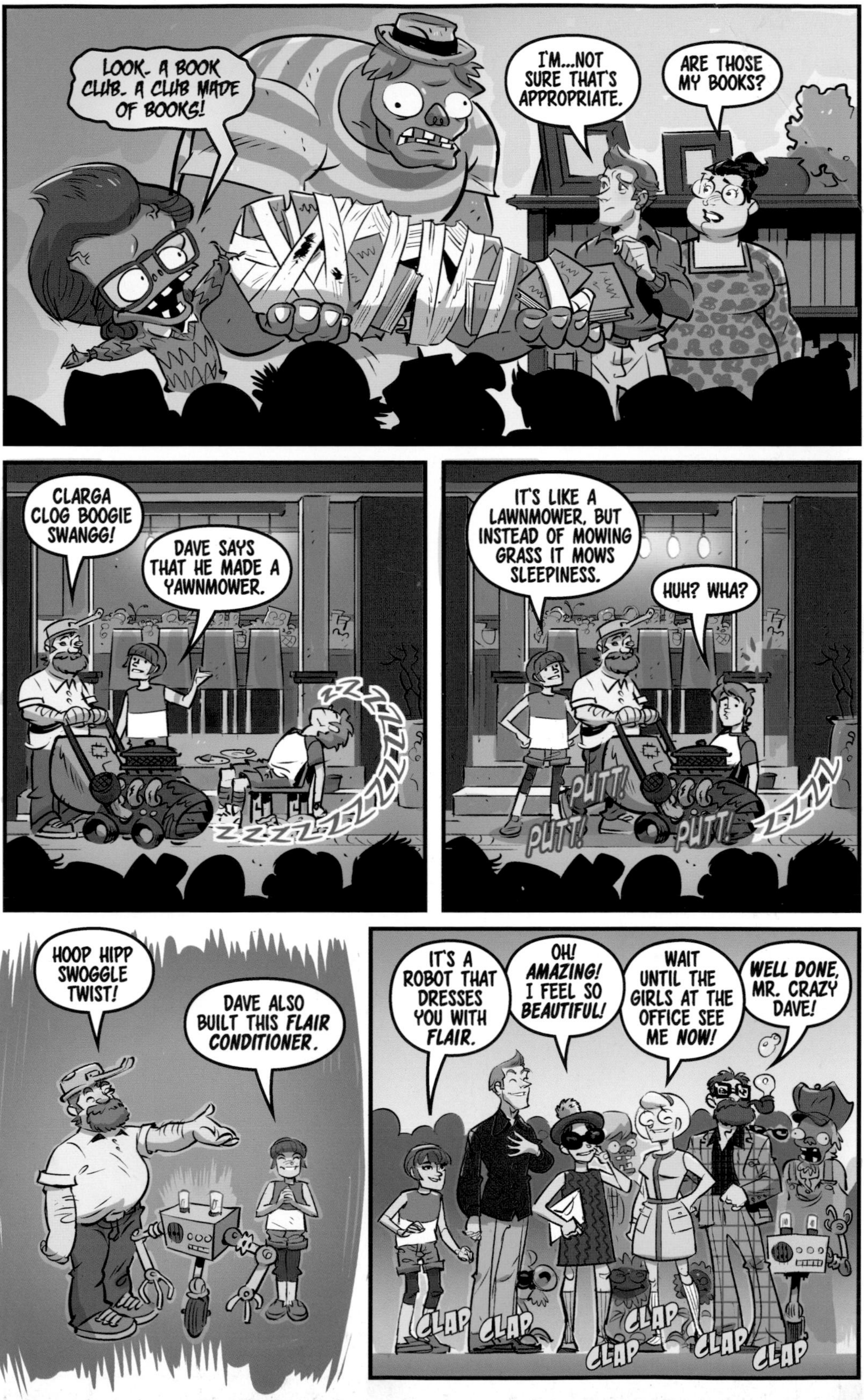
LOOK. A BOOK CLUB. A CLUB MADE OF BOOKS!
I'M...NOT SURE THAT'S APPROPRIATE.
ARE THOSE MY BOOKS?
CLARGA CLOG BOOGIE SWANGG!
DAVE SAYS THAT HE MADE A YAWNMOWER.
IT'S LIKE A LAWNMOWER, BUT INSTEAD OF MOWING GRASS IT MOWS SLEEPINESS.
HUH? WHA?
PUTT! PUTT! PUTT!
HOOP HIPP SWOGGLE TWIST!
DAVE ALSO BUILT THIS FLAIR CONDITIONER.
IT'S A ROBOT THAT DRESSES YOU WITH FLAIR.
OH! AMAZING! I FEEL SO BEAUTIFUL!
WAIT UNTIL THE GIRLS AT THE OFFICE SEE ME NOW!
WELL DONE, MR. CRAZY DAVE!
CLAP CLAP CLAP CLAP CLAP CLAP CLAP

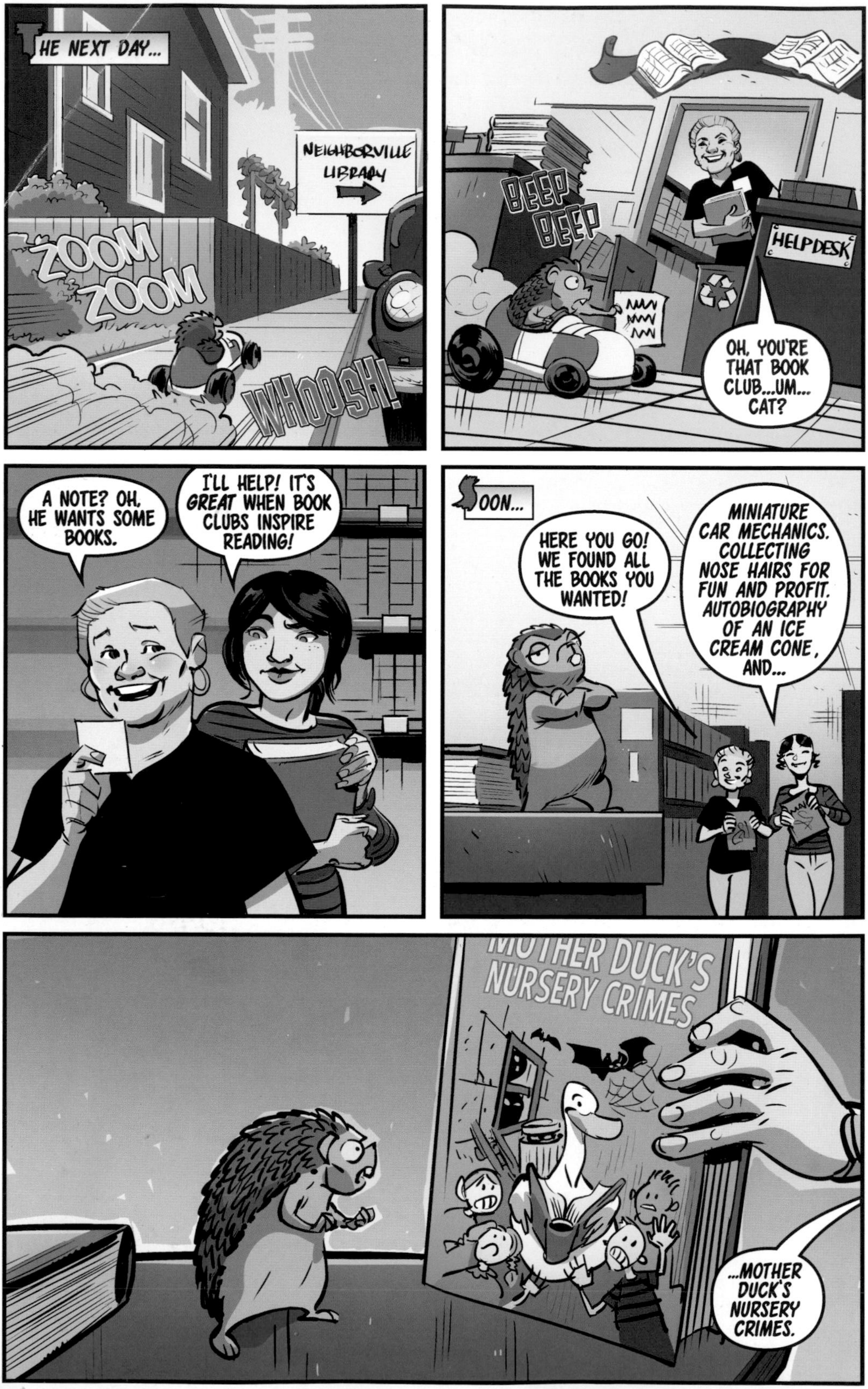
THE NEXT DAY...
NEIGHBORVILLE LIBRARY
ZOOM ZOOM
WHOOSH!
BEEP BEEP
HELPDESK
OH, YOU'RE THAT BOOK CLUB...UM... CAT?
A NOTE? OH, HE WANTS SOME BOOKS.
I'LL HELP! IT'S GREAT WHEN BOOK CLUBS INSPIRE READING!
SOON...
HERE YOU GO! WE FOUND ALL THE BOOKS YOU WANTED!
MINIATURE CAR MECHANICS. COLLECTING NOSE HAIRS FOR FUN AND PROFIT. AUTOBIOGRAPHY OF AN ICE CREAM CONE, AND...
MOTHER DUCK'S NURSERY CRIMES
...MOTHER DUCK'S NURSERY CRIMES.

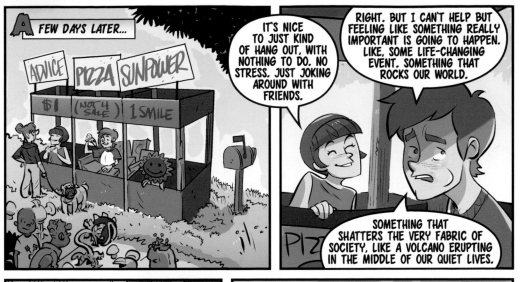

FEW DAYS LATER...

ADVICE $1

PIZZA (NOT 4 SALE)

SUNPOWER 1 SMILE

IT'S NICE TO JUST KIND OF HANG OUT, WITH NOTHING TO DO. NO STRESS. JUST JOKING AROUND WITH FRIENDS.

RIGHT. BUT I CAN'T HELP BUT FEELING LIKE SOMETHING REALLY IMPORTANT IS GOING TO HAPPEN. LIKE, SOME LIFE-CHANGING EVENT. SOMETHING THAT ROCKS OUR WORLD.

SOMETHING THAT SHATTERS THE VERY FABRIC OF SOCIETY, LIKE A VOLCANO ERUPTING IN THE MIDDLE OF OUR QUIET LIVES.

AND...

JOG JOG JOG

RUN RUN RUN

JOG JOG

RUN WHOOSH! JOG JOG

BLAP-TWANGG SPOOLY DRANG!

HUH? REALLY? WOW!

WELL, UNCLE DAVE SAYS THAT...

ADVICE PIZZ

$1

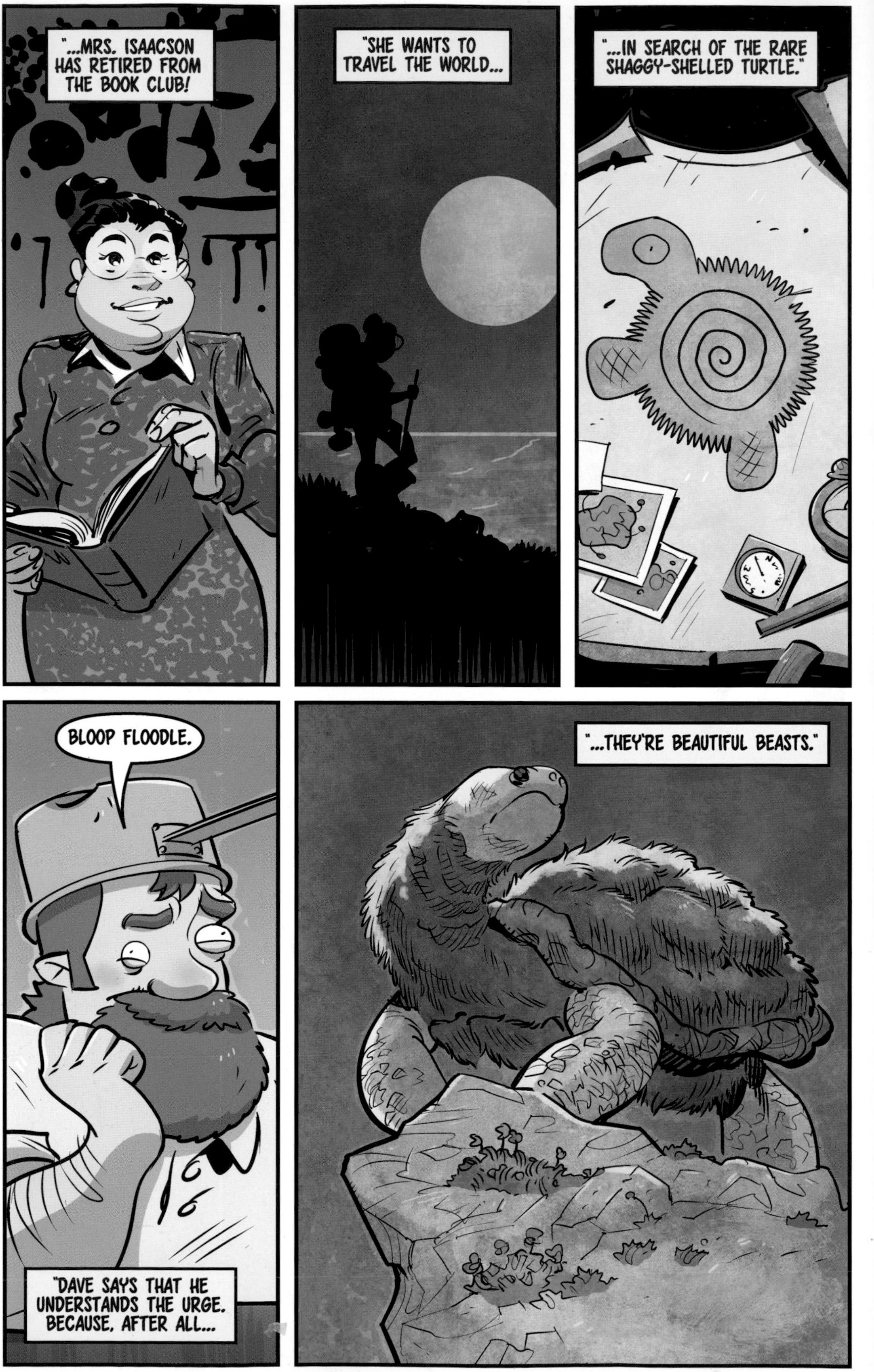
"...MRS. ISAACSON HAS RETIRED FROM THE BOOK CLUB!
"SHE WANTS TO TRAVEL THE WORLD...
"...IN SEARCH OF THE RARE SHAGGY-SHELLED TURTLE."
BLOOP FLOODLE.
"DAVE SAYS THAT HE UNDERSTANDS THE URGE. BECAUSE, AFTER ALL...
"...THEY'RE BEAUTIFUL BEASTS."

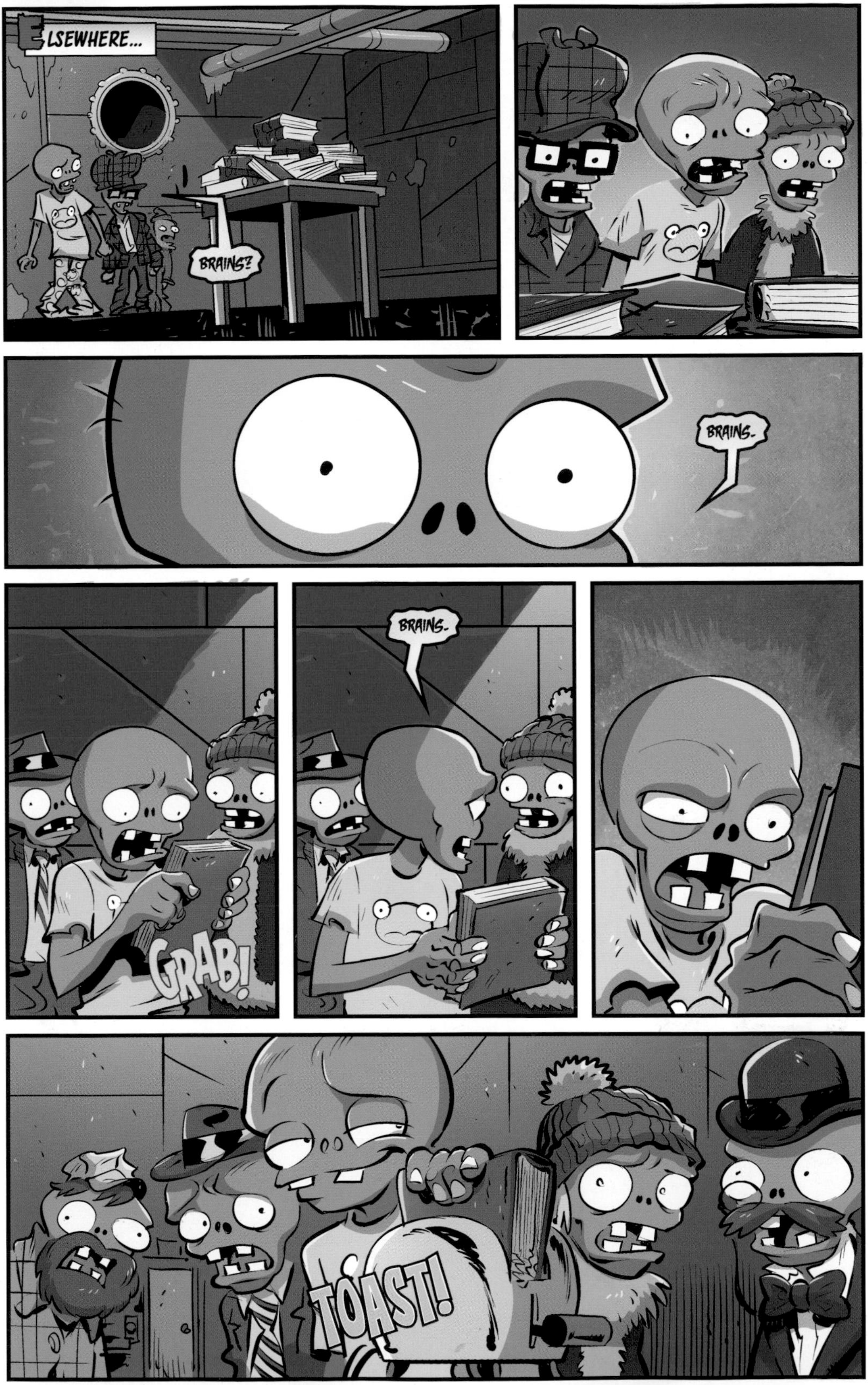
ELSEWHERE...
BRAINS?
BRAINS.
BRAINS.
GRAB!
TOAST!

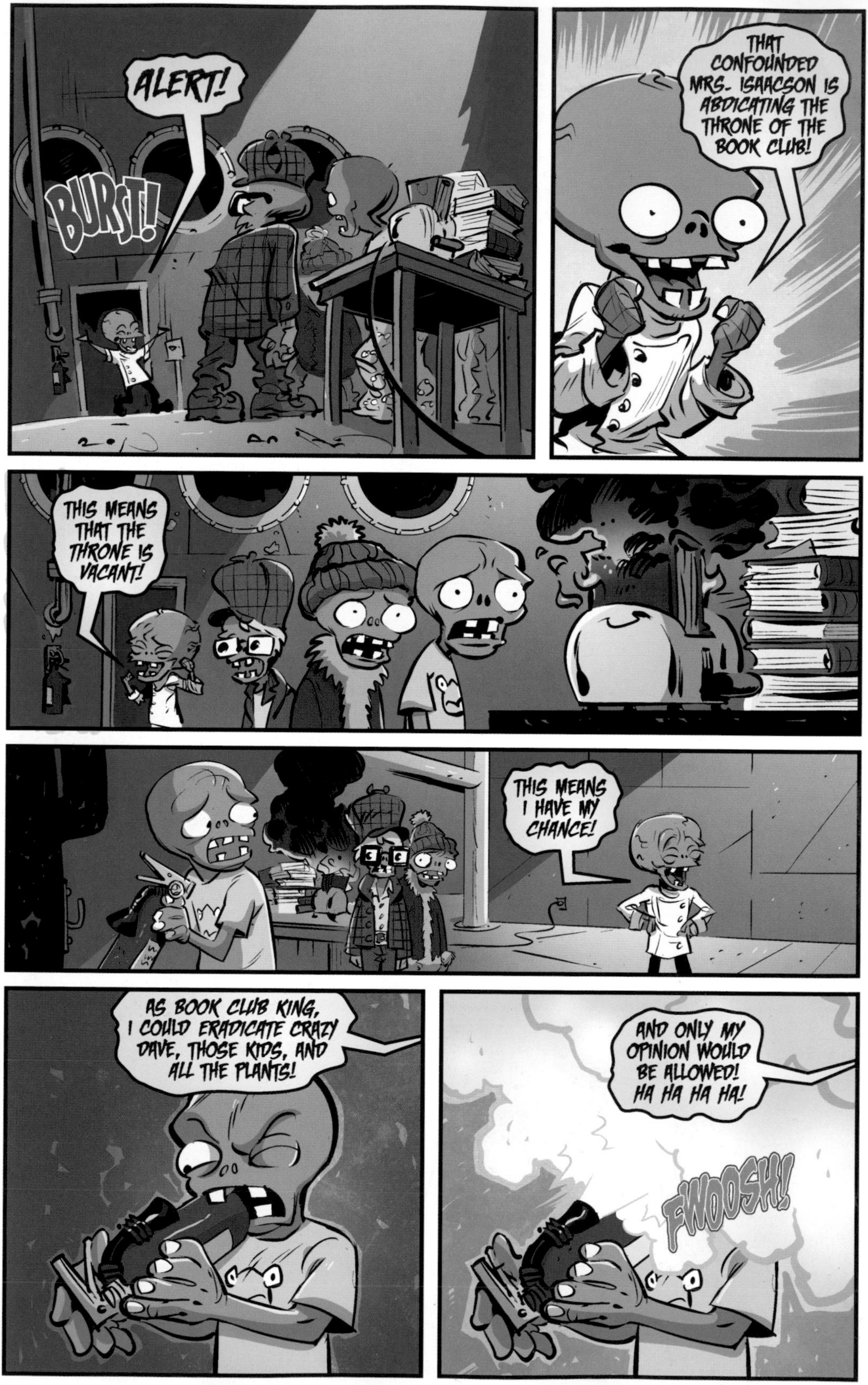
ALERT!
BURST!
THAT CONFOUNDED MRS. ISAACSON IS ABDICATING THE THRONE OF THE BOOK CLUB!
THIS MEANS THAT THE THRONE IS VACANT!
THIS MEANS I HAVE MY CHANCE!
AS BOOK CLUB KING, I COULD ERADICATE CRAZY DAVE, THOSE KIDS, AND ALL THE PLANTS!
AND ONLY MY OPINION WOULD BE ALLOWED! HA HA HA HA!
FWOOSH!

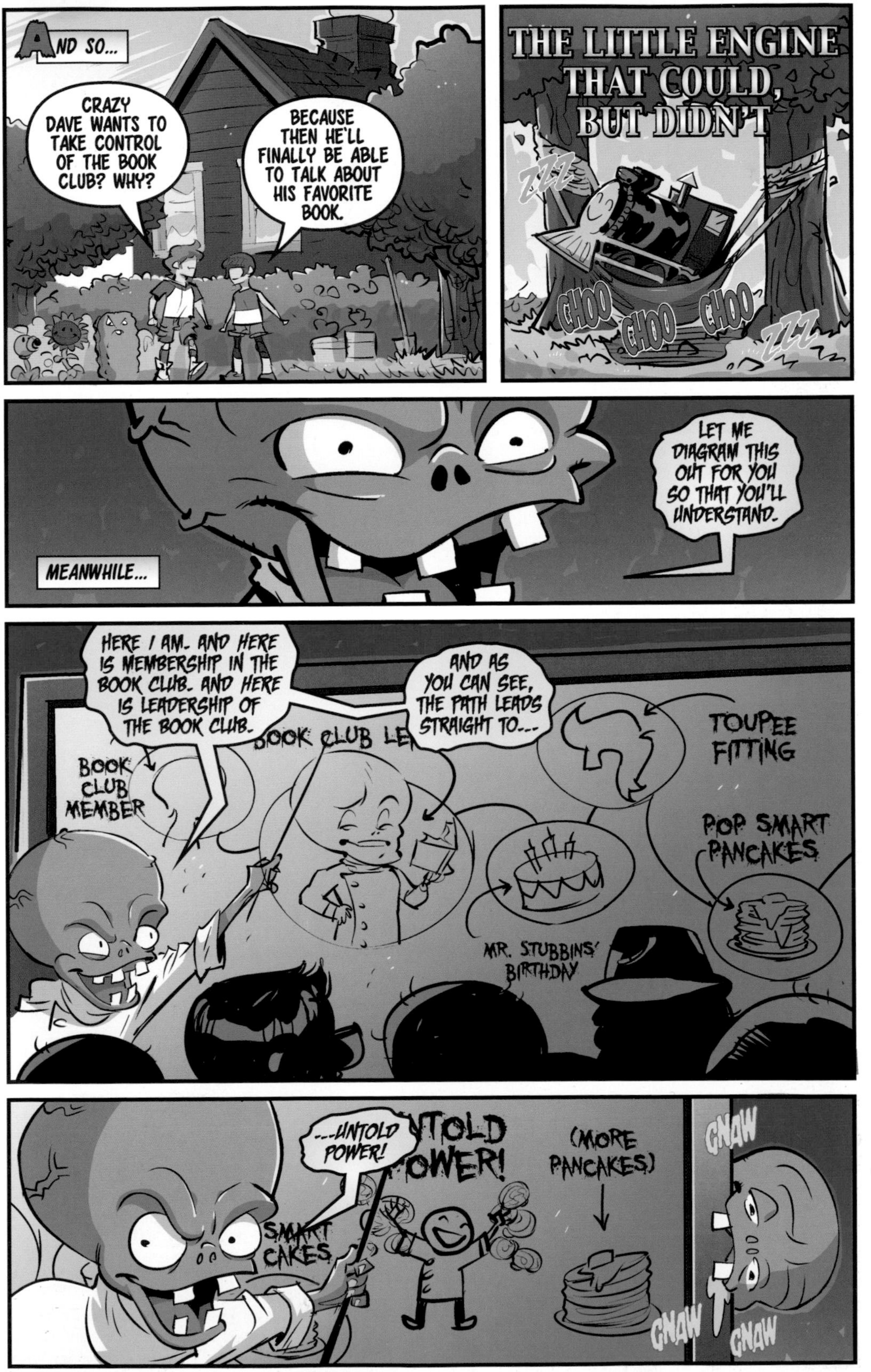
AND SO...
CRAZY DAVE WANTS TO TAKE CONTROL OF THE BOOK CLUB? WHY?
BECAUSE THEN HE'LL FINALLY BE ABLE TO TALK ABOUT HIS FAVORITE BOOK.
THE LITTLE ENGINE THAT COULD, BUT DIDN'T
ZZZ
CHOO
CHOO
CHOO
ZZZ
LET ME DIAGRAM THIS OUT FOR YOU SO THAT YOU'LL UNDERSTAND.
MEANWHILE...
HERE I AM. AND HERE IS MEMBERSHIP IN THE BOOK CLUB. AND HERE IS LEADERSHIP OF THE BOOK CLUB.
AND AS YOU CAN SEE, THE PATH LEADS STRAIGHT TO...
BOOK CLUB MEMBER
BOOK CLUB LE
TOUPEE FITTING
POP SMART PANCAKES
MR. STUBBINS' BIRTHDAY
...UNTOLD POWER!
UNTOLD POWER!
SMART CAKES
(MORE PANCAKES)
GNAW
GNAW
GNAW

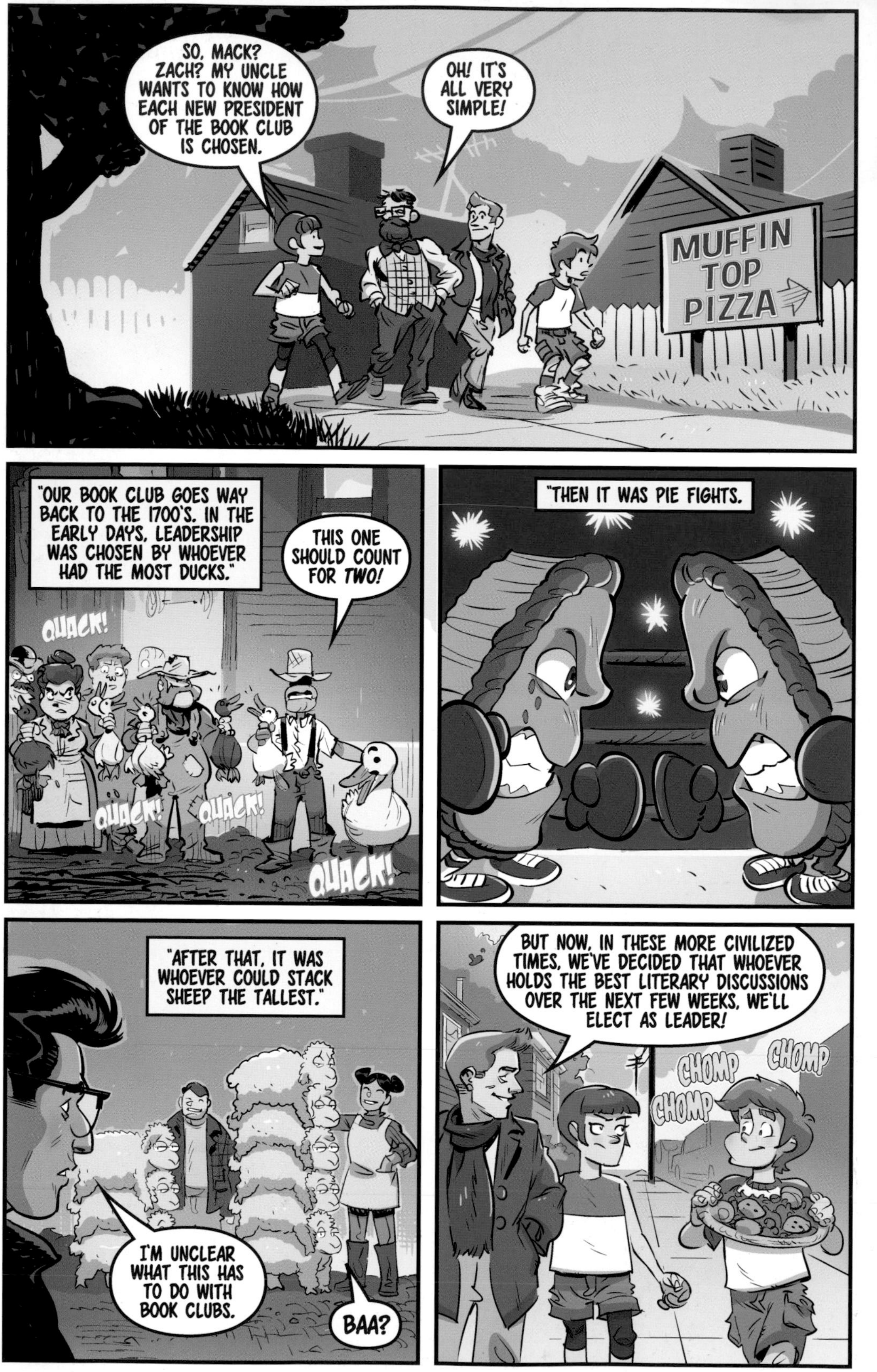
SO, MACK? ZACH? MY UNCLE WANTS TO KNOW HOW EACH NEW PRESIDENT OF THE BOOK CLUB IS CHOSEN.
OH! IT'S ALL VERY SIMPLE!
MUFFIN TOP PIZZA
"OUR BOOK CLUB GOES WAY BACK TO THE 1700'S. IN THE EARLY DAYS, LEADERSHIP WAS CHOSEN BY WHOEVER HAD THE MOST DUCKS."
THIS ONE SHOULD COUNT FOR *TWO!*
QUACK!
QUACK!
QUACK!
QUACK!
"THEN IT WAS PIE FIGHTS.
"AFTER THAT, IT WAS WHOEVER COULD STACK SHEEP THE TALLEST."
I'M UNCLEAR WHAT THIS HAS TO DO WITH BOOK CLUBS.
BAA?
BUT NOW, IN THESE MORE CIVILIZED TIMES, WE'VE DECIDED THAT WHOEVER HOLDS THE BEST LITERARY DISCUSSIONS OVER THE NEXT FEW WEEKS, WE'LL ELECT AS LEADER!
CHOMP
CHOMP
CHOMP

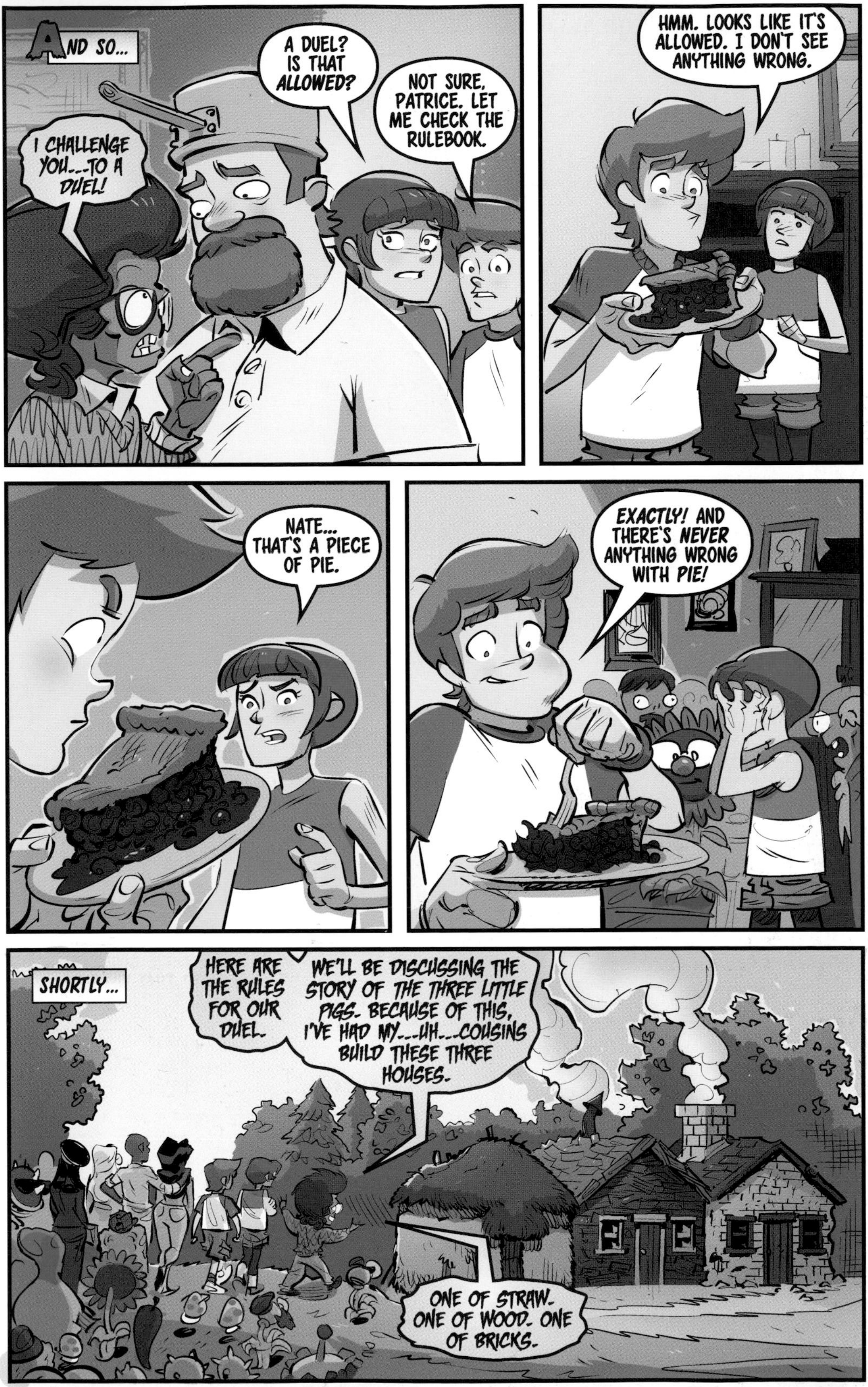
AND SO...
I CHALLENGE YOU...TO A DUEL!
A DUEL? IS THAT ALLOWED?
NOT SURE, PATRICE. LET ME CHECK THE RULEBOOK.
HMM. LOOKS LIKE IT'S ALLOWED. I DON'T SEE ANYTHING WRONG.
NATE... THAT'S A PIECE OF PIE.
EXACTLY! AND THERE'S NEVER ANYTHING WRONG WITH PIE!
SHORTLY...
HERE ARE THE RULES FOR OUR DUEL.
WE'LL BE DISCUSSING THE STORY OF THE THREE LITTLE PIGS. BECAUSE OF THIS, I'VE HAD MY...UH...COUSINS BUILD THESE THREE HOUSES.
ONE OF STRAW. ONE OF WOOD. ONE OF BRICKS.

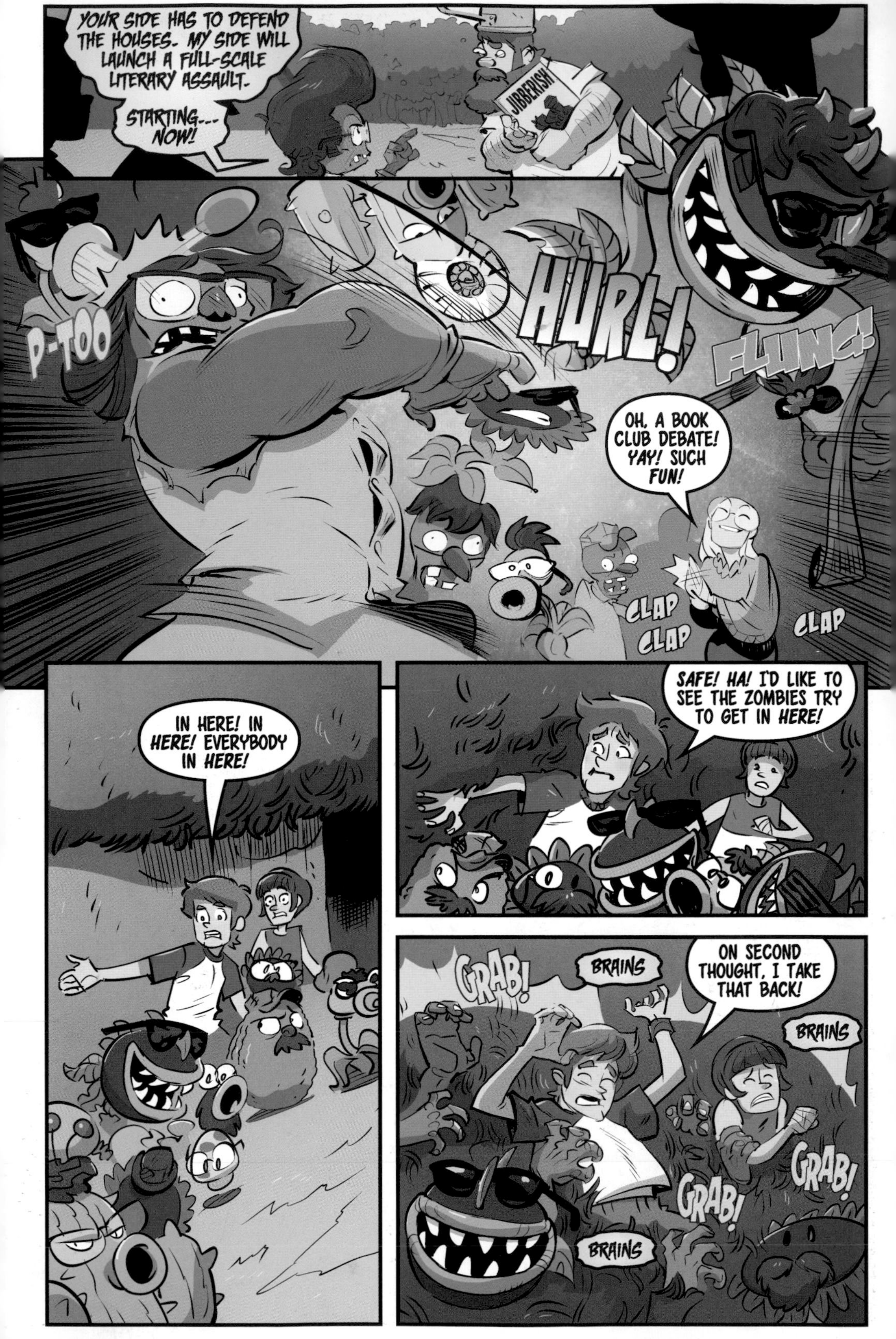
YOUR SIDE HAS TO DEFEND THE HOUSES. MY SIDE WILL LAUNCH A FULL-SCALE LITERARY ASSAULT.
STARTING... NOW!
JIBBERISH
P-TOO
HURL!
FLUNG!
OH, A BOOK CLUB DEBATE! YAY! SUCH FUN!
CLAP
CLAP
CLAP
IN HERE! IN HERE! EVERYBODY IN HERE!
SAFE! HA! I'D LIKE TO SEE THE ZOMBIES TRY TO GET IN HERE!
GRAB!
BRAINS
ON SECOND THOUGHT, I TAKE THAT BACK!
BRAINS
GRAB!
GRAB!
BRAINS

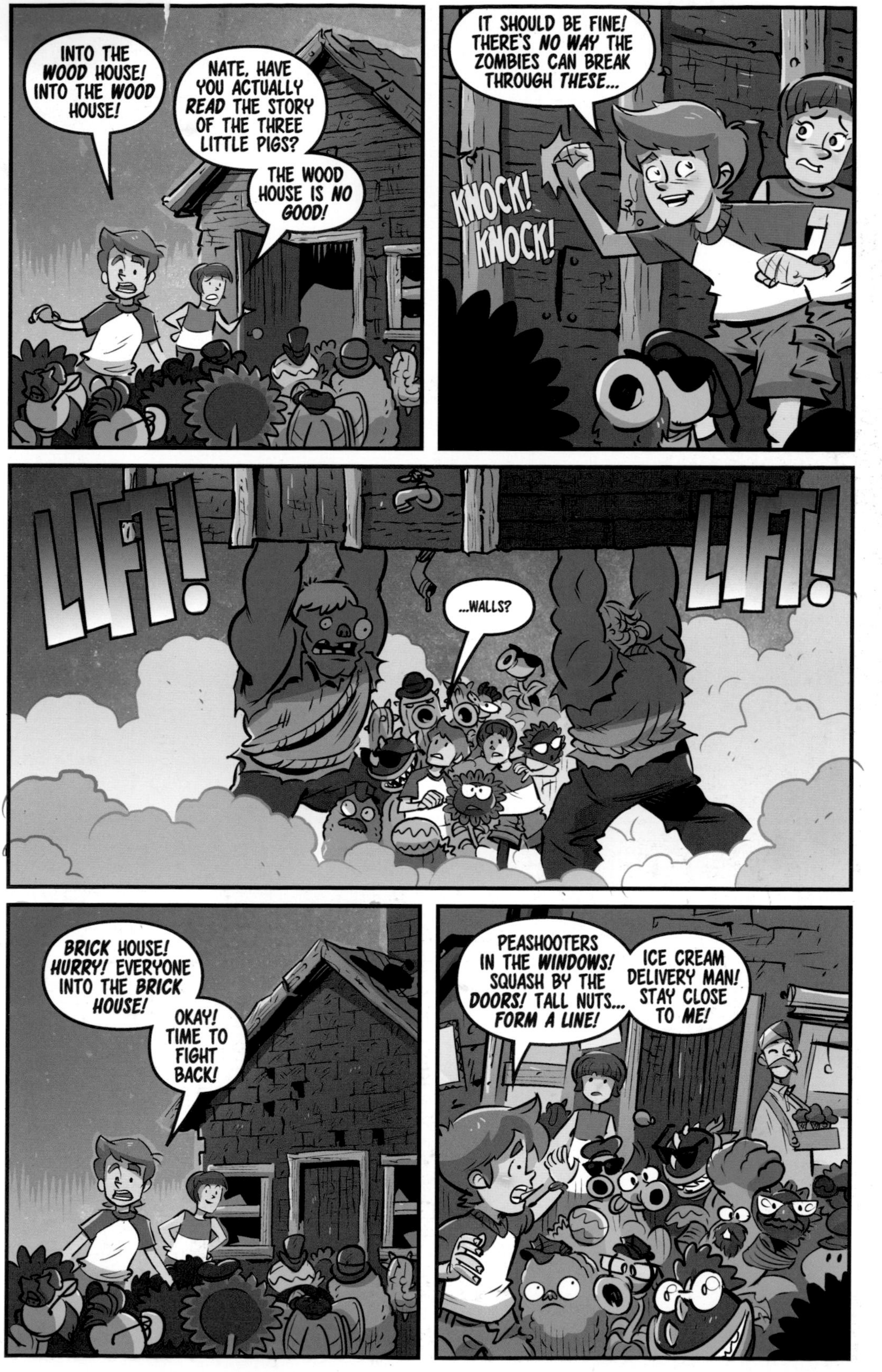
INTO THE WOOD HOUSE! INTO THE WOOD HOUSE!
NATE, HAVE YOU ACTUALLY READ THE STORY OF THE THREE LITTLE PIGS?
THE WOOD HOUSE IS NO GOOD!
IT SHOULD BE FINE! THERE'S NO WAY THE ZOMBIES CAN BREAK THROUGH THESE...
KNOCK! KNOCK!
LIFT!
LIFT!
...WALLS?
BRICK HOUSE! HURRY! EVERYONE INTO THE BRICK HOUSE!
OKAY! TIME TO FIGHT BACK!
PEASHOOTERS IN THE WINDOWS! SQUASH BY THE DOORS! TALL NUTS... FORM A LINE!
ICE CREAM DELIVERY MAN! STAY CLOSE TO ME!

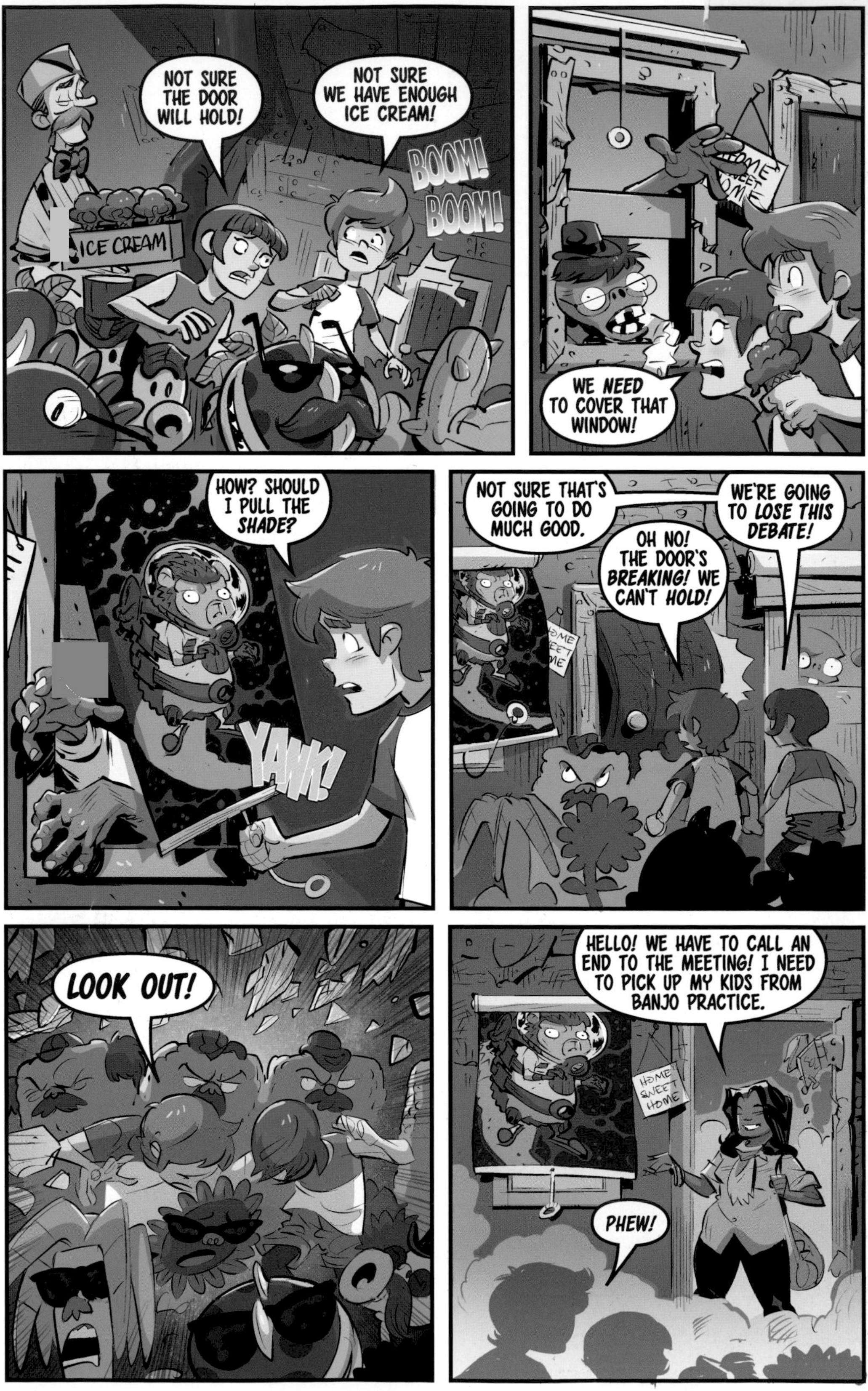
NOT SURE THE DOOR WILL HOLD!
NOT SURE WE HAVE ENOUGH ICE CREAM!
BOOM!
BOOM!
ICE CREAM
WE *NEED* TO COVER THAT WINDOW!
HOW? SHOULD I PULL THE *SHADE?*
YANK!
NOT SURE THAT'S GOING TO DO MUCH GOOD.
WE'RE GOING TO *LOSE THIS* DEBATE!
OH NO! THE DOOR'S *BREAKING!* WE CAN'T *HOLD!*
LOOK OUT!
HELLO! WE HAVE TO CALL AN END TO THE MEETING! I NEED TO PICK UP MY KIDS FROM BANJO PRACTICE.
HOME SWEET HOME
PHEW!

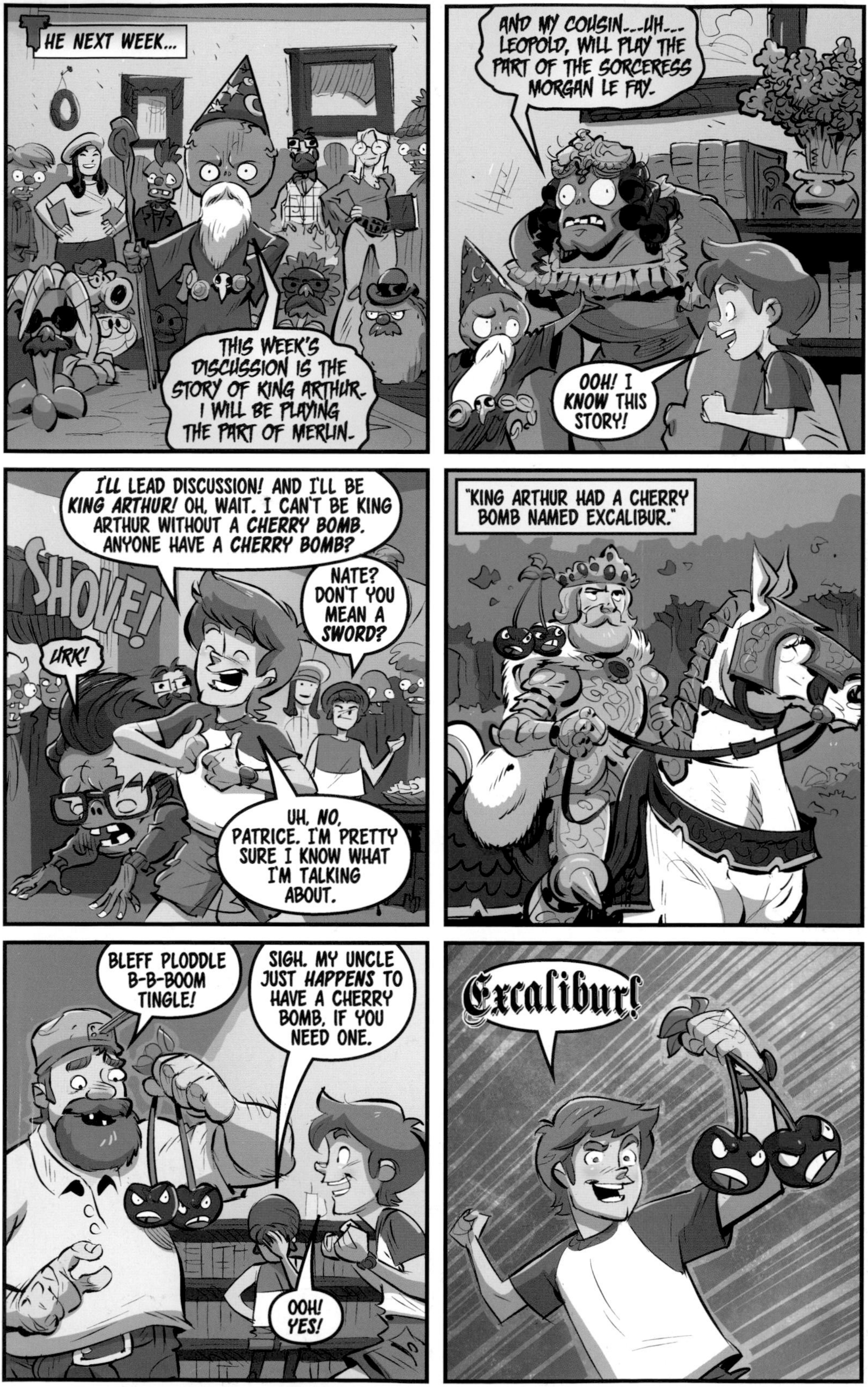
THE NEXT WEEK...
THIS WEEK'S DISCUSSION IS THE STORY OF KING ARTHUR. I WILL BE PLAYING THE PART OF MERLIN.
AND MY COUSIN...UH... LEOPOLD, WILL PLAY THE PART OF THE SORCERESS MORGAN LE FAY.
OOH! I KNOW THIS STORY!
I'LL LEAD DISCUSSION! AND I'LL BE KING ARTHUR! OH, WAIT. I CAN'T BE KING ARTHUR WITHOUT A CHERRY BOMB. ANYONE HAVE A CHERRY BOMB?
SHOVE!
URK!
NATE? DON'T YOU MEAN A SWORD?
UH, NO, PATRICE. I'M PRETTY SURE I KNOW WHAT I'M TALKING ABOUT.
"KING ARTHUR HAD A CHERRY BOMB NAMED EXCALIBUR."
BLEFF PLODDLE B-B-BOOM TINGLE!
SIGH. MY UNCLE JUST HAPPENS TO HAVE A CHERRY BOMB, IF YOU NEED ONE.
OOH! YES!
Excalibur!

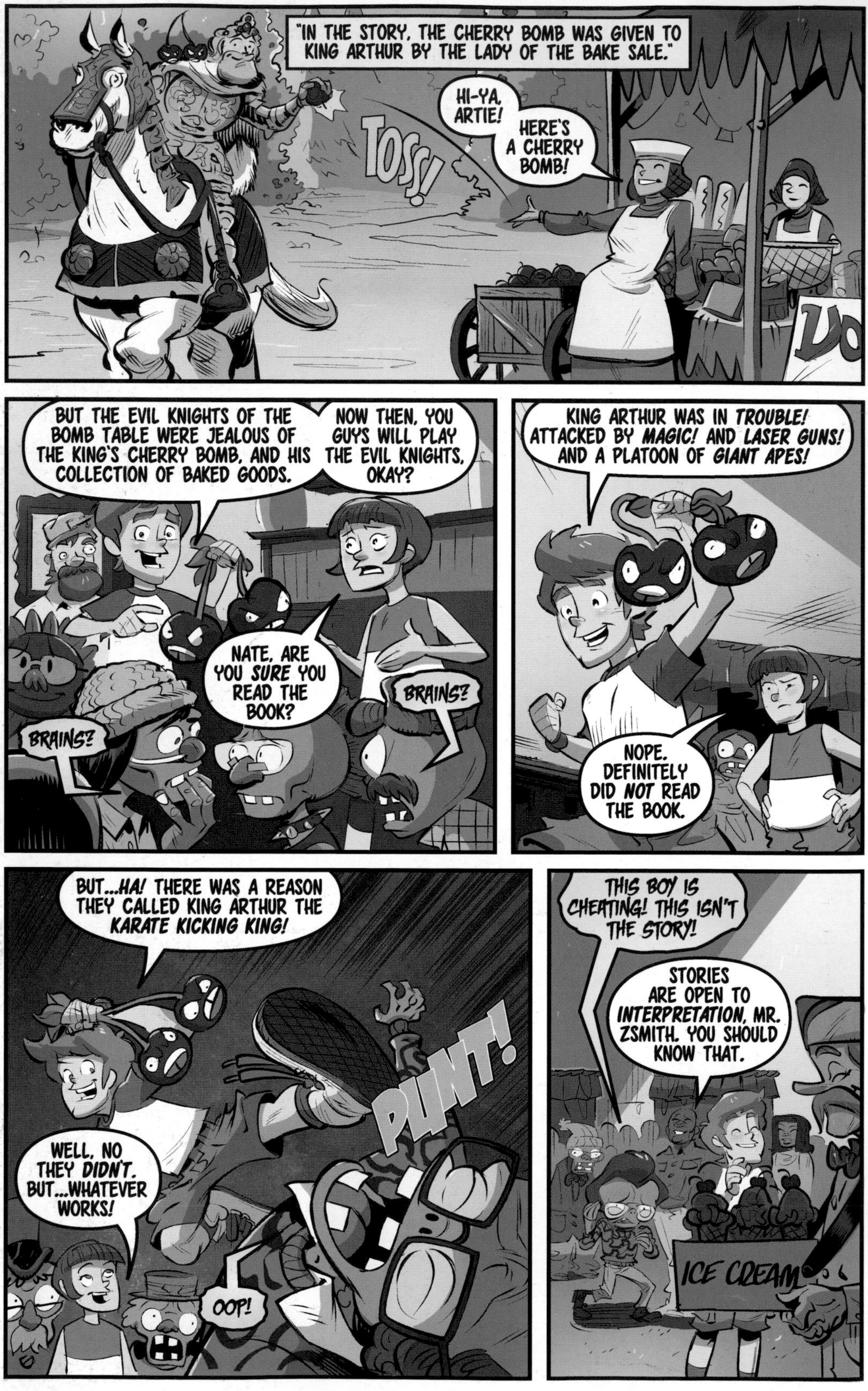
"IN THE STORY, THE CHERRY BOMB WAS GIVEN TO KING ARTHUR BY THE LADY OF THE BAKE SALE."
HI-YA, ARTIE!
HERE'S A CHERRY BOMB!
TOSS!
BUT THE EVIL KNIGHTS OF THE BOMB TABLE WERE JEALOUS OF THE KING'S CHERRY BOMB, AND HIS COLLECTION OF BAKED GOODS.
NOW THEN, YOU GUYS WILL PLAY THE EVIL KNIGHTS, OKAY?
NATE, ARE YOU SURE YOU READ THE BOOK?
BRAINS?
BRAINS?
KING ARTHUR WAS IN TROUBLE! ATTACKED BY MAGIC! AND LASER GUNS! AND A PLATOON OF GIANT APES!
NOPE. DEFINITELY DID NOT READ THE BOOK.
BUT...HA! THERE WAS A REASON THEY CALLED KING ARTHUR THE KARATE KICKING KING!
PUNT!
WELL, NO THEY DIDN'T. BUT...WHATEVER WORKS!
OOP!
THIS BOY IS CHEATING! THIS ISN'T THE STORY!
STORIES ARE OPEN TO INTERPRETATION, MR. ZSMITH. YOU SHOULD KNOW THAT.
ICE CREAM

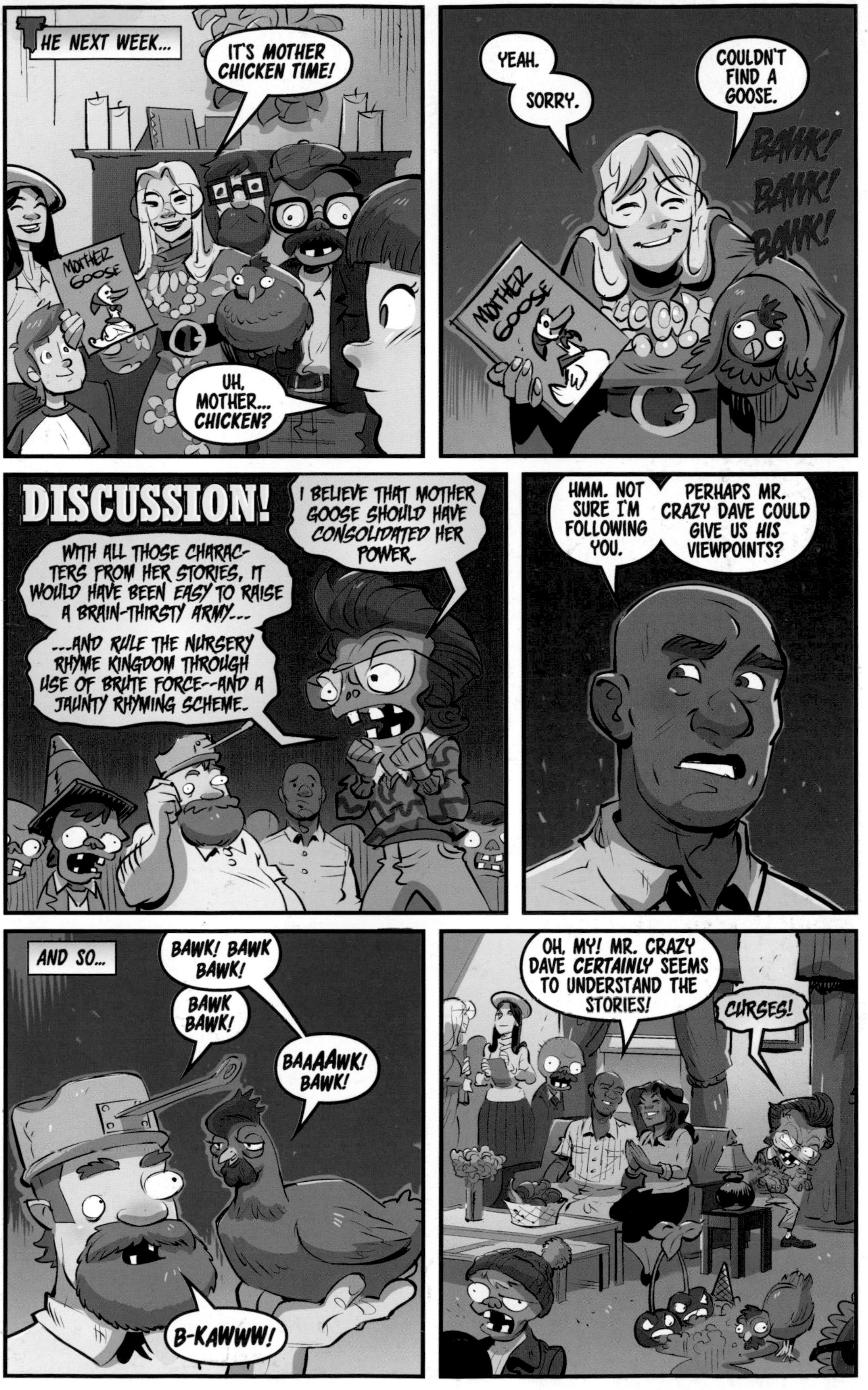
THE NEXT WEEK...
IT'S MOTHER CHICKEN TIME!
MOTHER GOOSE
UH, MOTHER... CHICKEN?
YEAH.
SORRY.
COULDN'T FIND A GOOSE.
BAWK! BAWK! BAWK!
MOTHER GOOSE
DISCUSSION!
I BELIEVE THAT MOTHER GOOSE SHOULD HAVE CONSOLIDATED HER POWER.
WITH ALL THOSE CHARACTERS FROM HER STORIES, IT WOULD HAVE BEEN EASY TO RAISE A BRAIN-THIRSTY ARMY...
...AND RULE THE NURSERY RHYME KINGDOM THROUGH USE OF BRUTE FORCE--AND A JAUNTY RHYMING SCHEME.
HMM. NOT SURE I'M FOLLOWING YOU.
PERHAPS MR. CRAZY DAVE COULD GIVE US HIS VIEWPOINTS?
AND SO...
BAWK! BAWK BAWK!
BAWK BAWK!
BAAAAWK! BAWK!
B-KAWWW!
OH, MY! MR. CRAZY DAVE CERTAINLY SEEMS TO UNDERSTAND THE STORIES!
CURSES!

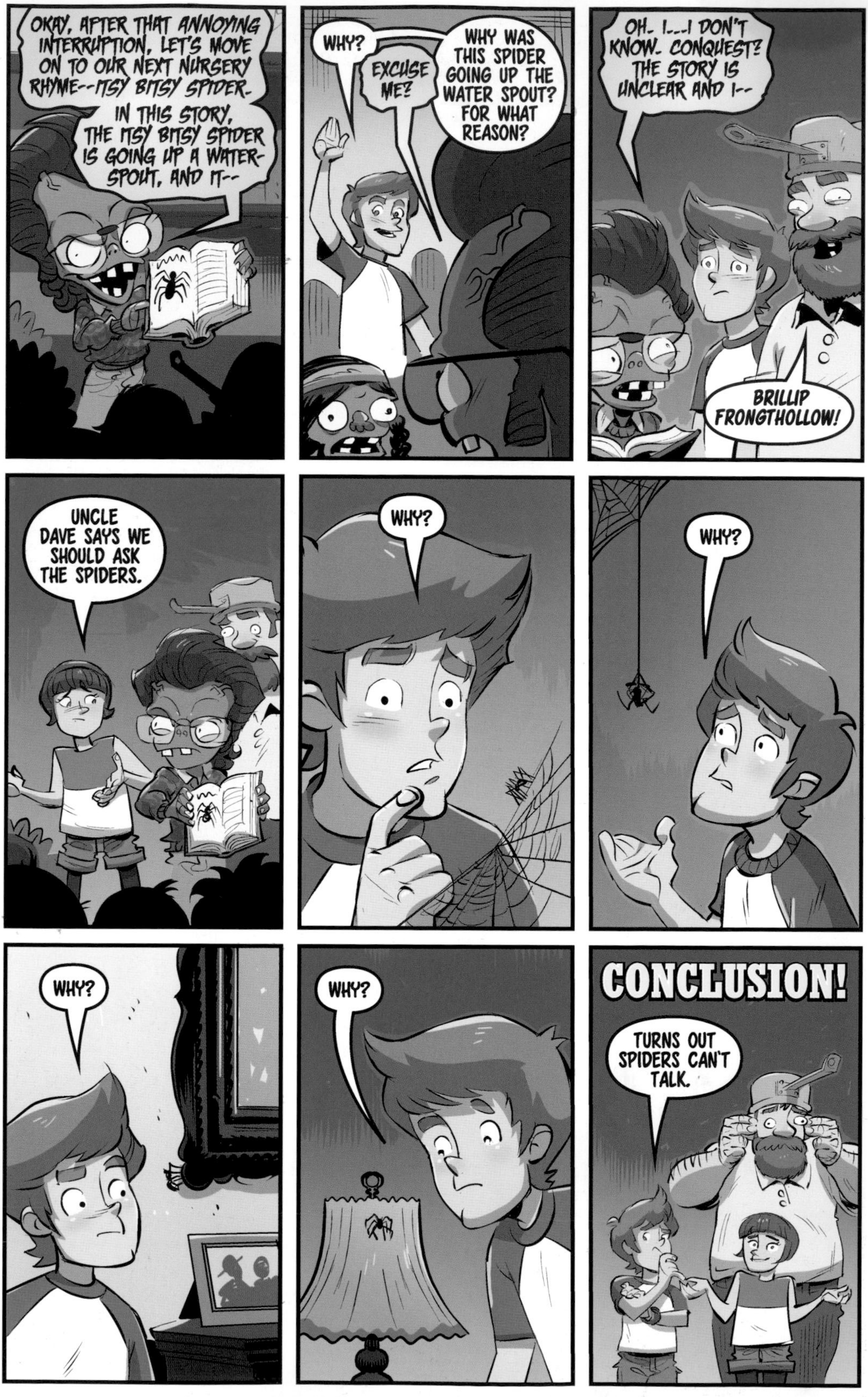
OKAY, AFTER THAT ANNOYING INTERRUPTION, LET'S MOVE ON TO OUR NEXT NURSERY RHYME--ITSY BITSY SPIDER.
IN THIS STORY, THE ITSY BITSY SPIDER IS GOING UP A WATER-SPOUT, AND IT--
WHY?
EXCUSE ME?
WHY WAS THIS SPIDER GOING UP THE WATER SPOUT? FOR WHAT REASON?
OH. I...I DON'T KNOW. CONQUEST? THE STORY IS UNCLEAR AND I--
BRILLIP FRONGTHOLLOW!
UNCLE DAVE SAYS WE SHOULD ASK THE SPIDERS.
WHY?
WHY?
WHY?
WHY?
CONCLUSION!
TURNS OUT SPIDERS CAN'T TALK.

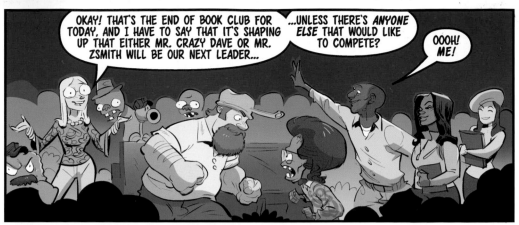

OKAY! THAT'S THE END OF BOOK CLUB FOR TODAY, AND I HAVE TO SAY THAT IT'S SHAPING UP THAT EITHER MR. CRAZY DAVE OR MR. ZSMITH WILL BE OUR NEXT LEADER...

...UNLESS THERE'S *ANYONE ELSE* THAT WOULD LIKE TO COMPETE?

OOOH! ME!

I'VE ALWAYS THOUGHT IT WOULD BE JUST *GRAND* TO LEAD THE BOOK CLUB!

MY VISION IS THAT WE COULD EACH WRITE ESSAYS TO PRESENT ON A WEEKLY BASIS, AND WE...

...WE...

BRAINS?

UH...

...AS I WAS SAYING, I THINK MR. ZSMITH WOULD BE AN EXCELLENT CANDIDATE FOR PRESIDENT OF BOOK CLUB.

CLAP CLAP

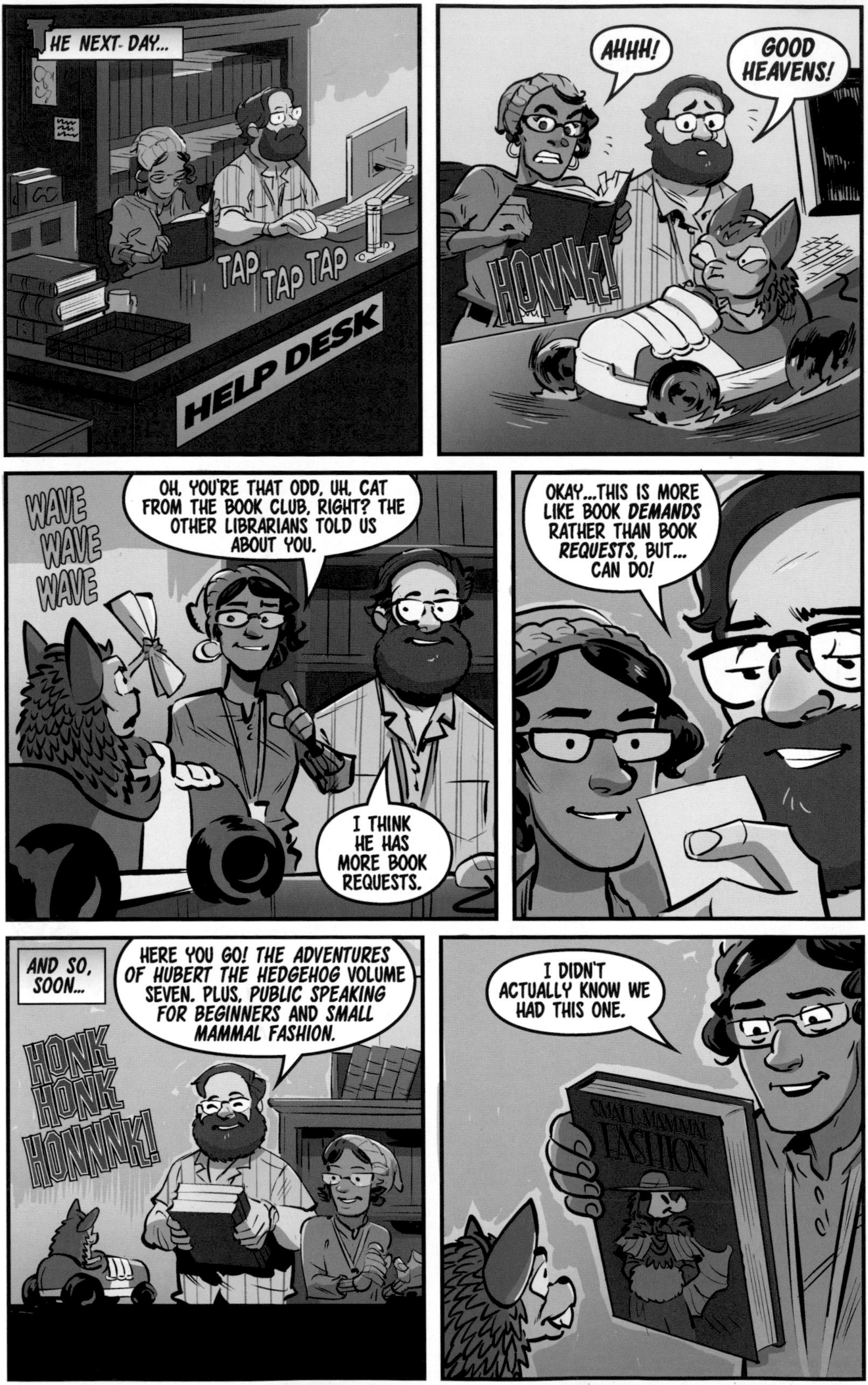
THE NEXT DAY...
TAP TAP TAP
HELP DESK
AHHH!
GOOD HEAVENS!
HONNK!
WAVE WAVE WAVE
OH, YOU'RE THAT ODD, UH, CAT FROM THE BOOK CLUB, RIGHT? THE OTHER LIBRARIANS TOLD US ABOUT YOU.
I THINK HE HAS MORE BOOK REQUESTS.
OKAY...THIS IS MORE LIKE BOOK DEMANDS RATHER THAN BOOK REQUESTS, BUT... CAN DO!
AND SO, SOON...
HERE YOU GO! THE ADVENTURES OF HUBERT THE HEDGEHOG VOLUME SEVEN. PLUS, PUBLIC SPEAKING FOR BEGINNERS AND SMALL MAMMAL FASHION.
HONK HONK HONNNK!
I DIDN'T ACTUALLY KNOW WE HAD THIS ONE.
SMALL MAMMAL FASHION

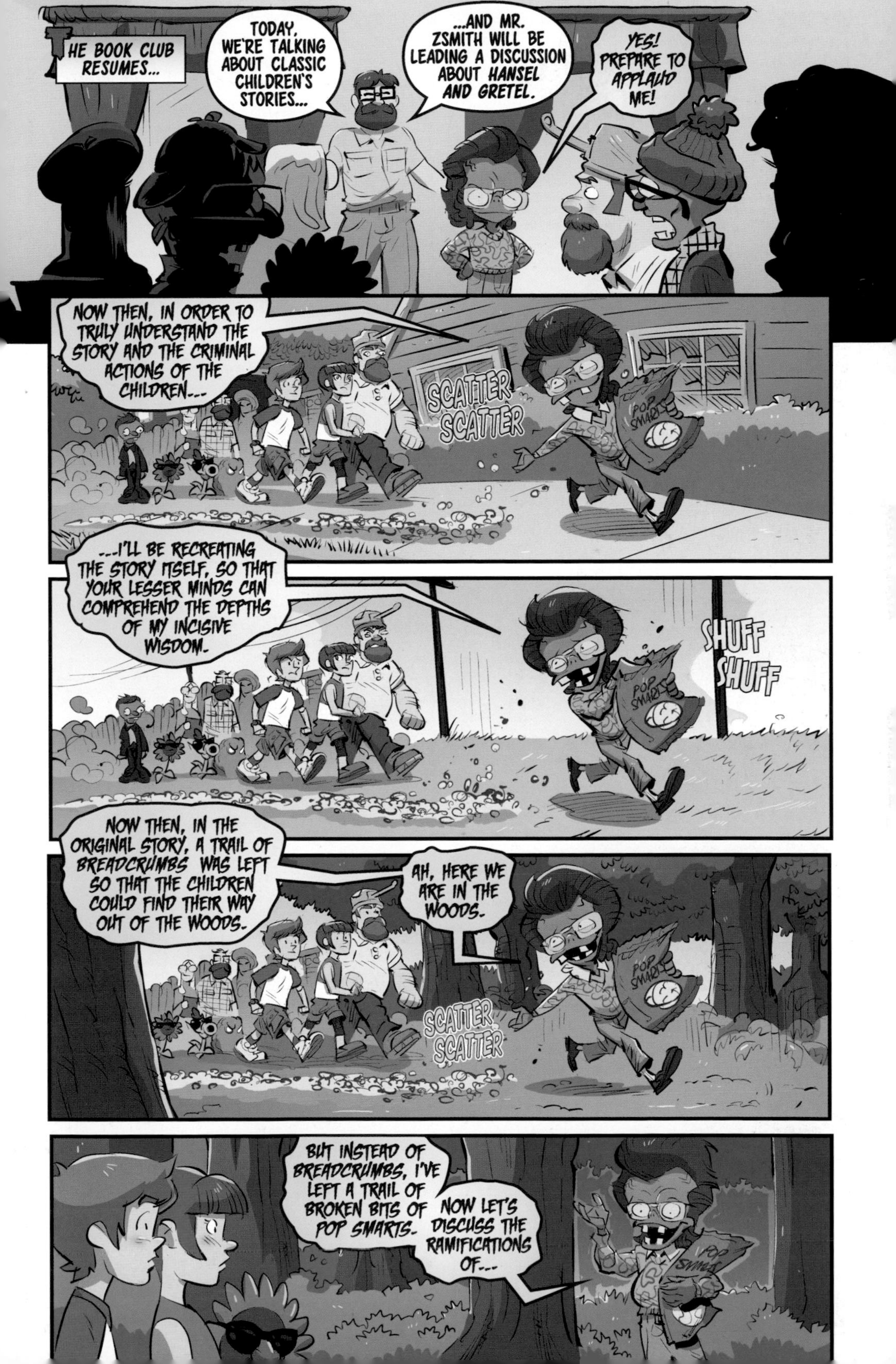
THE BOOK CLUB RESUMES...
TODAY, WE'RE TALKING ABOUT CLASSIC CHILDREN'S STORIES...
...AND MR. ZSMITH WILL BE LEADING A DISCUSSION ABOUT HANSEL AND GRETEL.
YES! PREPARE TO APPLAUD ME!
NOW THEN, IN ORDER TO TRULY UNDERSTAND THE STORY AND THE CRIMINAL ACTIONS OF THE CHILDREN...
SCATTER SCATTER
POP SMARTS
...I'LL BE RECREATING THE STORY ITSELF, SO THAT YOUR LESSER MINDS CAN COMPREHEND THE DEPTHS OF MY INCISIVE WISDOM.
SHUFF SHUFF
NOW THEN, IN THE ORIGINAL STORY, A TRAIL OF BREADCRUMBS WAS LEFT SO THAT THE CHILDREN COULD FIND THEIR WAY OUT OF THE WOODS.
AH, HERE WE ARE IN THE WOODS.
SCATTER SCATTER
BUT INSTEAD OF BREADCRUMBS, I'VE LEFT A TRAIL OF BROKEN BITS OF POP SMARTS.
NOW LET'S DISCUSS THE RAMIFICATIONS OF...

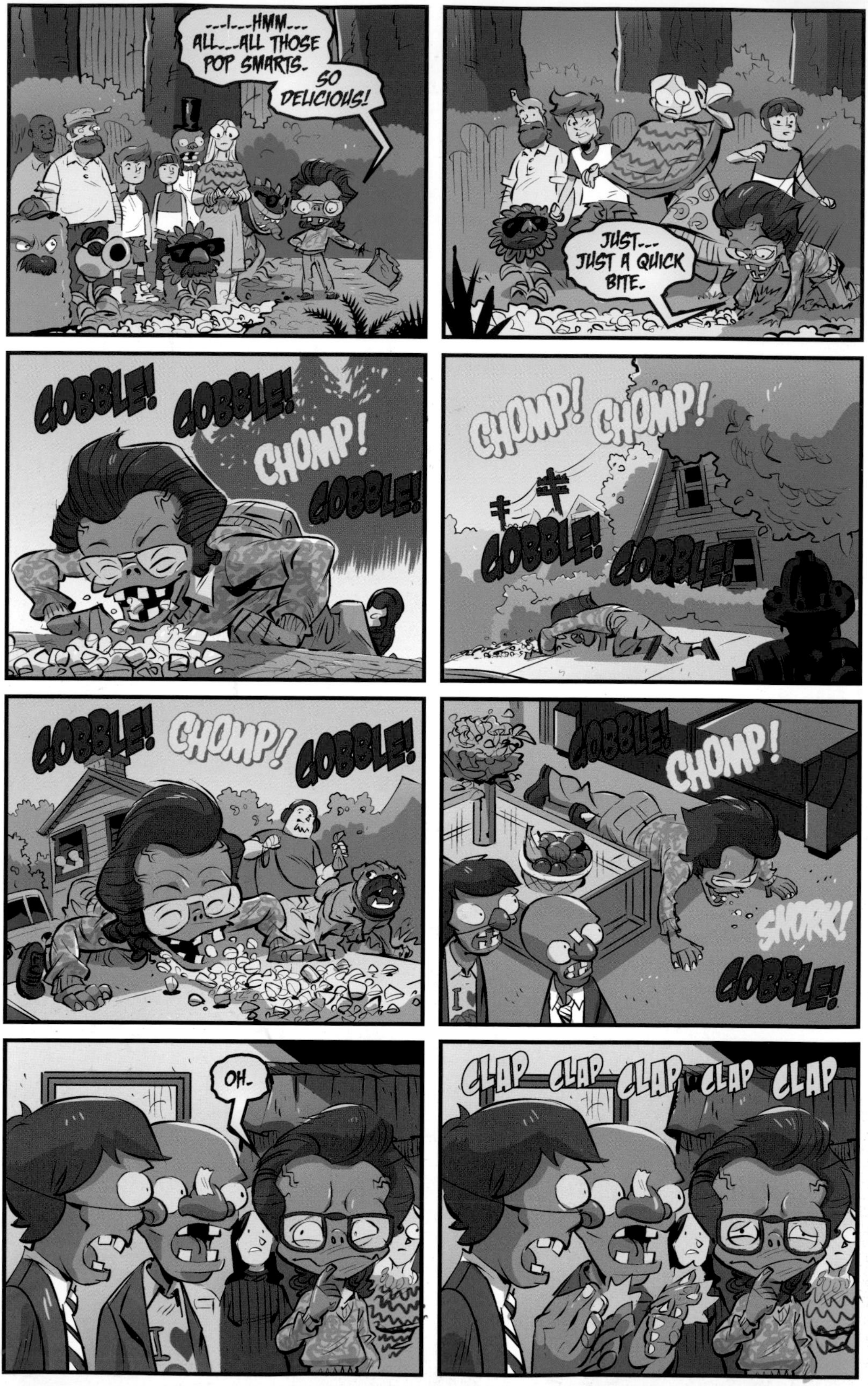
...I...HMM...
ALL...ALL THOSE POP SMARTS.
SO DELICIOUS!
JUST... JUST A QUICK BITE.
GOBBLE! GOBBLE!
CHOMP!
GOBBLE!
CHOMP! CHOMP!
GOBBLE! GOBBLE!
GOBBLE! CHOMP! GOBBLE!
GOBBLE!
CHOMP!
SNORK!
GOBBLE!
OH.
CLAP CLAP CLAP CLAP CLAP

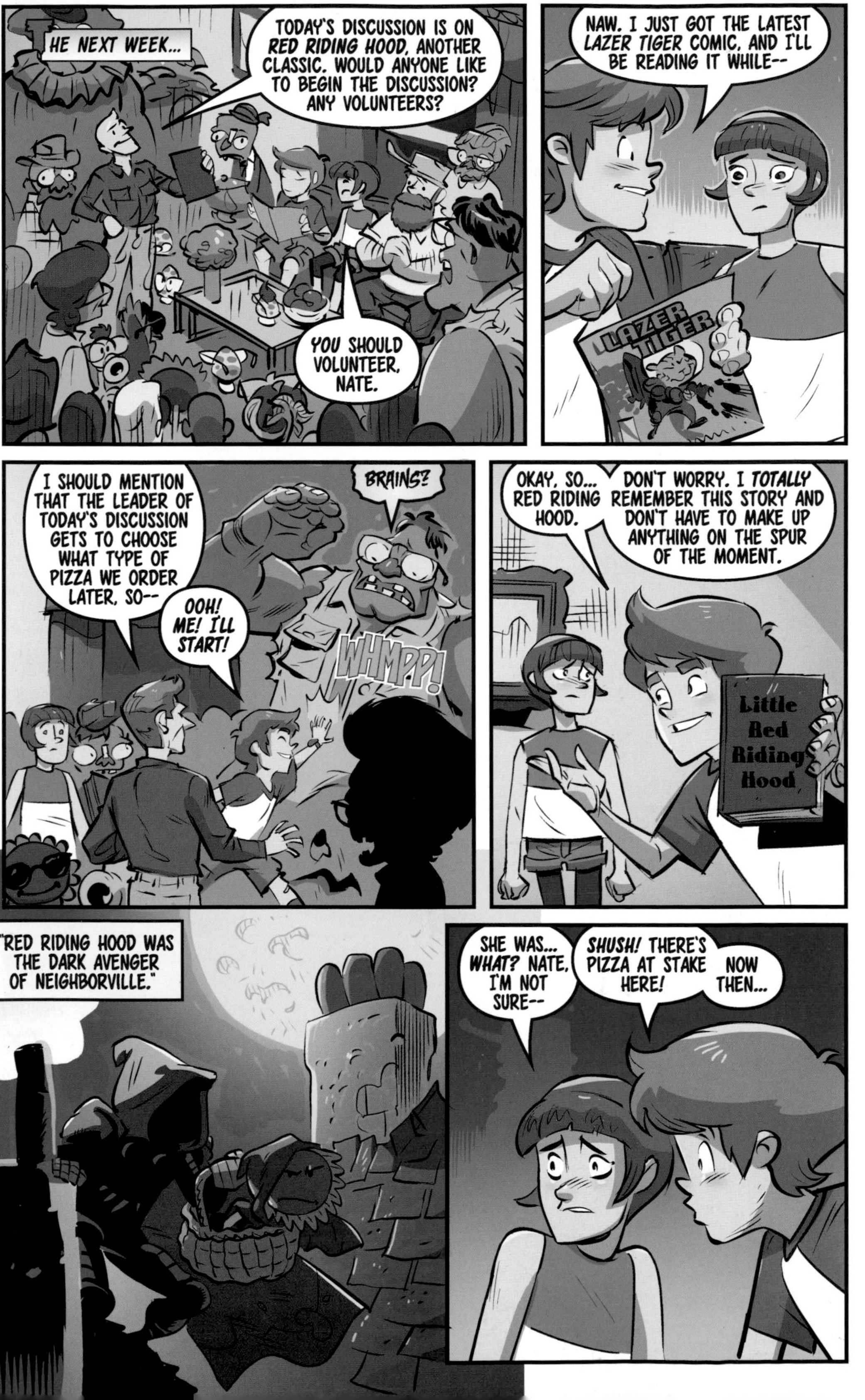
HE NEXT WEEK...
TODAY'S DISCUSSION IS ON RED RIDING HOOD, ANOTHER CLASSIC. WOULD ANYONE LIKE TO BEGIN THE DISCUSSION? ANY VOLUNTEERS?
YOU SHOULD VOLUNTEER, NATE.
NAW. I JUST GOT THE LATEST LAZER TIGER COMIC, AND I'LL BE READING IT WHILE--
LAZER TIGER
I SHOULD MENTION THAT THE LEADER OF TODAY'S DISCUSSION GETS TO CHOOSE WHAT TYPE OF PIZZA WE ORDER LATER, SO--
BRAINS?
OOH! ME! I'LL START!
WHMPP!
OKAY, SO... RED RIDING HOOD.
DON'T WORRY. I TOTALLY REMEMBER THIS STORY AND DON'T HAVE TO MAKE UP ANYTHING ON THE SPUR OF THE MOMENT.
Little Red Riding Hood
"RED RIDING HOOD WAS THE DARK AVENGER OF NEIGHBORVILLE."
SHE WAS... WHAT? NATE, I'M NOT SURE--
SHUSH! THERE'S PIZZA AT STAKE HERE!
NOW THEN...

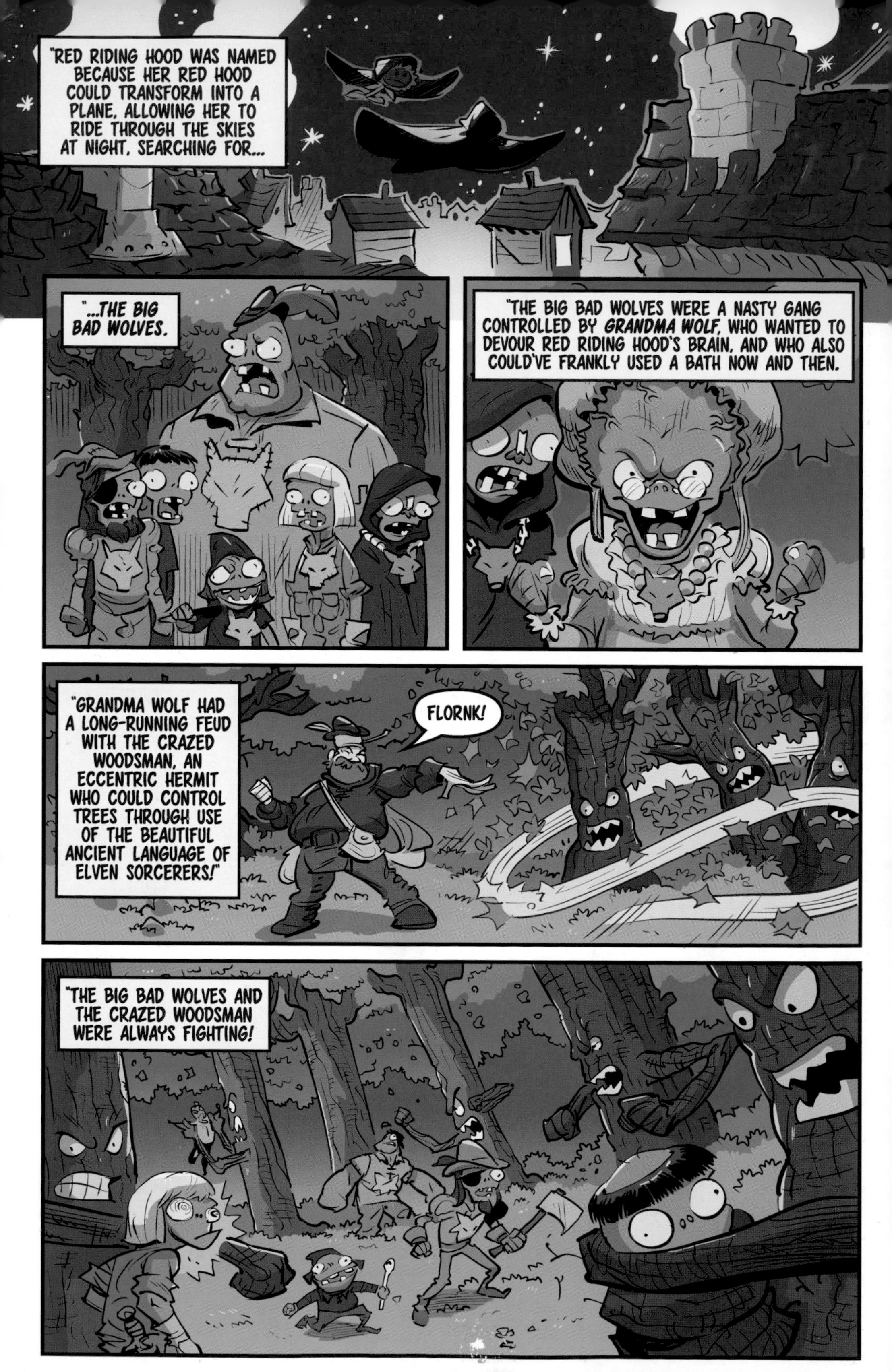
"RED RIDING HOOD WAS NAMED BECAUSE HER RED HOOD COULD TRANSFORM INTO A PLANE, ALLOWING HER TO RIDE THROUGH THE SKIES AT NIGHT, SEARCHING FOR...
"...THE BIG BAD WOLVES.
"THE BIG BAD WOLVES WERE A NASTY GANG CONTROLLED BY GRANDMA WOLF, WHO WANTED TO DEVOUR RED RIDING HOOD'S BRAIN, AND WHO ALSO COULD'VE FRANKLY USED A BATH NOW AND THEN.
"GRANDMA WOLF HAD A LONG-RUNNING FEUD WITH THE CRAZED WOODSMAN, AN ECCENTRIC HERMIT WHO COULD CONTROL TREES THROUGH USE OF THE BEAUTIFUL ANCIENT LANGUAGE OF ELVEN SORCERERS!"
FLORNK!
"THE BIG BAD WOLVES AND THE CRAZED WOODSMAN WERE ALWAYS FIGHTING!

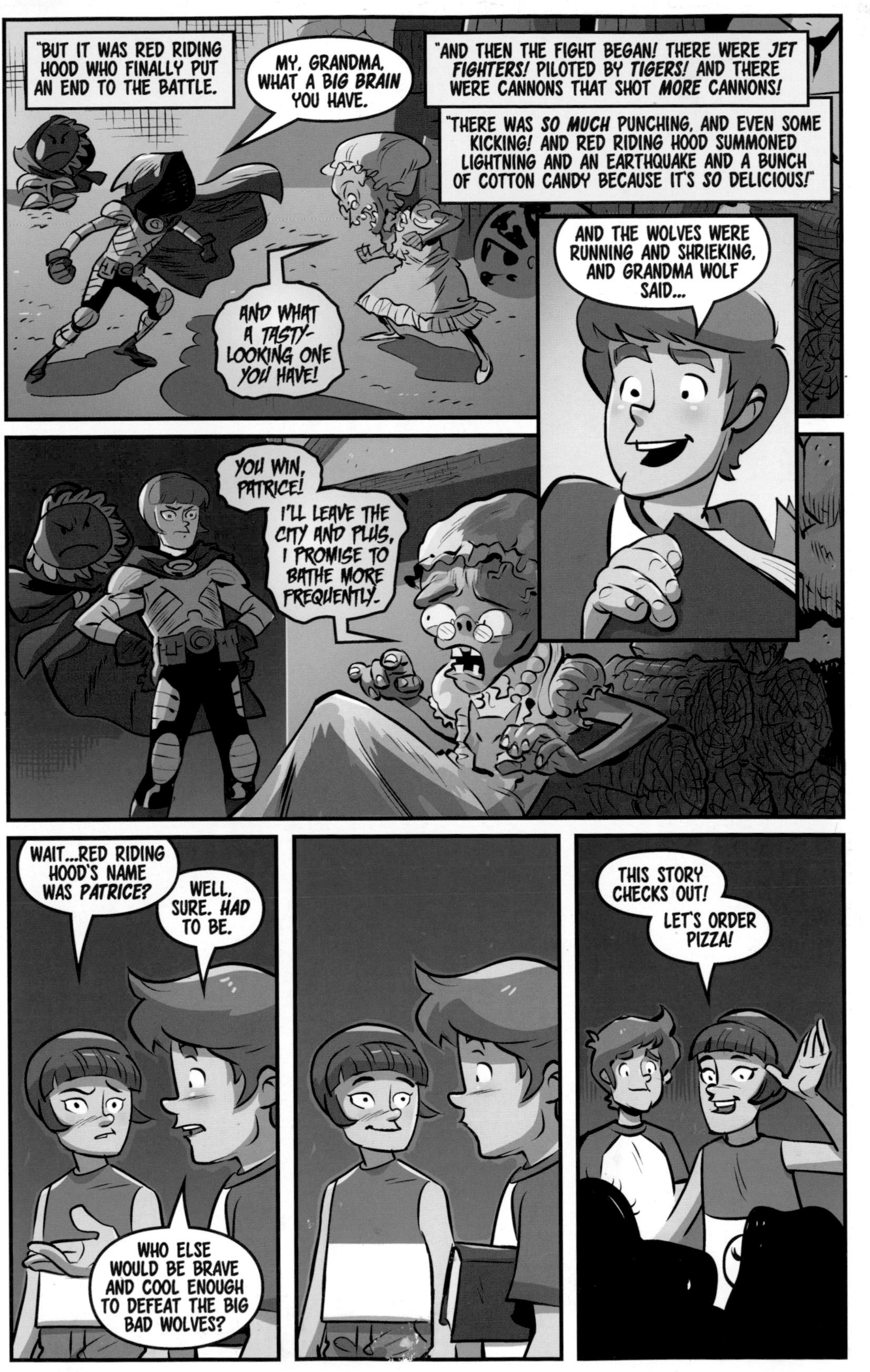
"BUT IT WAS RED RIDING HOOD WHO FINALLY PUT AN END TO THE BATTLE.
MY, GRANDMA, WHAT A BIG BRAIN YOU HAVE.
AND WHAT A TASTY-LOOKING ONE YOU HAVE!
"AND THEN THE FIGHT BEGAN! THERE WERE JET FIGHTERS! PILOTED BY TIGERS! AND THERE WERE CANNONS THAT SHOT MORE CANNONS!
"THERE WAS SO MUCH PUNCHING, AND EVEN SOME KICKING! AND RED RIDING HOOD SUMMONED LIGHTNING AND AN EARTHQUAKE AND A BUNCH OF COTTON CANDY BECAUSE IT'S SO DELICIOUS!"
AND THE WOLVES WERE RUNNING AND SHRIEKING, AND GRANDMA WOLF SAID...
YOU WIN, PATRICE!
I'LL LEAVE THE CITY AND PLUS, I PROMISE TO BATHE MORE FREQUENTLY.
WAIT...RED RIDING HOOD'S NAME WAS PATRICE?
WELL, SURE. HAD TO BE.
WHO ELSE WOULD BE BRAVE AND COOL ENOUGH TO DEFEAT THE BIG BAD WOLVES?
THIS STORY CHECKS OUT!
LET'S ORDER PIZZA!

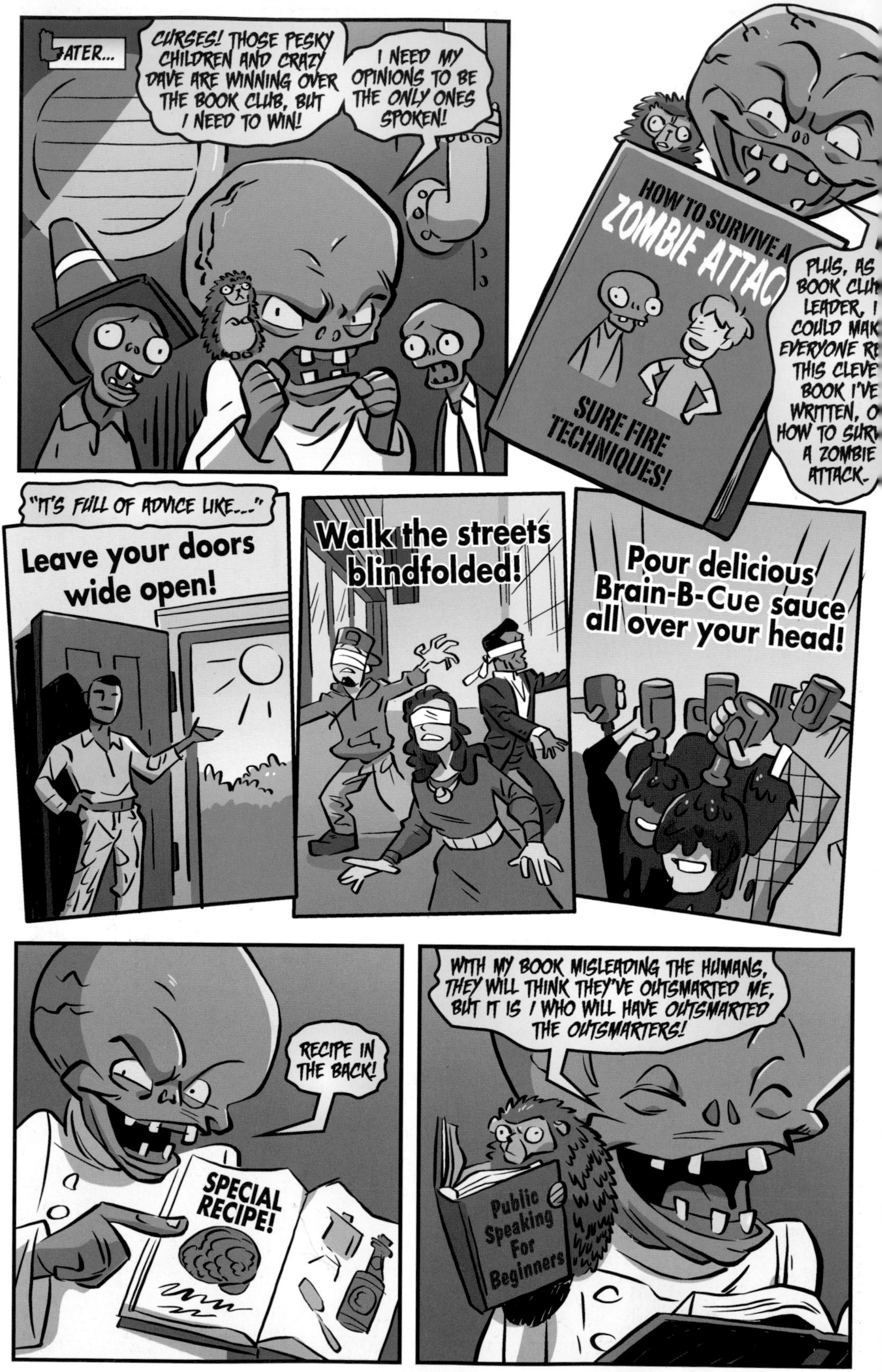
LATER...
CURSES! THOSE PESKY CHILDREN AND CRAZY DAVE ARE WINNING OVER THE BOOK CLUB, BUT I NEED TO WIN!
I NEED MY OPINIONS TO BE THE ONLY ONES SPOKEN!
HOW TO SURVIVE A ZOMBIE ATTAC
SURE FIRE TECHNIQUES!
PLUS, AS BOOK CLU LEADER, I COULD MAK EVERYONE RE THIS CLEVE BOOK I'VE WRITTEN, O HOW TO SURV A ZOMBIE ATTACK.
"IT'S FULL OF ADVICE LIKE..."
Leave your doors wide open!
Walk the streets blindfolded!
Pour delicious Brain-B-Cue sauce all over your head!
RECIPE IN THE BACK!
SPECIAL RECIPE!
WITH MY BOOK MISLEADING THE HUMANS, THEY WILL THINK THEY'VE OUTSMARTED ME, BUT IT IS I WHO WILL HAVE OUTSMARTED THE OUTSMARTERS!
Public Speaking For Beginners

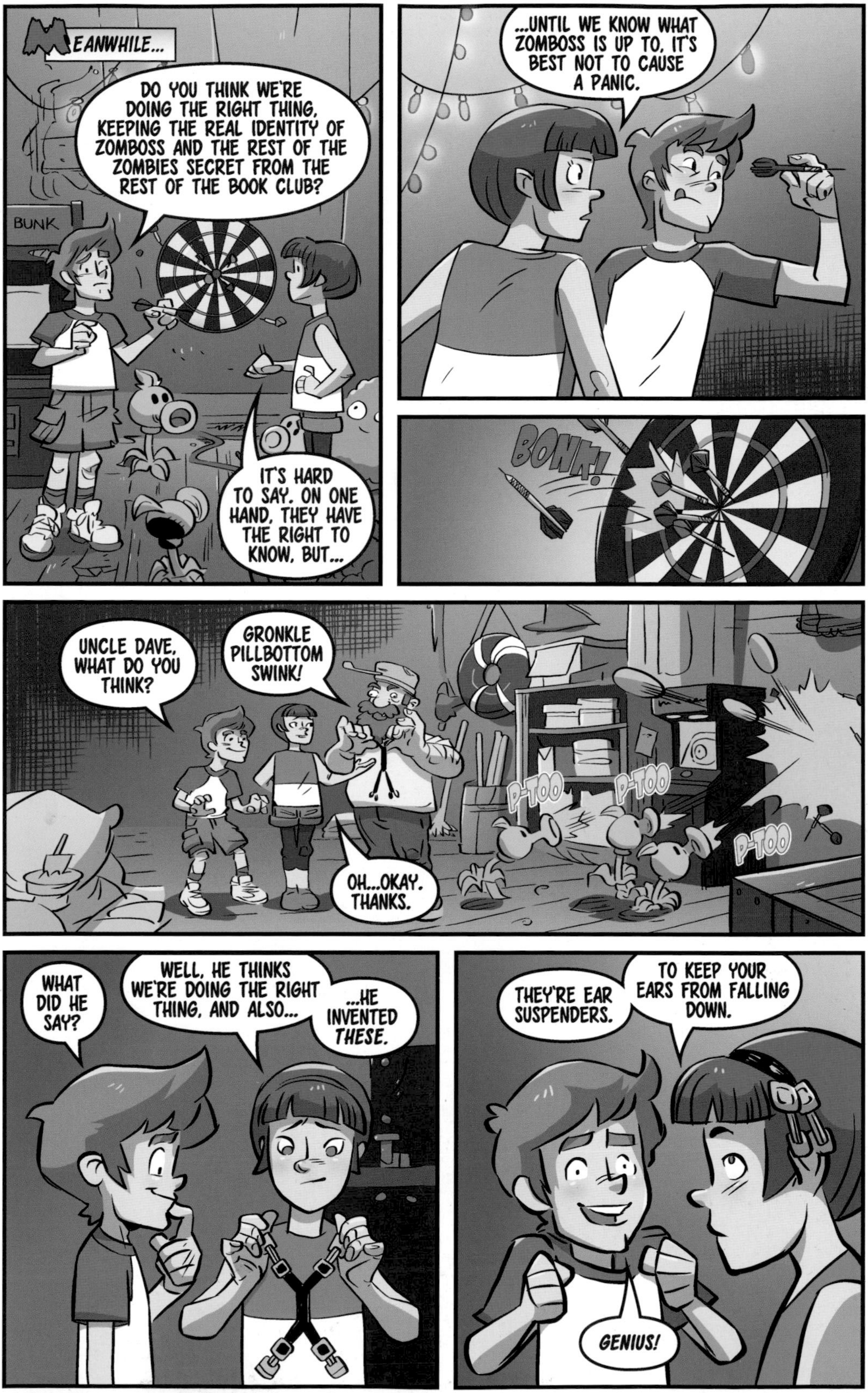
MEANWHILE...
DO YOU THINK WE'RE DOING THE RIGHT THING, KEEPING THE REAL IDENTITY OF ZOMBOSS AND THE REST OF THE ZOMBIES SECRET FROM THE REST OF THE BOOK CLUB?
BUNK
IT'S HARD TO SAY. ON ONE HAND, THEY HAVE THE RIGHT TO KNOW, BUT...
...UNTIL WE KNOW WHAT ZOMBOSS IS UP TO, IT'S BEST NOT TO CAUSE A PANIC.
BONK!
UNCLE DAVE, WHAT DO YOU THINK?
GRONKLE PILLBOTTOM SWINK!
OH...OKAY. THANKS.
P-TOO
P-TOO
P-TOO
WHAT DID HE SAY?
WELL, HE THINKS WE'RE DOING THE RIGHT THING, AND ALSO...
...HE INVENTED THESE.
THEY'RE EAR SUSPENDERS.
TO KEEP YOUR EARS FROM FALLING DOWN.
GENIUS!

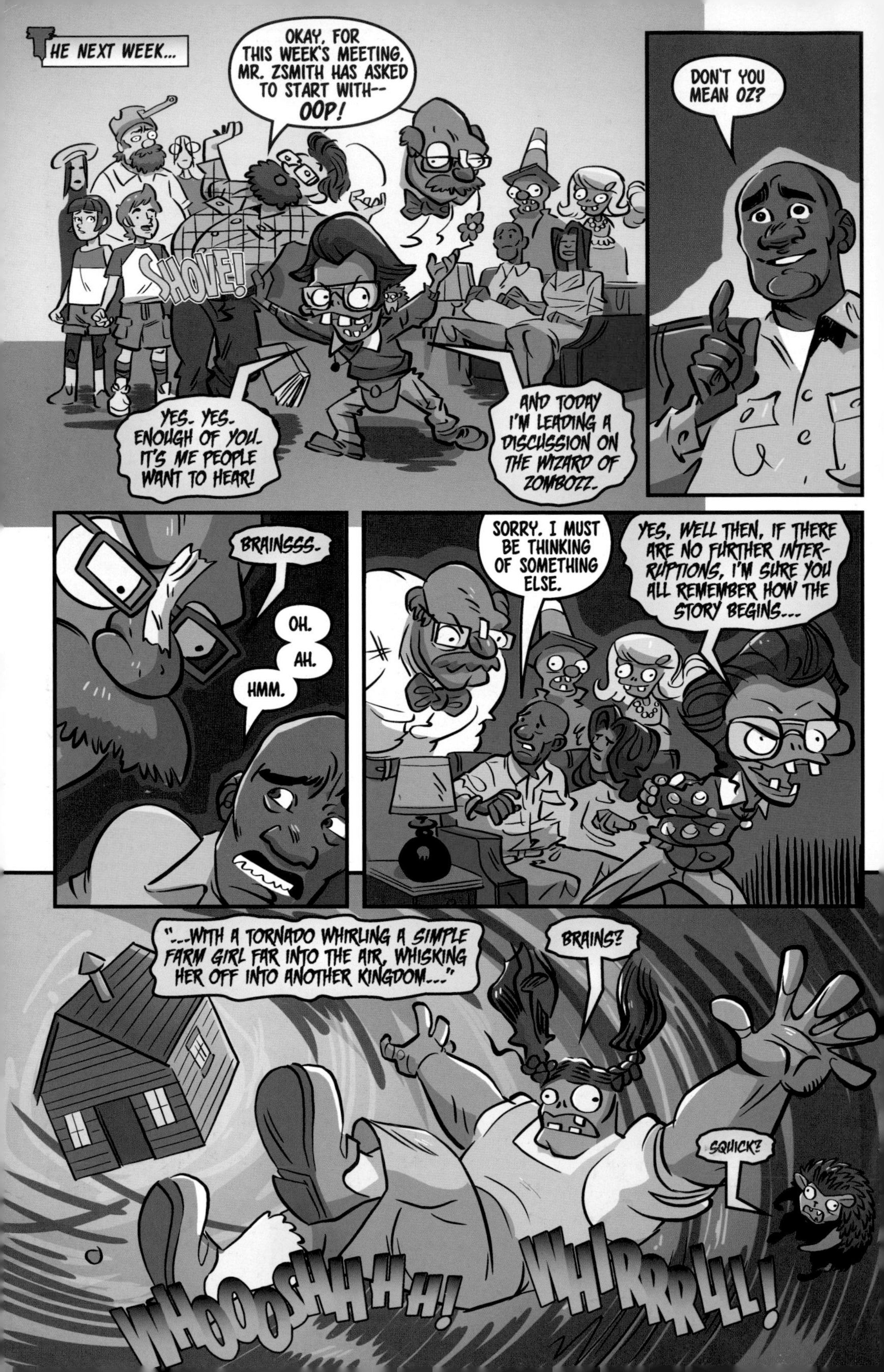
THE NEXT WEEK...
OKAY, FOR THIS WEEK'S MEETING, MR. ZSMITH HAS ASKED TO START WITH-- OOP!
SHOVE!
YES. YES. ENOUGH OF YOU. IT'S ME PEOPLE WANT TO HEAR!
AND TODAY I'M LEADING A DISCUSSION ON THE WIZARD OF ZOMBOZZ.
DON'T YOU MEAN OZ?
BRAINSSS.
OH.
AH.
HMM.
SORRY. I MUST BE THINKING OF SOMETHING ELSE.
YES, WELL THEN, IF THERE ARE NO FURTHER INTER-RUPTIONS, I'M SURE YOU ALL REMEMBER HOW THE STORY BEGINS...
"...WITH A TORNADO WHIRLING A SIMPLE FARM GIRL FAR INTO THE AIR, WHISKING HER OFF INTO ANOTHER KINGDOM..."
BRAINS?
SQUICK?
WHOOOSHHHHH!
WHIRRRRLL!

"WHERE SHE LANDED IN DAINTY FASHION, AND THEN..."

FWHOOOSH

OH, DARN IT.

"...JUST BY CHANCE FOUND A PAIR OF BEAUTIFUL SHOES!"

"THEY FIT PERFECTLY!"

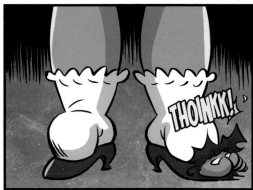

THOINKK!

"THE FARM GIRL SOON SET OFF TO FIND THE WIZARD OF ZOMBOZZ..."

OH, SUCH BEAUTIFUL SHOES!

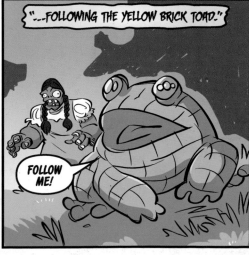

"...FOLLOWING THE YELLOW BRICK TOAD."

FOLLOW ME!

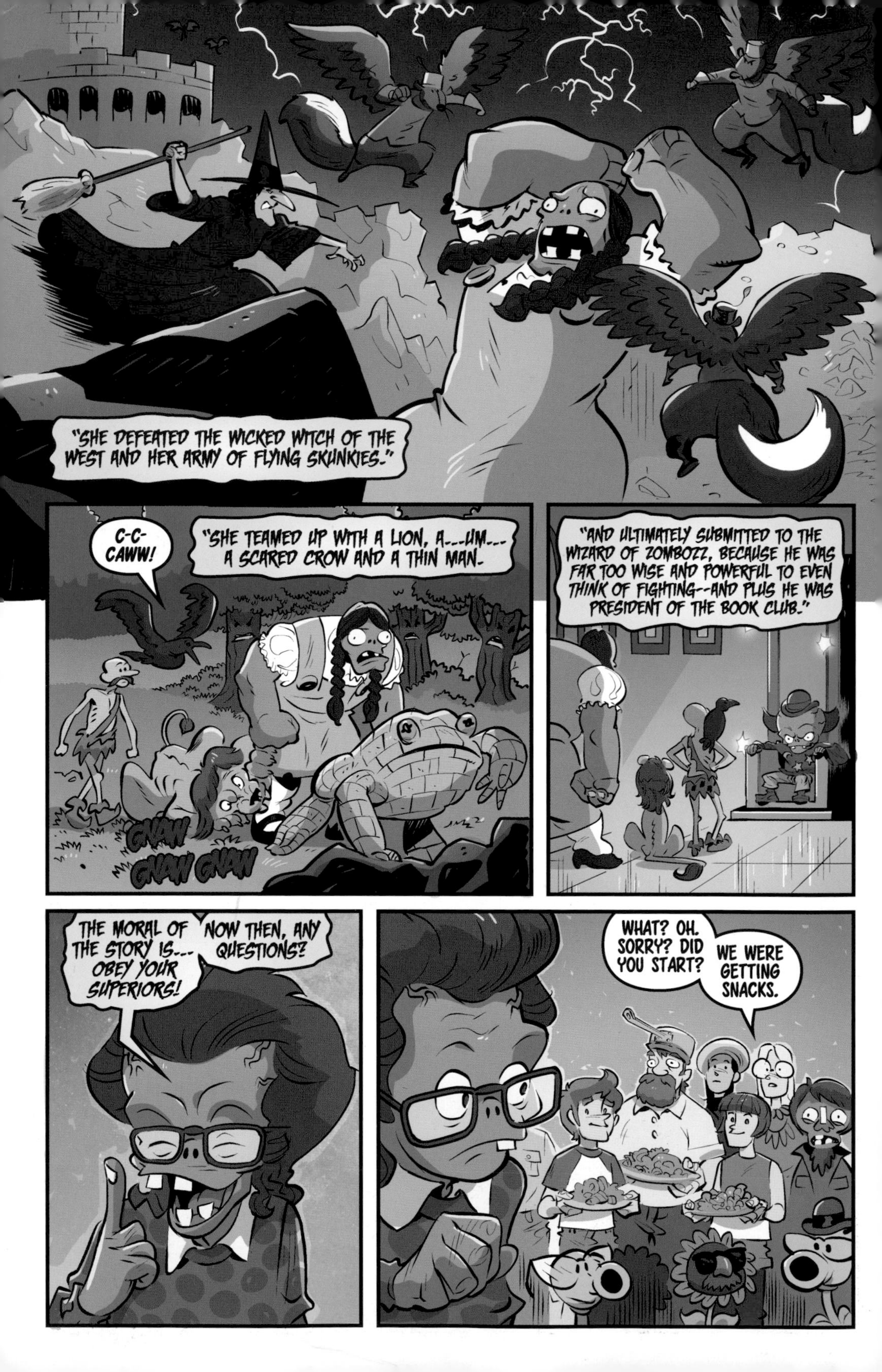
"SHE DEFEATED THE WICKED WITCH OF THE WEST AND HER ARMY OF FLYING SKUNKIES."
C-C-CAWW!
"SHE TEAMED UP WITH A LION, A---UM--- A SCARED CROW AND A THIN MAN.
GNAW GNAW GNAW
"AND ULTIMATELY SUBMITTED TO THE WIZARD OF ZOMBOZZ, BECAUSE HE WAS FAR TOO WISE AND POWERFUL TO EVEN THINK OF FIGHTING--AND PLUS HE WAS PRESIDENT OF THE BOOK CLUB."
THE MORAL OF THE STORY IS... OBEY YOUR SUPERIORS!
NOW THEN, ANY QUESTIONS?
WHAT? OH. SORRY? DID YOU START?
WE WERE GETTING SNACKS.

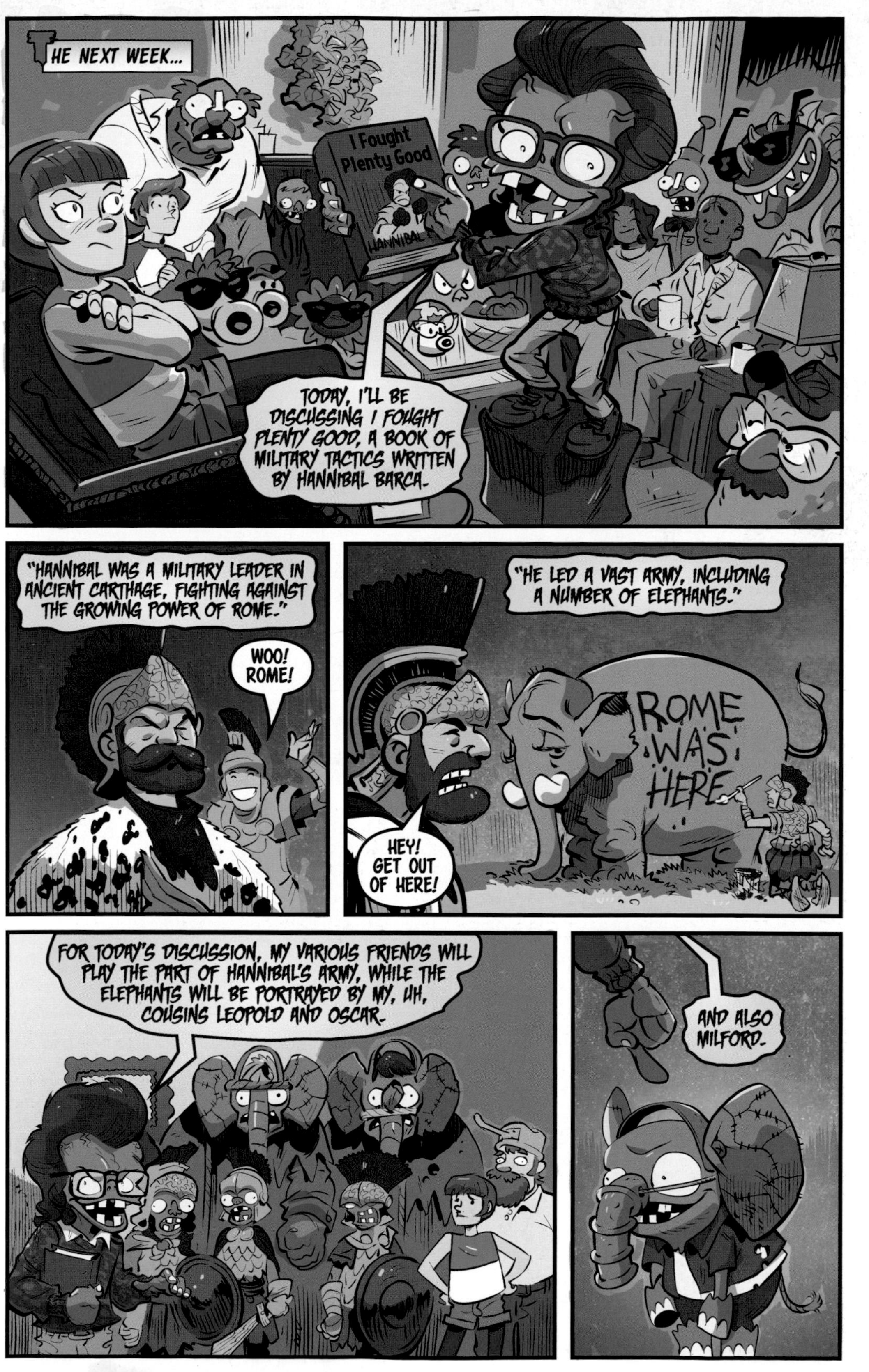
THE NEXT WEEK...
I Fought Plenty Good
HANNIBAL
TODAY, I'LL BE DISCUSSING I FOUGHT PLENTY GOOD, A BOOK OF MILITARY TACTICS WRITTEN BY HANNIBAL BARCA.
"HANNIBAL WAS A MILITARY LEADER IN ANCIENT CARTHAGE, FIGHTING AGAINST THE GROWING POWER OF ROME."
WOO! ROME!
"HE LED A VAST ARMY, INCLUDING A NUMBER OF ELEPHANTS."
ROME WAS HERE
HEY! GET OUT OF HERE!
FOR TODAY'S DISCUSSION, MY VARIOUS FRIENDS WILL PLAY THE PART OF HANNIBAL'S ARMY, WHILE THE ELEPHANTS WILL BE PORTRAYED BY MY, UH, COUSINS LEOPOLD AND OSCAR.
AND ALSO MILFORD.

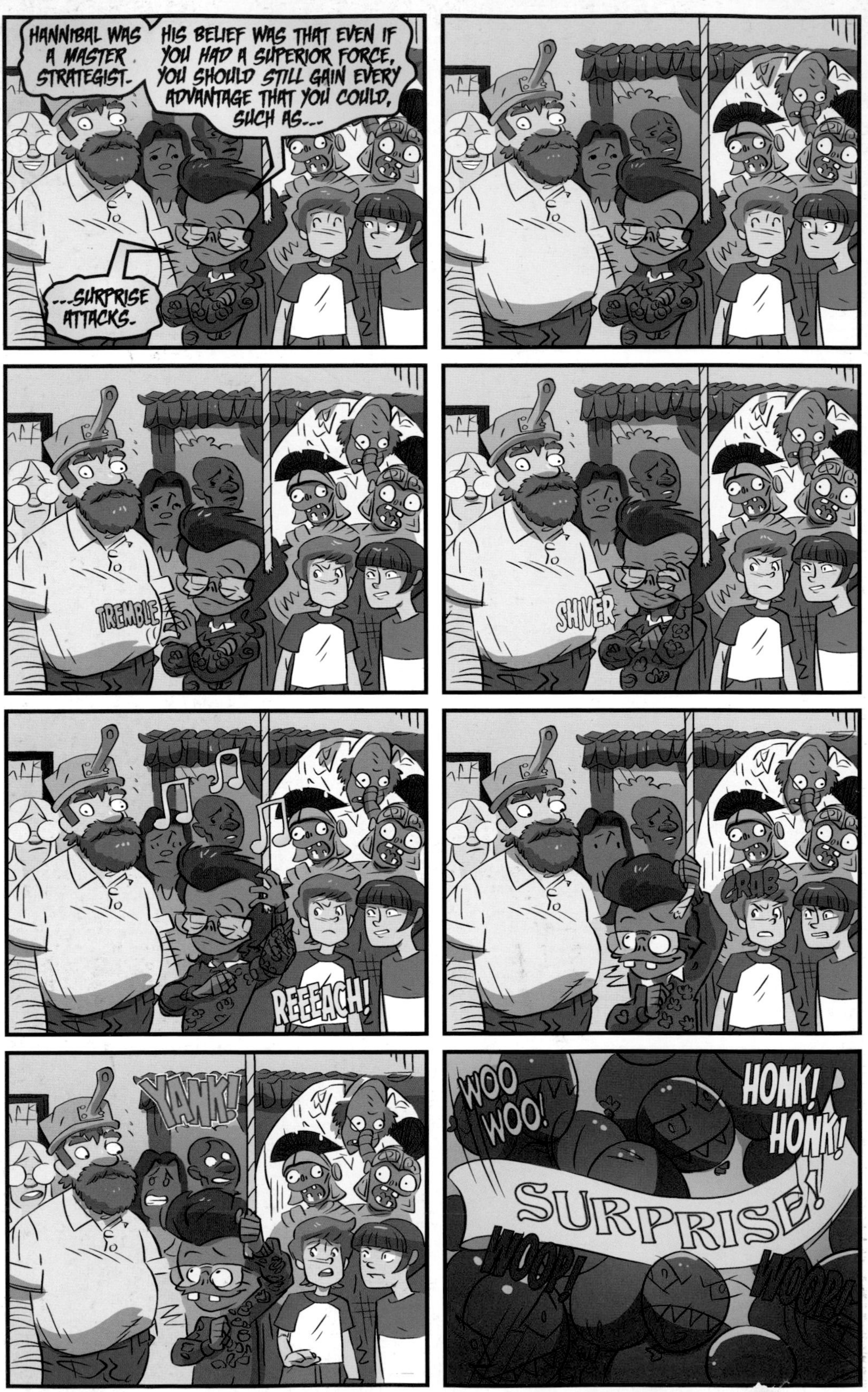
HANNIBAL WAS A MASTER STRATEGIST.
HIS BELIEF WAS THAT EVEN IF YOU HAD A SUPERIOR FORCE, YOU SHOULD STILL GAIN EVERY ADVANTAGE THAT YOU COULD, SUCH AS...
...SURPRISE ATTACKS.
TREMBLE
SHIVER
REEEACH!
GRAB
YANK!
WOO WOO!
HONK! HONK!
SURPRISE!
WOOP!
WOOP!

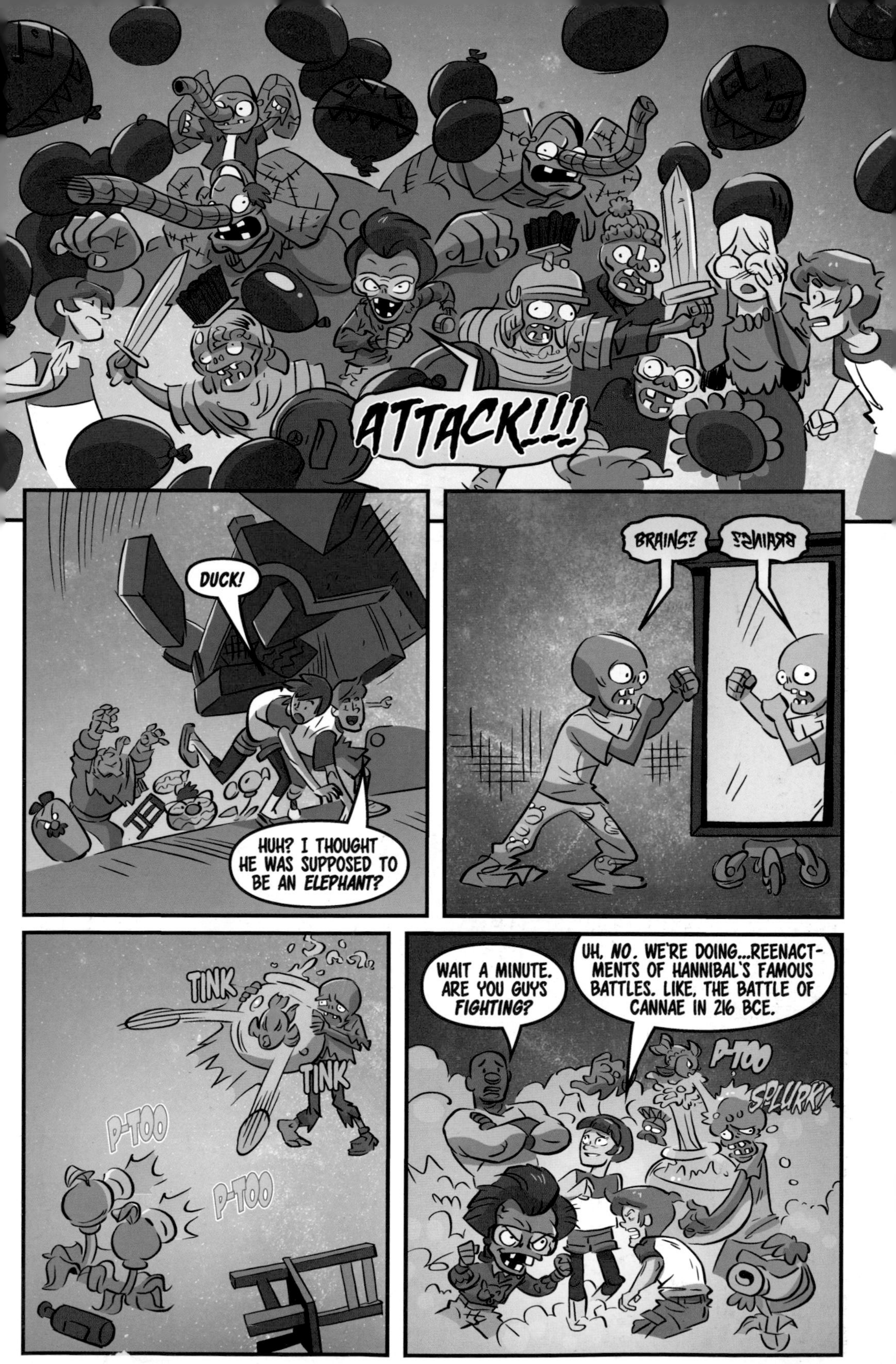
ATTACK!!!
DUCK!
HUH? I THOUGHT HE WAS SUPPOSED TO BE AN *ELEPHANT?*
BRAINS?
BRAINS?
TINK
TINK
P-TOO
P-TOO
WAIT A MINUTE. ARE YOU GUYS *FIGHTING?*
UH, *NO*. WE'RE DOING...REENACTMENTS OF HANNIBAL'S FAMOUS BATTLES. LIKE, THE BATTLE OF CANNAE IN 216 BCE.
P-TOO
SPLURK!

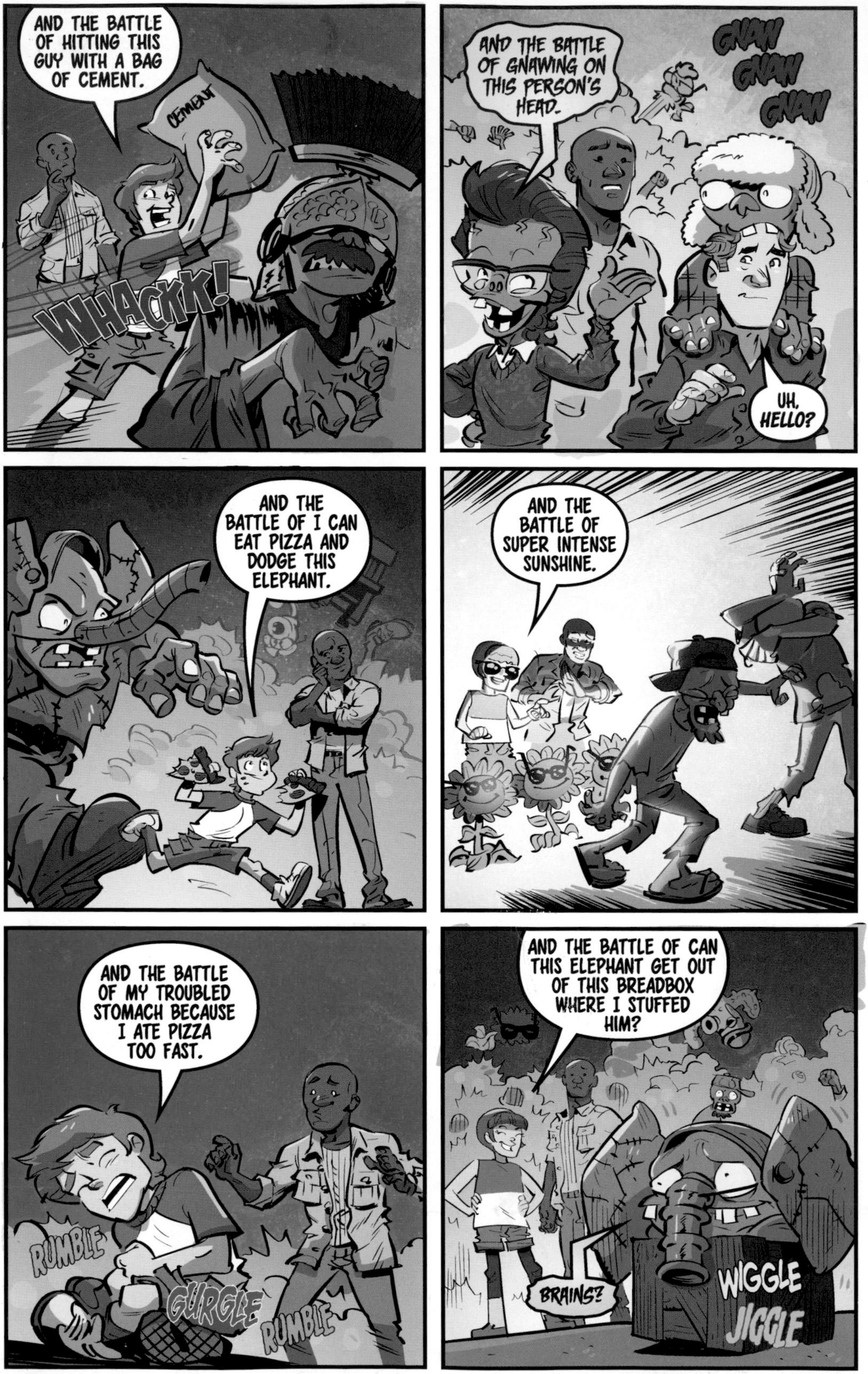

AND THE BATTLE OF HITTING THIS GUY WITH A BAG OF CEMENT.
CEMENT
WHACKK!
AND THE BATTLE OF GNAWING ON THIS PERSON'S HEAD.
GNAW GNAW GNAW
UH, HELLO?
AND THE BATTLE OF I CAN EAT PIZZA AND DODGE THIS ELEPHANT.
AND THE BATTLE OF SUPER INTENSE SUNSHINE.
AND THE BATTLE OF MY TROUBLED STOMACH BECAUSE I ATE PIZZA TOO FAST.
RUMBLE
GURGLE
RUMBLE
AND THE BATTLE OF CAN THIS ELEPHANT GET OUT OF THIS BREADBOX WHERE I STUFFED HIM?
BRAINS?
WIGGLE
JIGGLE

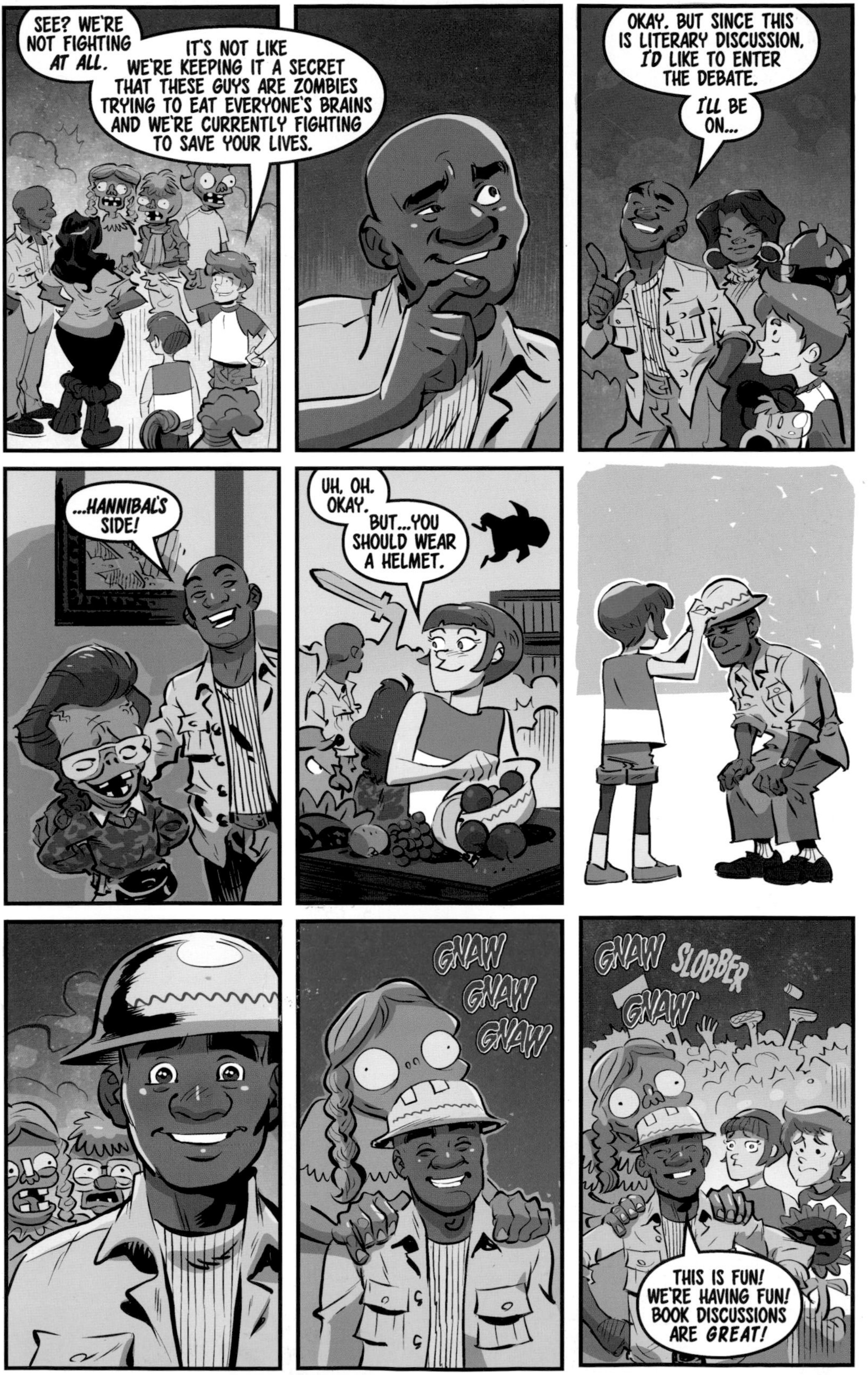
SEE? WE'RE NOT FIGHTING *AT ALL.*
IT'S NOT LIKE WE'RE KEEPING IT A SECRET THAT THESE GUYS ARE ZOMBIES TRYING TO EAT EVERYONE'S BRAINS AND WE'RE CURRENTLY FIGHTING TO SAVE YOUR LIVES.
OKAY. BUT SINCE THIS IS LITERARY DISCUSSION, *I'D* LIKE TO ENTER THE DEBATE.
I'LL BE ON...
...HANNIBAL'S SIDE!
UH, OH. OKAY.
BUT...YOU SHOULD WEAR A HELMET.
GNAW GNAW GNAW
GNAW SLOBBER GNAW
THIS IS FUN! WE'RE HAVING FUN! BOOK DISCUSSIONS ARE *GREAT!*

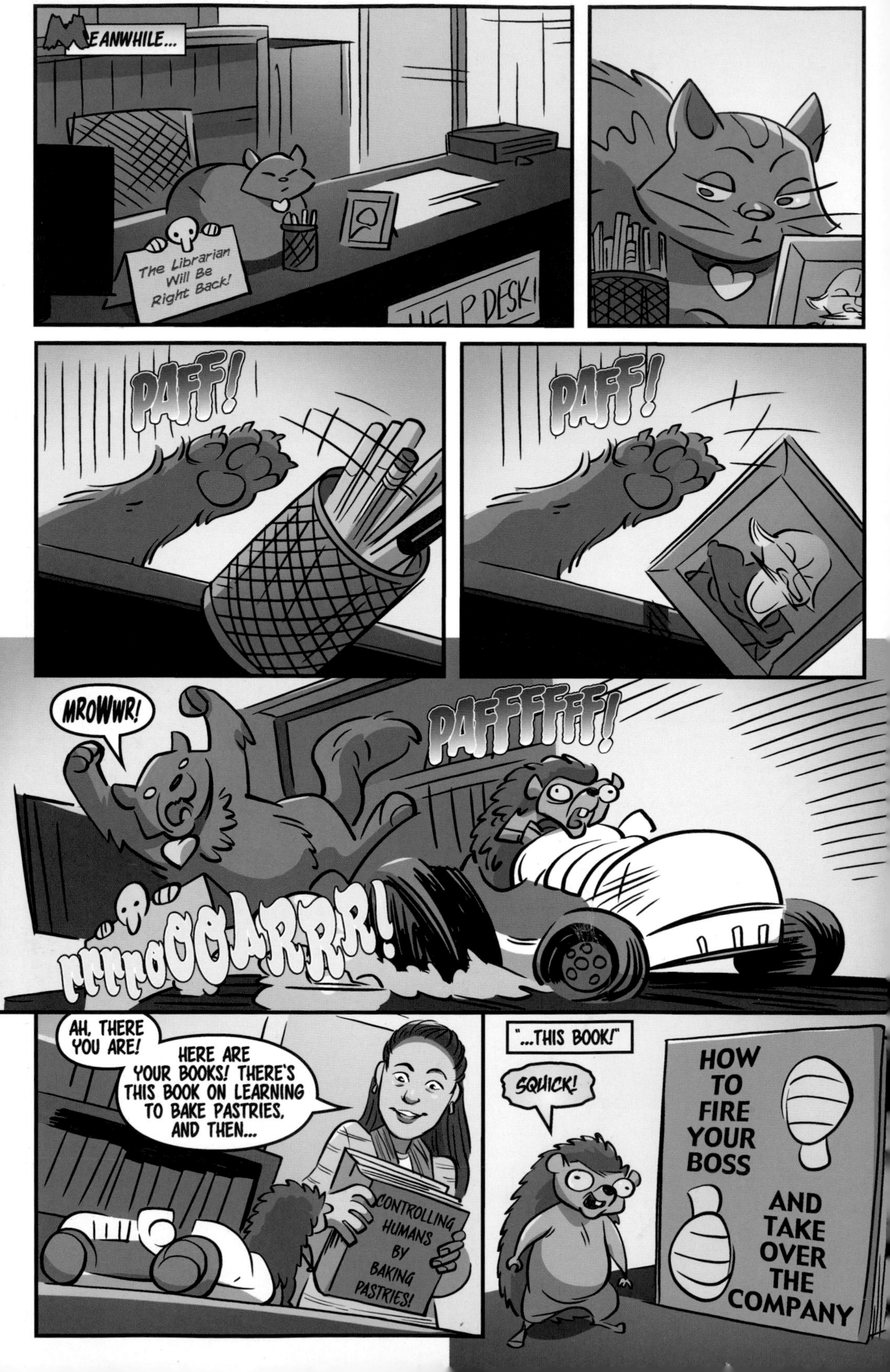
MEANWHILE...
The Librarian Will Be Right Back!
HELP DESK!
PAFF!
PAFF!
MROWWR!
PAFFFFFF!
rrrroOOARRR!
AH, THERE YOU ARE!
HERE ARE YOUR BOOKS! THERE'S THIS BOOK ON LEARNING TO BAKE PASTRIES, AND THEN...
CONTROLLING HUMANS BY BAKING PASTRIES!
"...THIS BOOK!"
SQUICK!
HOW TO FIRE YOUR BOSS AND TAKE OVER THE COMPANY

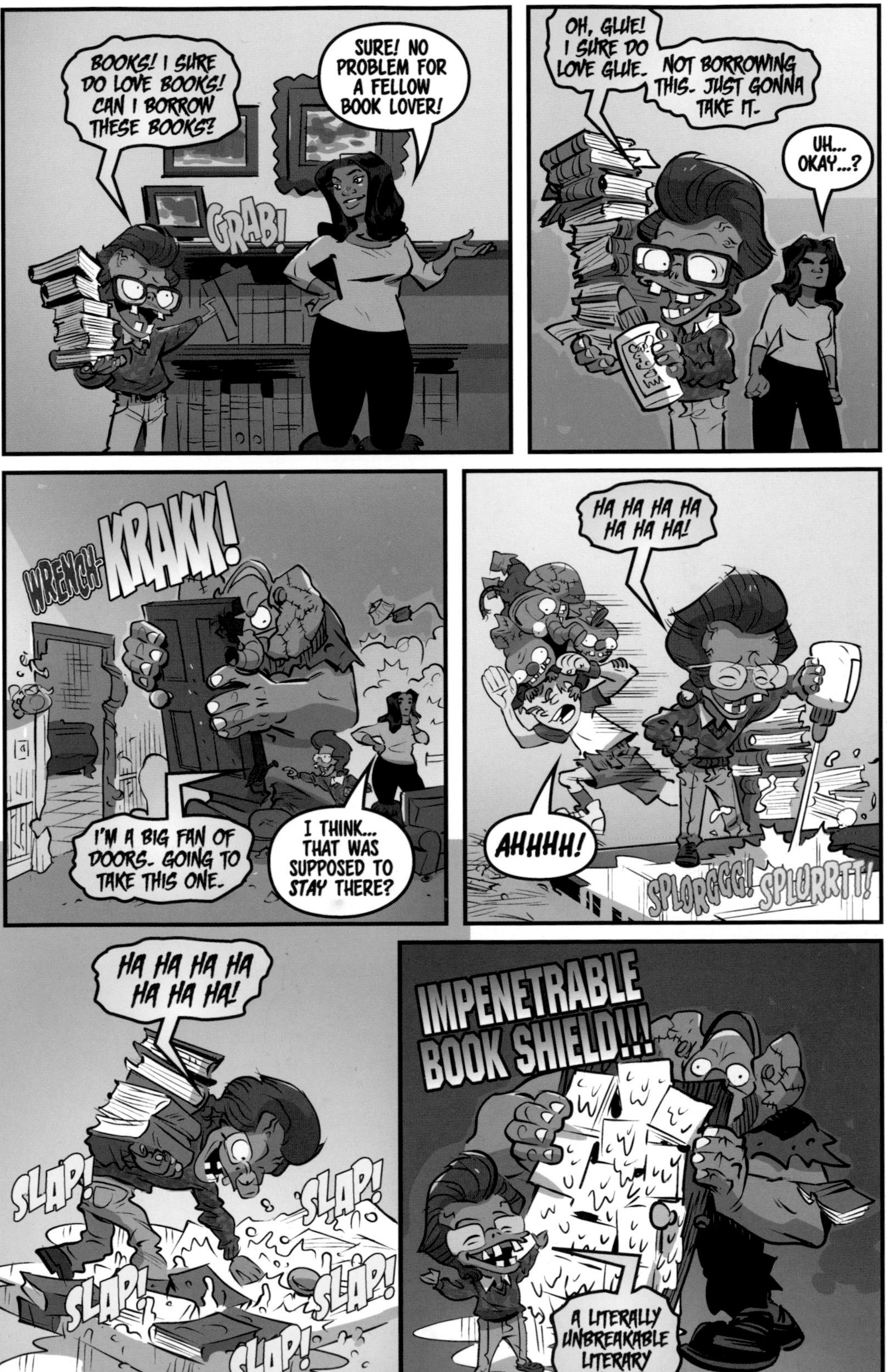
BOOKS! I SURE DO LOVE BOOKS! CAN I BORROW THESE BOOKS?
GRAB!
SURE! NO PROBLEM FOR A FELLOW BOOK LOVER!
OH, GLUE! I SURE DO LOVE GLUE.
NOT BORROWING THIS. JUST GONNA TAKE IT.
UH... OKAY...?
WRENCH-KRAKK!
I'M A BIG FAN OF DOORS. GOING TO TAKE THIS ONE.
I THINK... THAT WAS SUPPOSED TO STAY THERE?
HA HA HA HA HA HA HA!
AHHHH!
SPLORGGG! SPLURRTT!
HA HA HA HA HA HA HA!
SLAP! SLAP! SLAP! SLAP! SLAP!
IMPENETRABLE BOOK SHIELD!!!
A LITERALLY UNBREAKABLE LITERARY SHIELD!

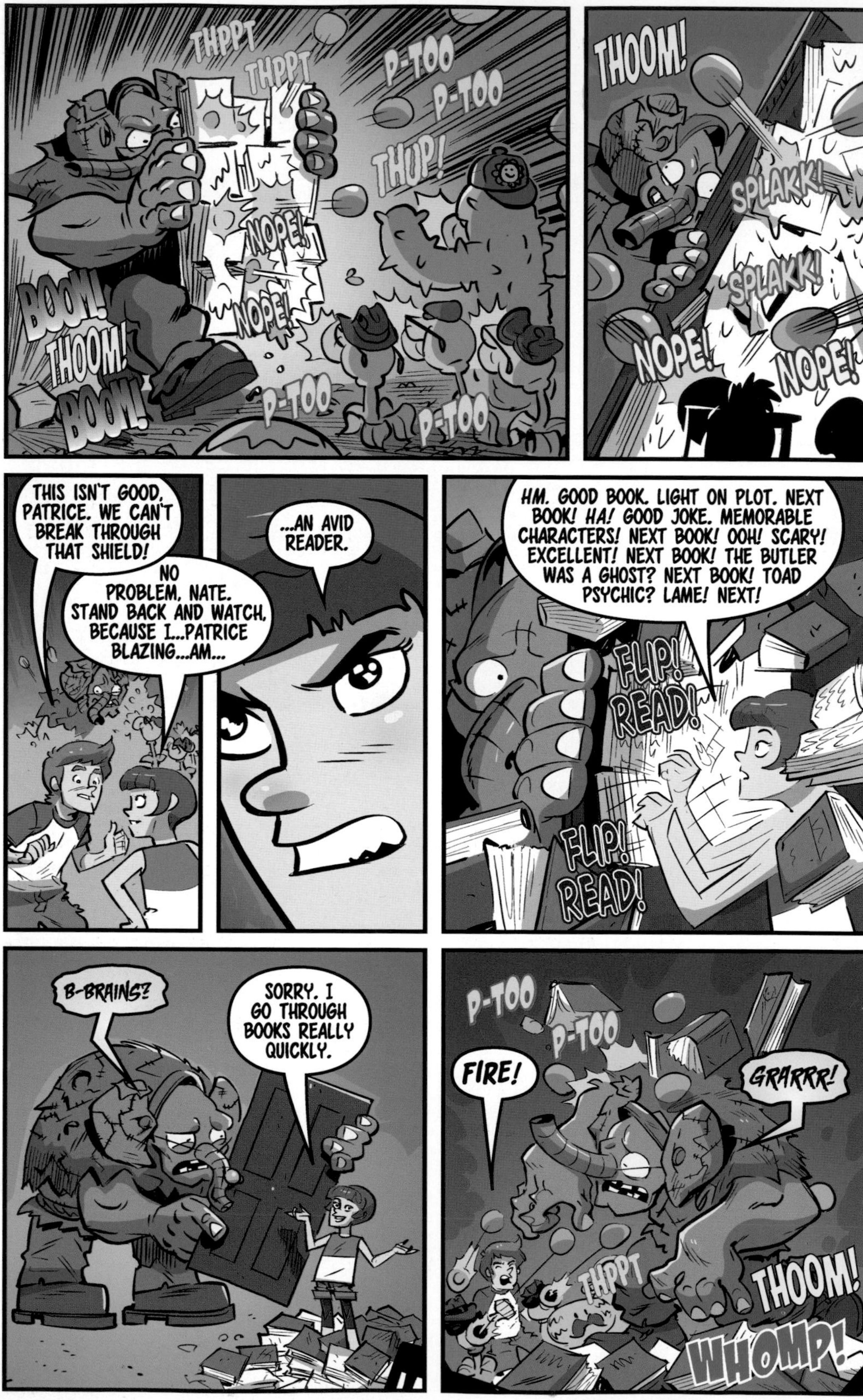
THPPT
THPPT
P-TOO
P-TOO
THUP!
NOPE!
NOPE!
BOOM!
THOOM!
BOOM!
P-TOO
P-TOO
THOOM!
SPLAKK!
SPLAKK!
NOPE!
NOPE!
THIS ISN'T GOOD, PATRICE. WE CAN'T BREAK THROUGH THAT SHIELD!
NO PROBLEM, NATE. STAND BACK AND WATCH, BECAUSE I...PATRICE BLAZING...AM...
...AN AVID READER.
HM. GOOD BOOK. LIGHT ON PLOT. NEXT BOOK! HA! GOOD JOKE. MEMORABLE CHARACTERS! NEXT BOOK! OOH! SCARY! EXCELLENT! NEXT BOOK! THE BUTLER WAS A GHOST? NEXT BOOK! TOAD PSYCHIC? LAME! NEXT!
FLIP! READ!
FLIP! READ!
B-BRAINS?
SORRY. I GO THROUGH BOOKS REALLY QUICKLY.
P-TOO
P-TOO
FIRE!
GRARRR!
THPPT
THOOM!
WHOMP!

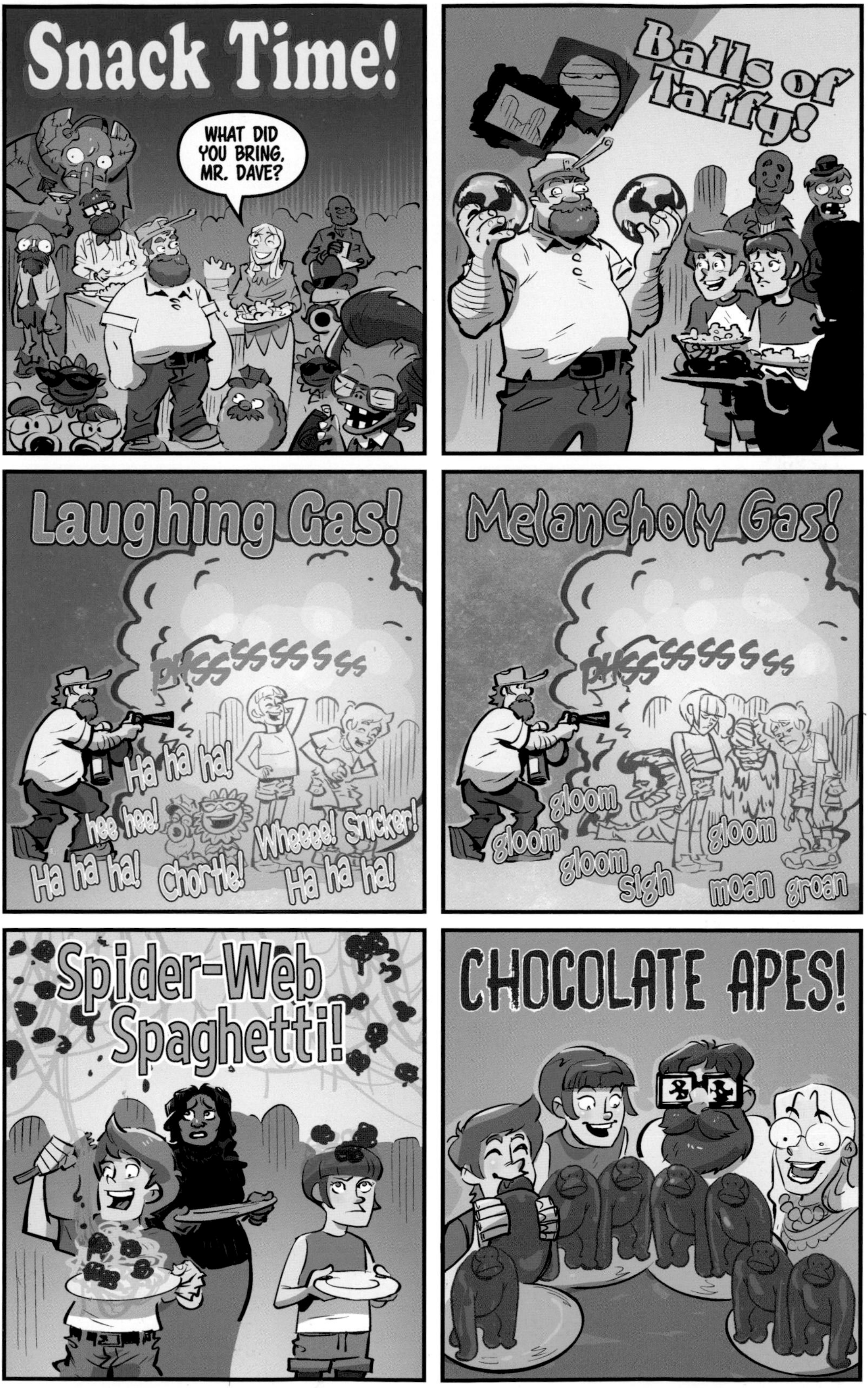
Snack Time!
WHAT DID YOU BRING, MR. DAVE?
Balls of Taffy!
Laughing Gas!
PHSSSSSSSSSS
Ha ha ha!
hee hee!
Ha ha ha!
Chortle!
Wheeee! Snicker!
Ha ha ha!
Melancholy Gas!
PHSSSSSSSSSS
gloom
gloom
gloom
sigh
gloom
moan
groan
Spider-Web Spaghetti!
CHOCOLATE APES!

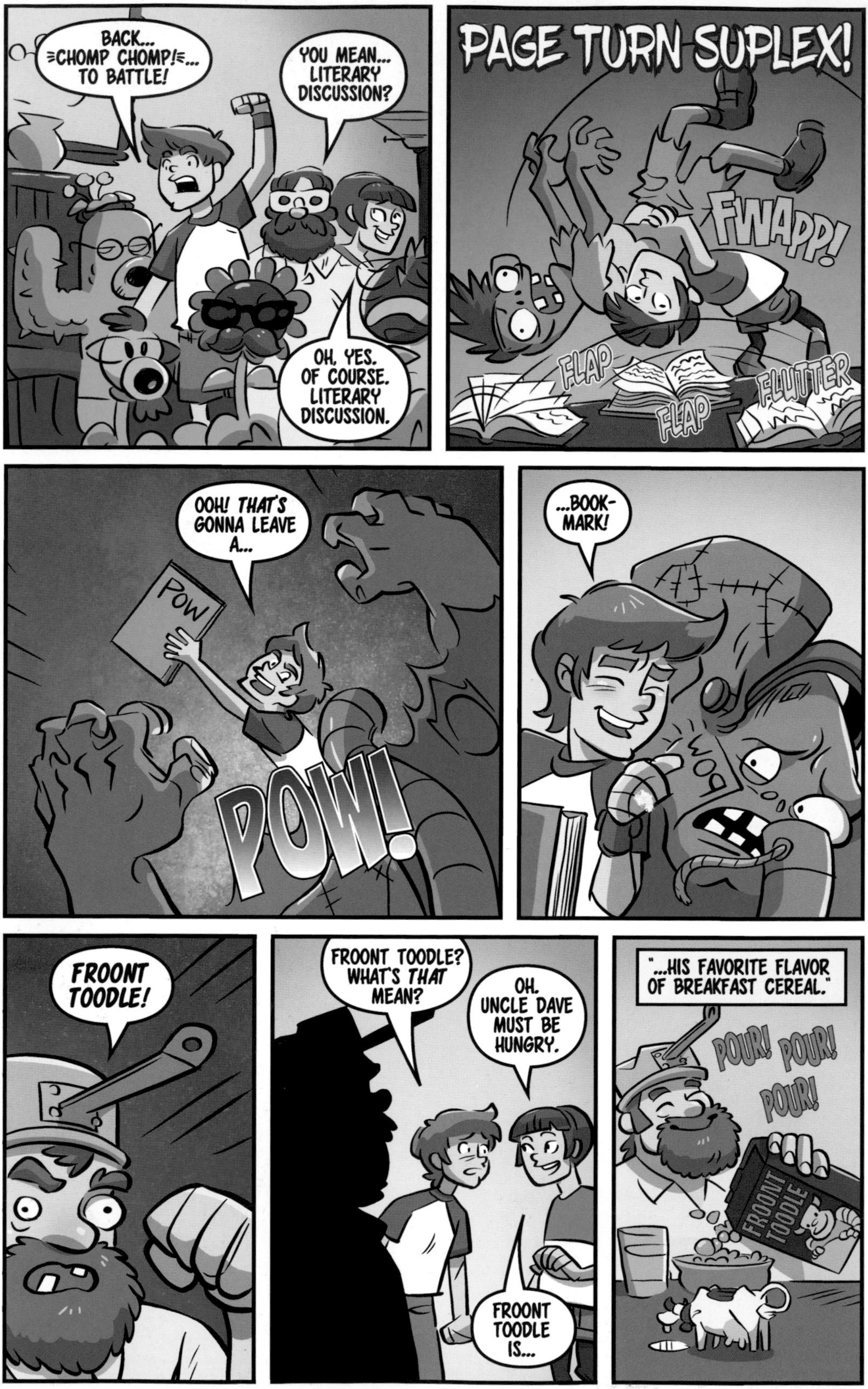
BACK... ≡CHOMP CHOMP!≡... TO BATTLE!
YOU MEAN... LITERARY DISCUSSION?
OH, YES. OF COURSE. LITERARY DISCUSSION.
PAGE TURN SUPLEX!
FWAPP!
FLAP
FLAP
FLUTTER
OOH! THAT'S GONNA LEAVE A...
POW
POW!
...BOOK-MARK!
POW
FROONT TOODLE!
FROONT TOODLE? WHAT'S THAT MEAN?
OH. UNCLE DAVE MUST BE HUNGRY.
FROONT TOODLE IS...
"...HIS FAVORITE FLAVOR OF BREAKFAST CEREAL."
POUR! POUR! POUR!
FROONT TOODLE

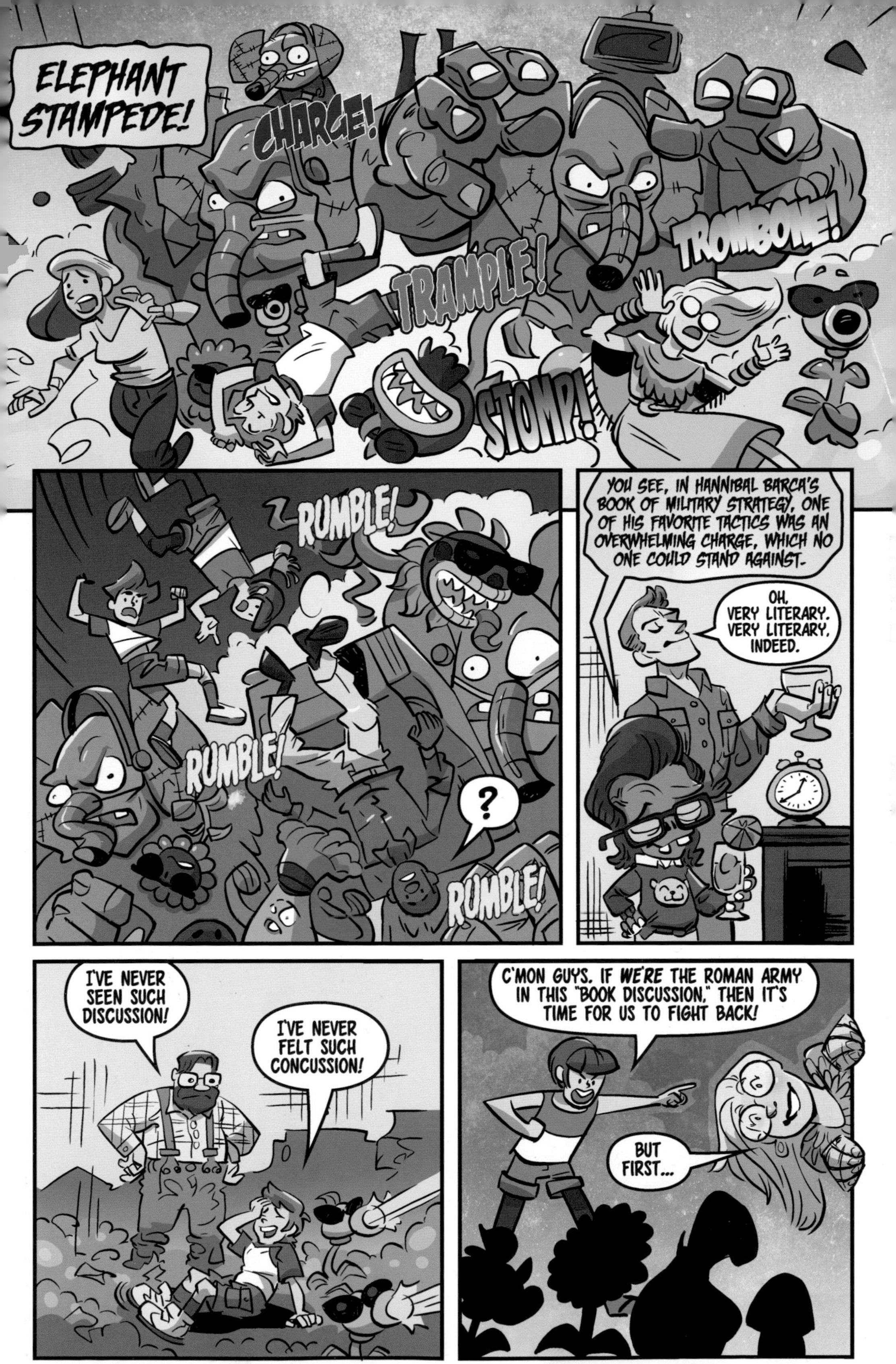
ELEPHANT STAMPEDE!
CHARGE!
TRAMPLE!
TROMBONE!
STOMP!
RUMBLE!
RUMBLE!
?
RUMBLE!
YOU SEE, IN HANNIBAL BARCA'S BOOK OF MILITARY STRATEGY, ONE OF HIS FAVORITE TACTICS WAS AN OVERWHELMING CHARGE, WHICH NO ONE COULD STAND AGAINST.
OH, VERY LITERARY. VERY LITERARY, INDEED.
I'VE NEVER SEEN SUCH DISCUSSION!
I'VE NEVER FELT SUCH CONCUSSION!
C'MON GUYS. IF *WE'RE* THE ROMAN ARMY IN THIS "BOOK DISCUSSION," THEN IT'S TIME FOR US TO FIGHT BACK!
BUT FIRST...

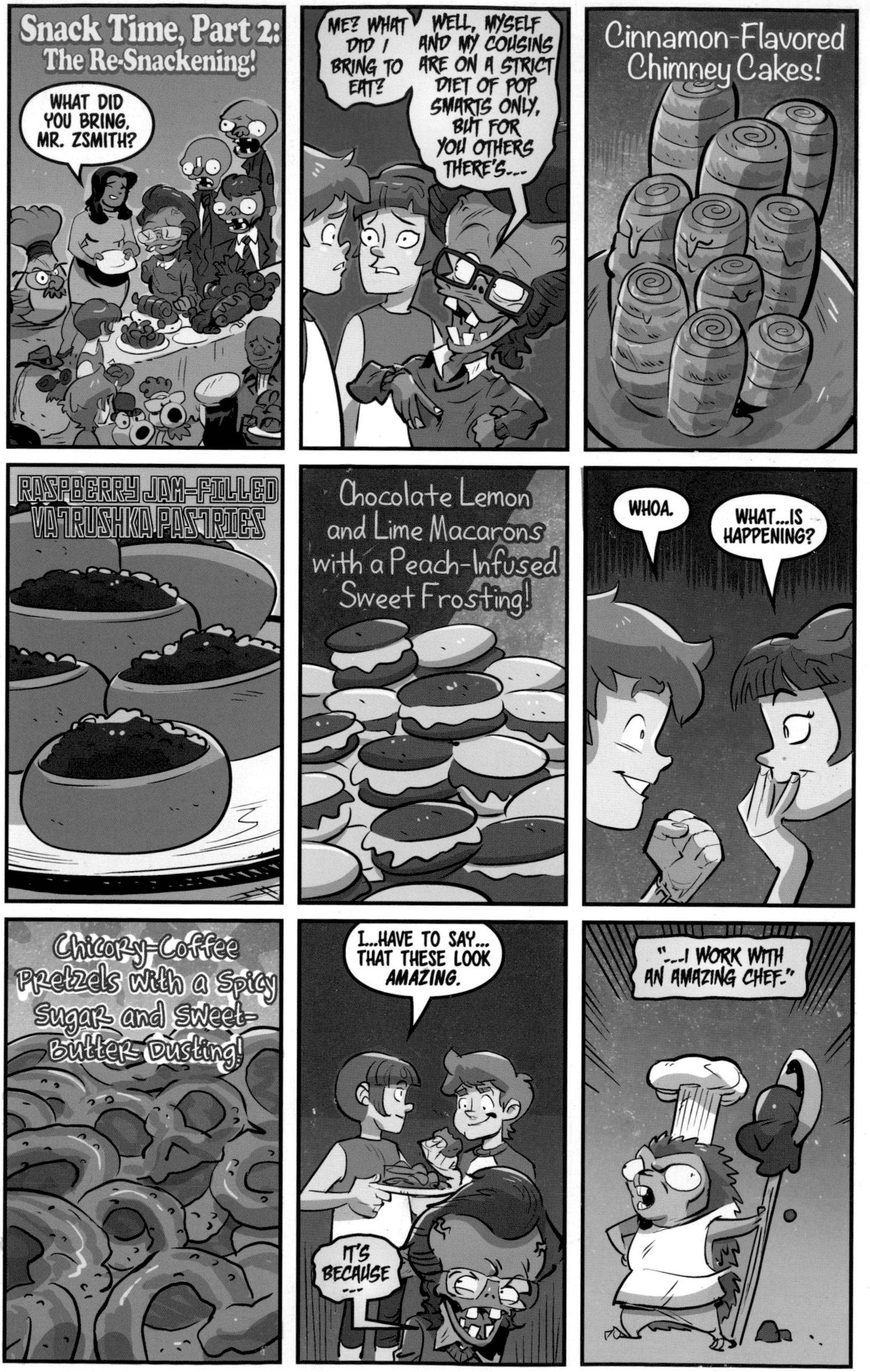
Snack Time, Part 2: The Re-Snackening!
WHAT DID YOU BRING, MR. ZSMITH?
ME? WHAT DID I BRING TO EAT?
WELL, MYSELF AND MY COUSINS ARE ON A STRICT DIET OF POP SMARTS ONLY, BUT FOR YOU OTHERS THERE'S...
Cinnamon-Flavored Chimney Cakes!
RASPBERRY JAM-FILLED VATRUSHKA PASTRIES
Chocolate Lemon and Lime Macarons with a Peach-Infused Sweet Frosting!
WHOA.
WHAT...IS HAPPENING?
Chicory-Coffee Pretzels with a Spicy Sugar and Sweet-Butter Dusting!
I...HAVE TO SAY... THAT THESE LOOK AMAZING.
IT'S BECAUSE ...
"...I WORK WITH AN AMAZING CHEF."

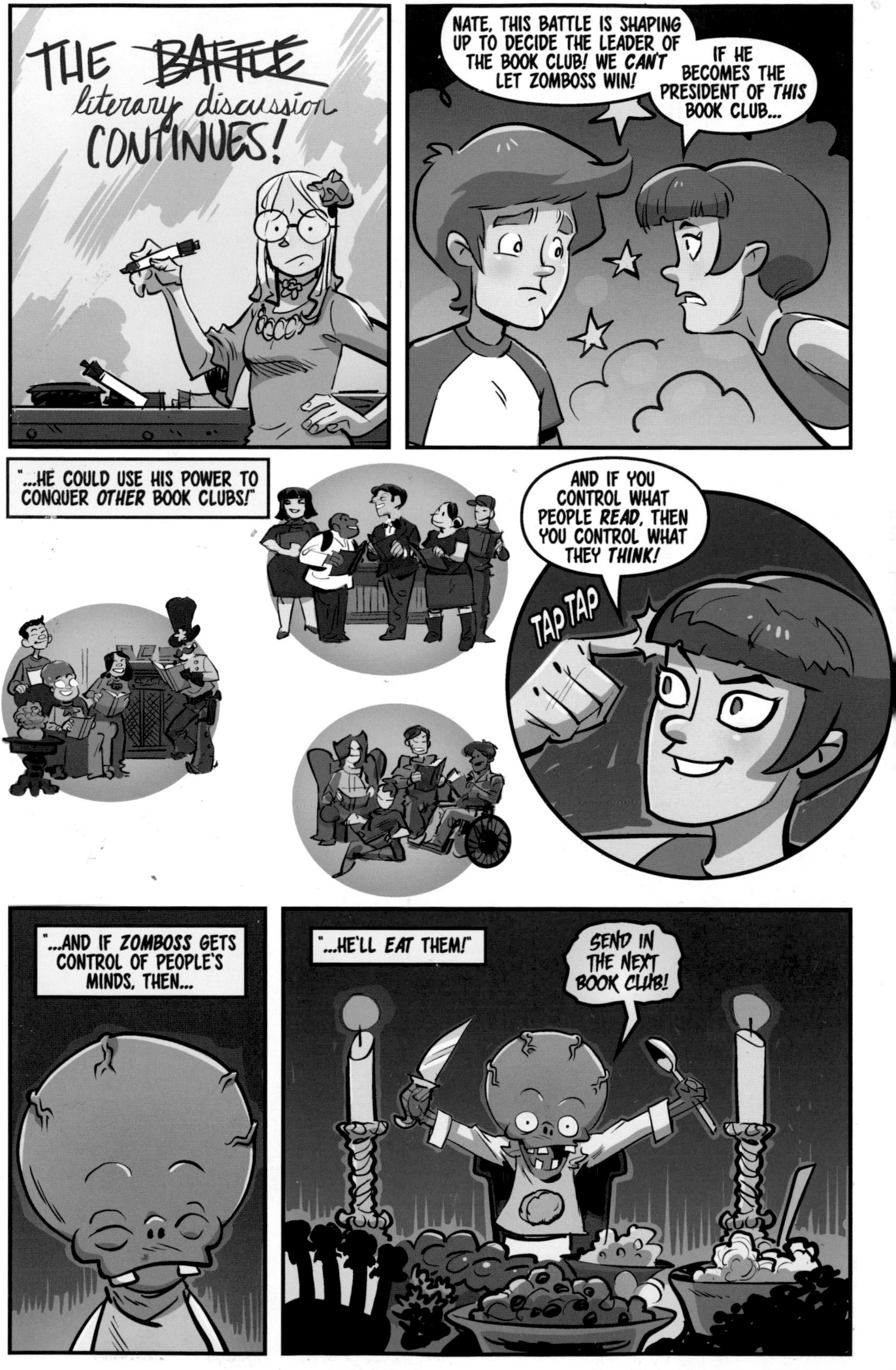
THE ~~BATTLE~~ literary discussion CONTINUES!
NATE, THIS BATTLE IS SHAPING UP TO DECIDE THE LEADER OF THE BOOK CLUB! WE CAN'T LET ZOMBOSS WIN!
IF HE BECOMES THE PRESIDENT OF THIS BOOK CLUB...
"...HE COULD USE HIS POWER TO CONQUER OTHER BOOK CLUBS!"
AND IF YOU CONTROL WHAT PEOPLE READ, THEN YOU CONTROL WHAT THEY THINK!
TAP TAP
"...AND IF ZOMBOSS GETS CONTROL OF PEOPLE'S MINDS, THEN...
"...HE'LL EAT THEM!"
SEND IN THE NEXT BOOK CLUB!

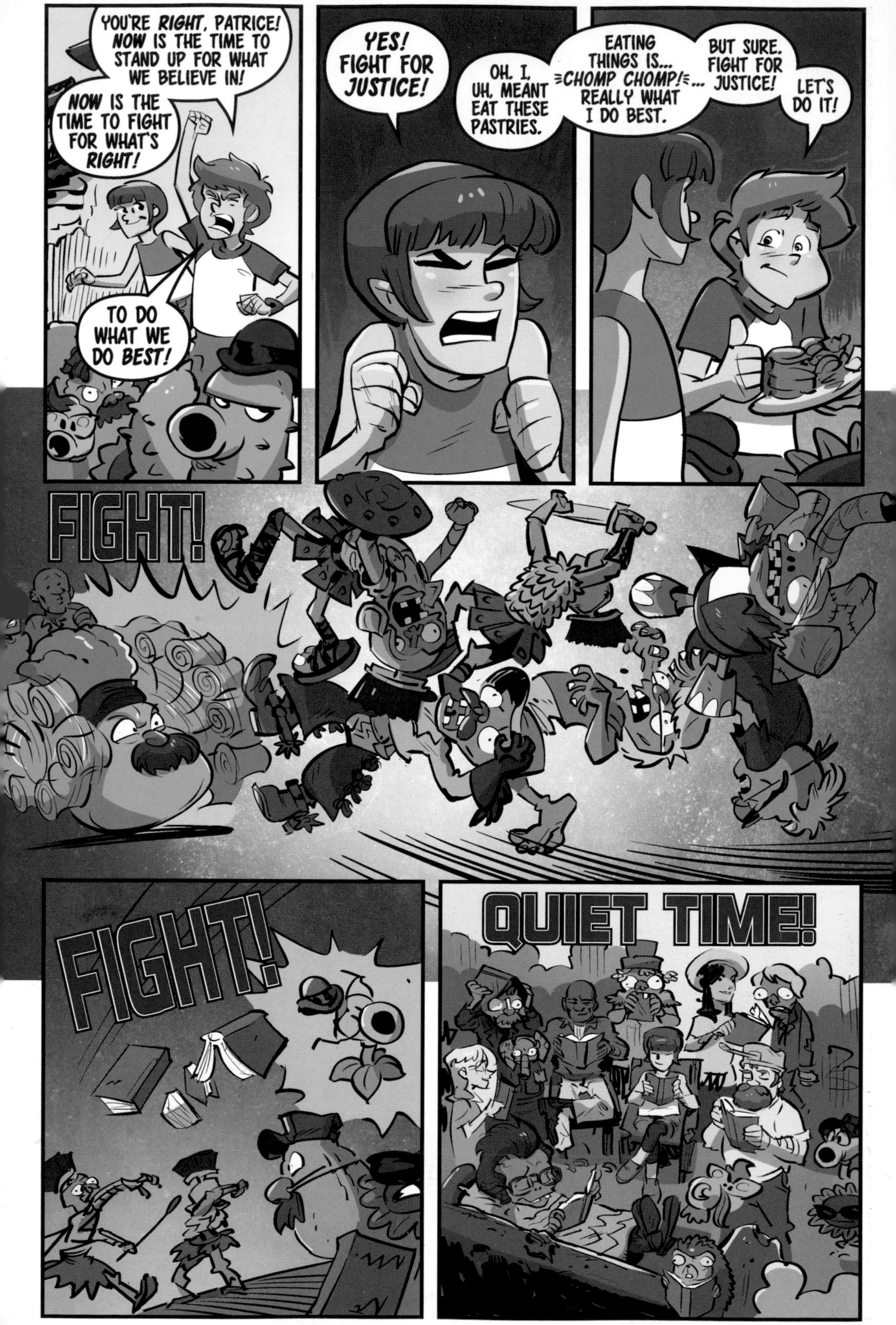
YOU'RE RIGHT, PATRICE! NOW IS THE TIME TO STAND UP FOR WHAT WE BELIEVE IN!
NOW IS THE TIME TO FIGHT FOR WHAT'S RIGHT!
TO DO WHAT WE DO BEST!
YES! FIGHT FOR JUSTICE!
OH. I, UH, MEANT EAT THESE PASTRIES.
EATING THINGS IS... CHOMP CHOMP!... REALLY WHAT I DO BEST.
BUT SURE. FIGHT FOR JUSTICE!
LET'S DO IT!
FIGHT!
FIGHT!
QUIET TIME!

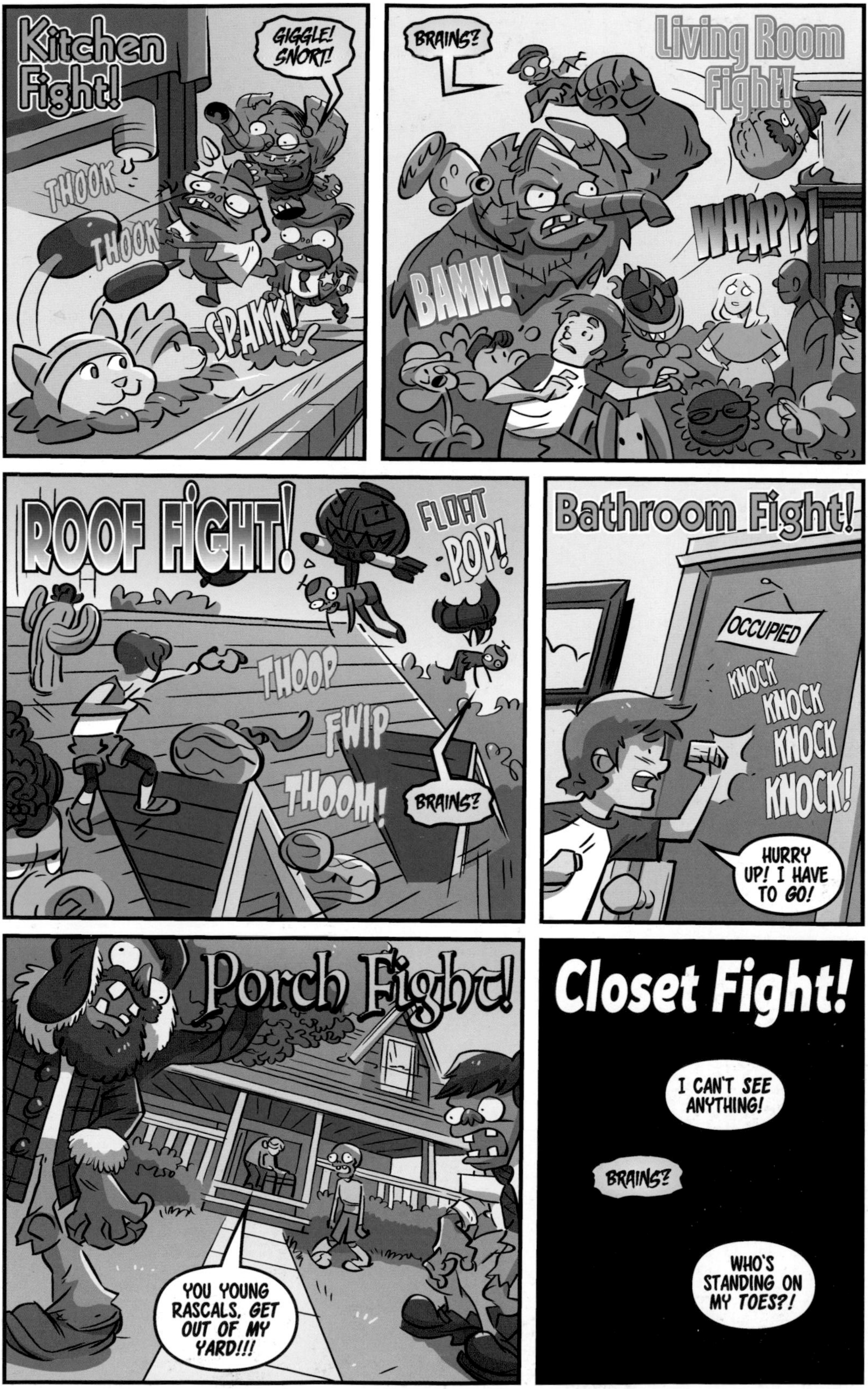
Kitchen Fight!
GIGGLE! SNORT!
THOOK
THOOK
SPAKK!
BRAINS?
Living Room Fight!
WHAPP!
BAMM!
ROOF FIGHT!
FLOAT
POP!
THOOP
FWIP
THOOM!
BRAINS?
Bathroom Fight!
OCCUPIED
KNOCK
KNOCK
KNOCK
KNOCK!
HURRY UP! I HAVE TO GO!
Porch Fight!
YOU YOUNG RASCALS, GET OUT OF MY YARD!!!
Closet Fight!
I CAN'T SEE ANYTHING!
BRAINS?
WHO'S STANDING ON MY TOES?!

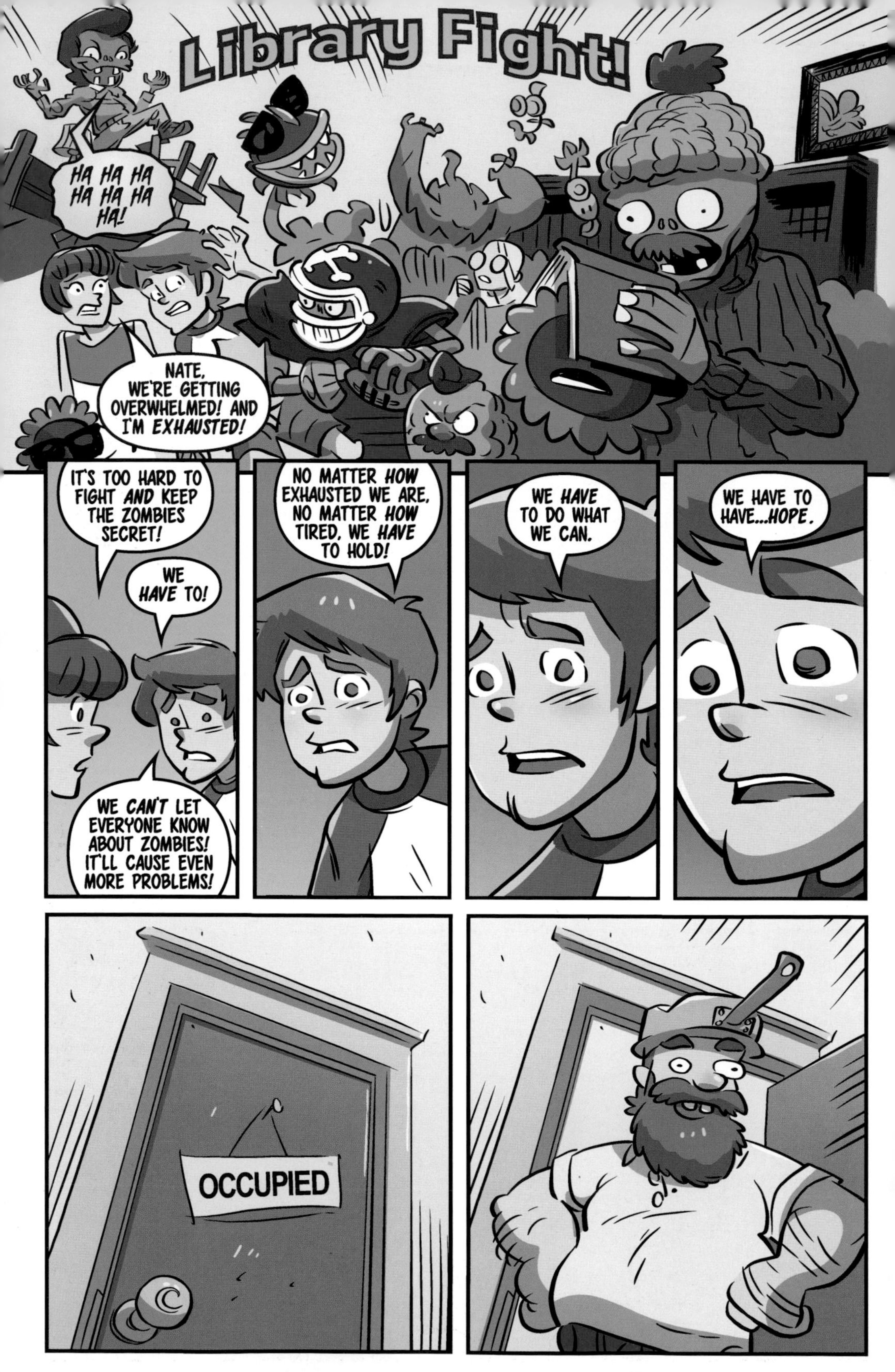
Library Fight!
HA HA HA HA HA HA HA!
NATE, WE'RE GETTING OVERWHELMED! AND I'M EXHAUSTED!
IT'S TOO HARD TO FIGHT AND KEEP THE ZOMBIES SECRET!
WE HAVE TO!
WE CAN'T LET EVERYONE KNOW ABOUT ZOMBIES! IT'LL CAUSE EVEN MORE PROBLEMS!
NO MATTER HOW EXHAUSTED WE ARE, NO MATTER HOW TIRED, WE HAVE TO HOLD!
WE HAVE TO DO WHAT WE CAN.
WE HAVE TO HAVE...HOPE.
OCCUPIED

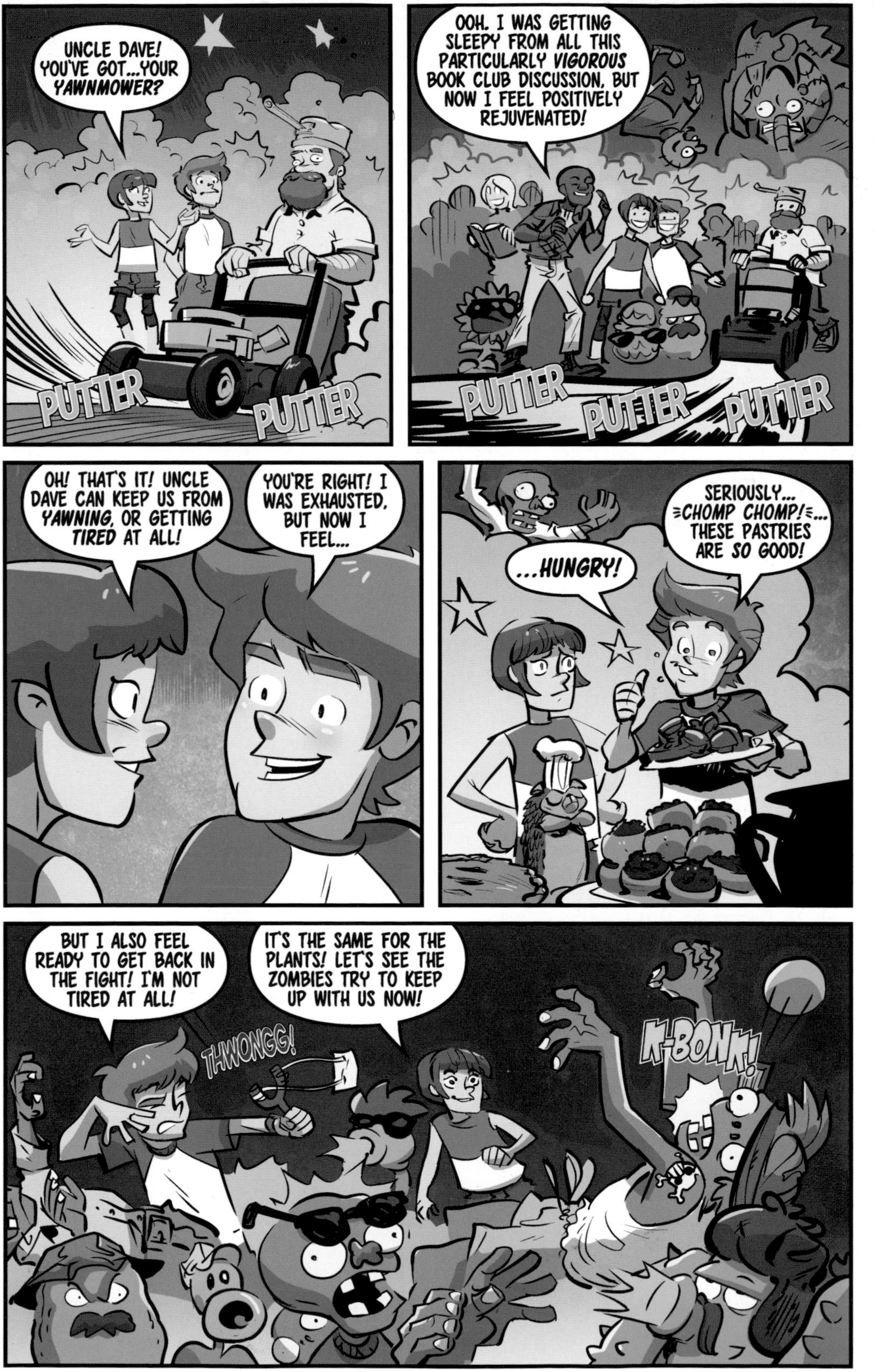
UNCLE DAVE! YOU'VE GOT...YOUR YAWNMOWER?
PUTTER
PUTTER
OOH, I WAS GETTING SLEEPY FROM ALL THIS PARTICULARLY VIGOROUS BOOK CLUB DISCUSSION, BUT NOW I FEEL POSITIVELY REJUVENATED!
PUTTER
PUTTER
PUTTER
OH! THAT'S IT! UNCLE DAVE CAN KEEP US FROM YAWNING, OR GETTING TIRED AT ALL!
YOU'RE RIGHT! I WAS EXHAUSTED, BUT NOW I FEEL...
...HUNGRY!
SERIOUSLY... CHOMP CHOMP!... THESE PASTRIES ARE SO GOOD!
BUT I ALSO FEEL READY TO GET BACK IN THE FIGHT! I'M NOT TIRED AT ALL!
IT'S THE SAME FOR THE PLANTS! LET'S SEE THE ZOMBIES TRY TO KEEP UP WITH US NOW!
THWONGG!
K-BONK!

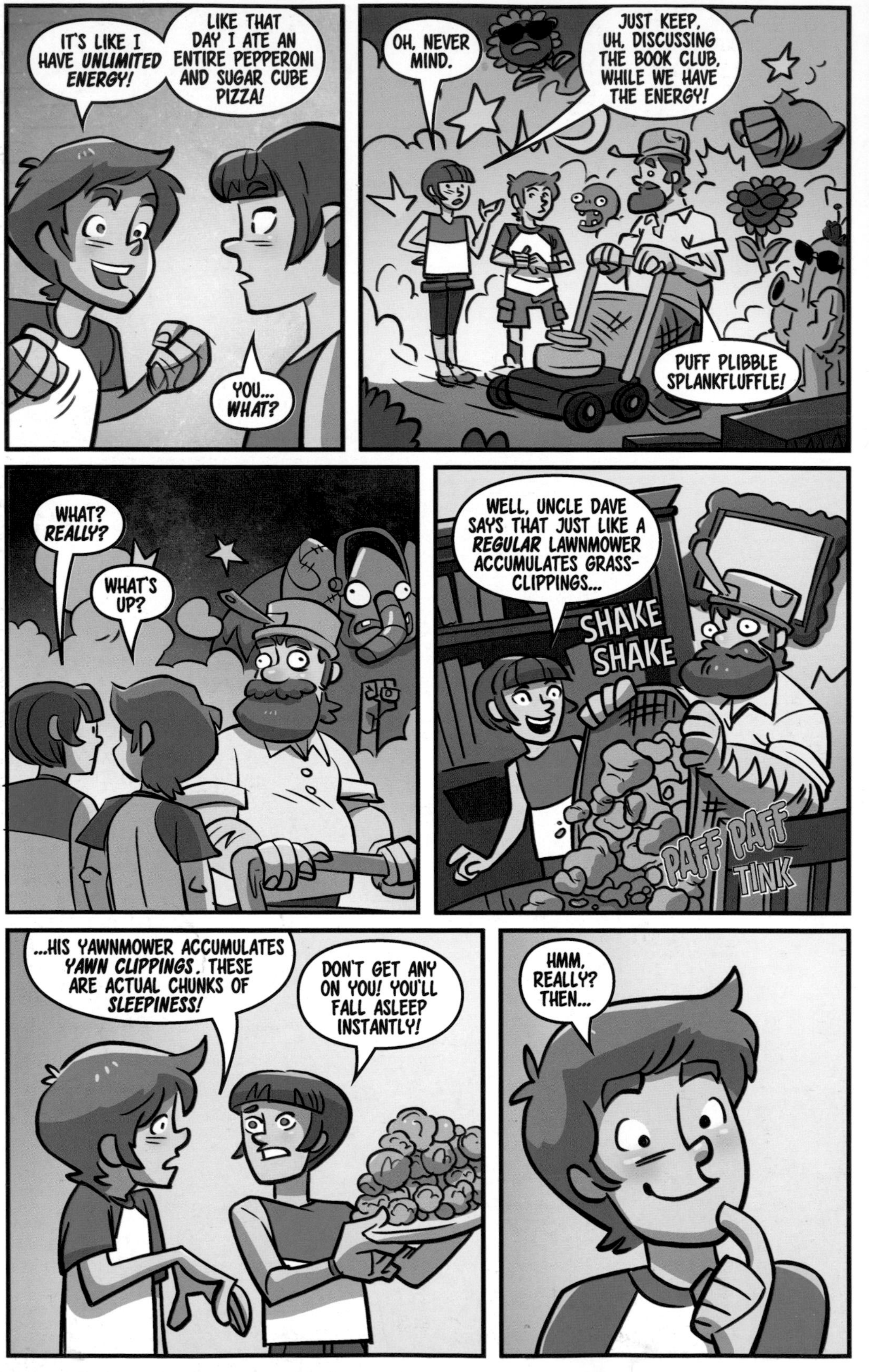
IT'S LIKE I HAVE UNLIMITED ENERGY!
LIKE THAT DAY I ATE AN ENTIRE PEPPERONI AND SUGAR CUBE PIZZA!
YOU... WHAT?
OH, NEVER MIND.
JUST KEEP, UH, DISCUSSING THE BOOK CLUB, WHILE WE HAVE THE ENERGY!
PUFF PLIBBLE SPLANKFLUFFLE!
WHAT? REALLY?
WHAT'S UP?
WELL, UNCLE DAVE SAYS THAT JUST LIKE A REGULAR LAWNMOWER ACCUMULATES GRASS-CLIPPINGS...
SHAKE
SHAKE
PAFF PAFF
TINK
...HIS YAWNMOWER ACCUMULATES YAWN CLIPPINGS. THESE ARE ACTUAL CHUNKS OF SLEEPINESS!
DON'T GET ANY ON YOU! YOU'LL FALL ASLEEP INSTANTLY!
HMM, REALLY? THEN...

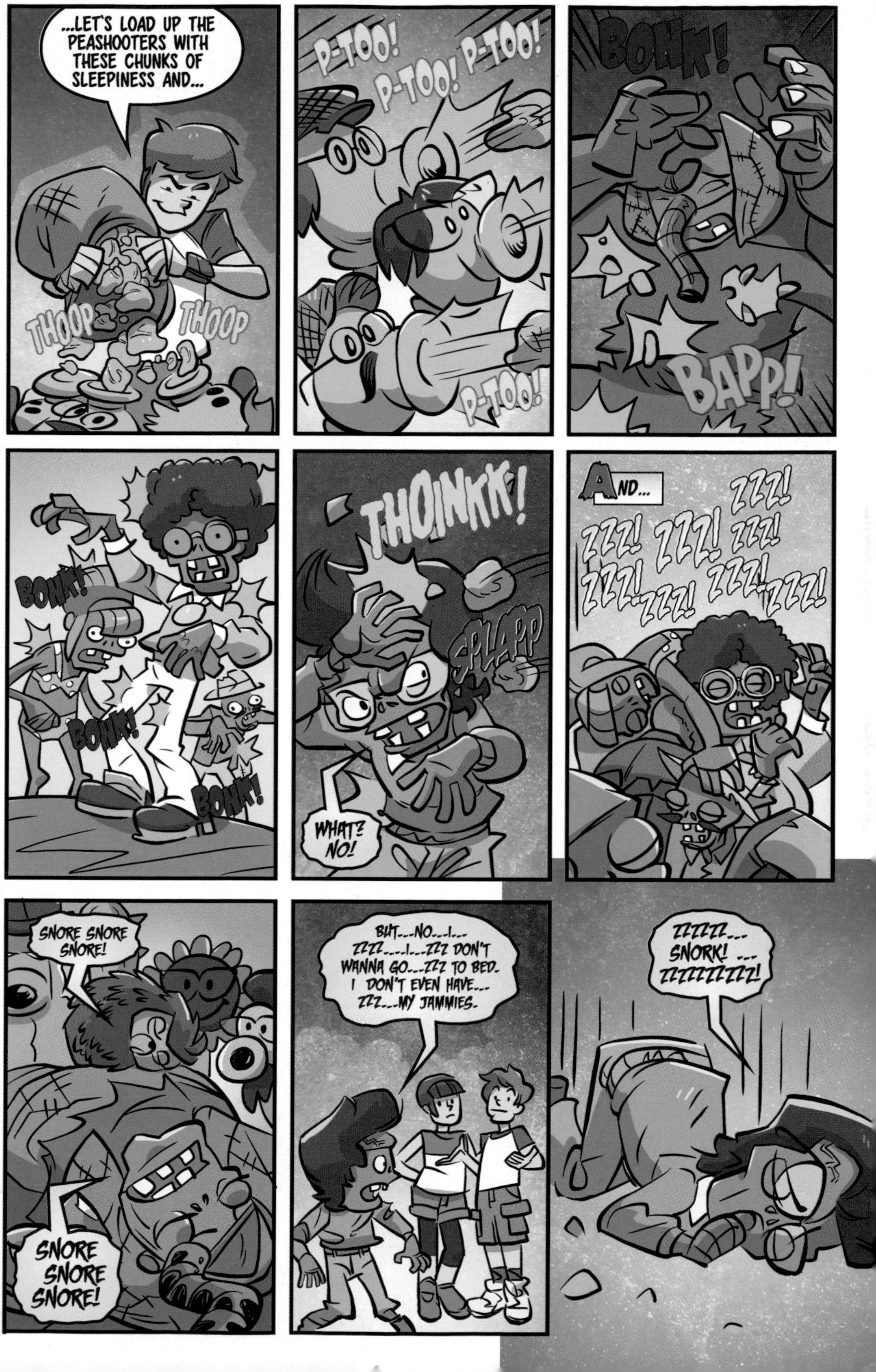
...LET'S LOAD UP THE PEASHOOTERS WITH THESE CHUNKS OF SLEEPINESS AND...
THOOP
THOOP
P-TOO!
P-TOO!
P-TOO!
P-TOO!
BONK!
BAPP!
BONK!
BONK!
BONK!
THOINKK!
SPLAPP
WHAT? NO!
AND...
ZZZ! ZZZ! ZZZ! ZZZ! ZZZ! ZZZ! ZZZ! ZZZ!
SNORE SNORE SNORE!
SNORE SNORE SNORE!
BUT...NO...I... ZZZ...I...ZZZ DON'T WANNA GO...ZZZ TO BED. I DON'T EVEN HAVE... ZZZ...MY JAMMIES.
ZZZZZZ... SNORK! ... ZZZZZZZZZZ!

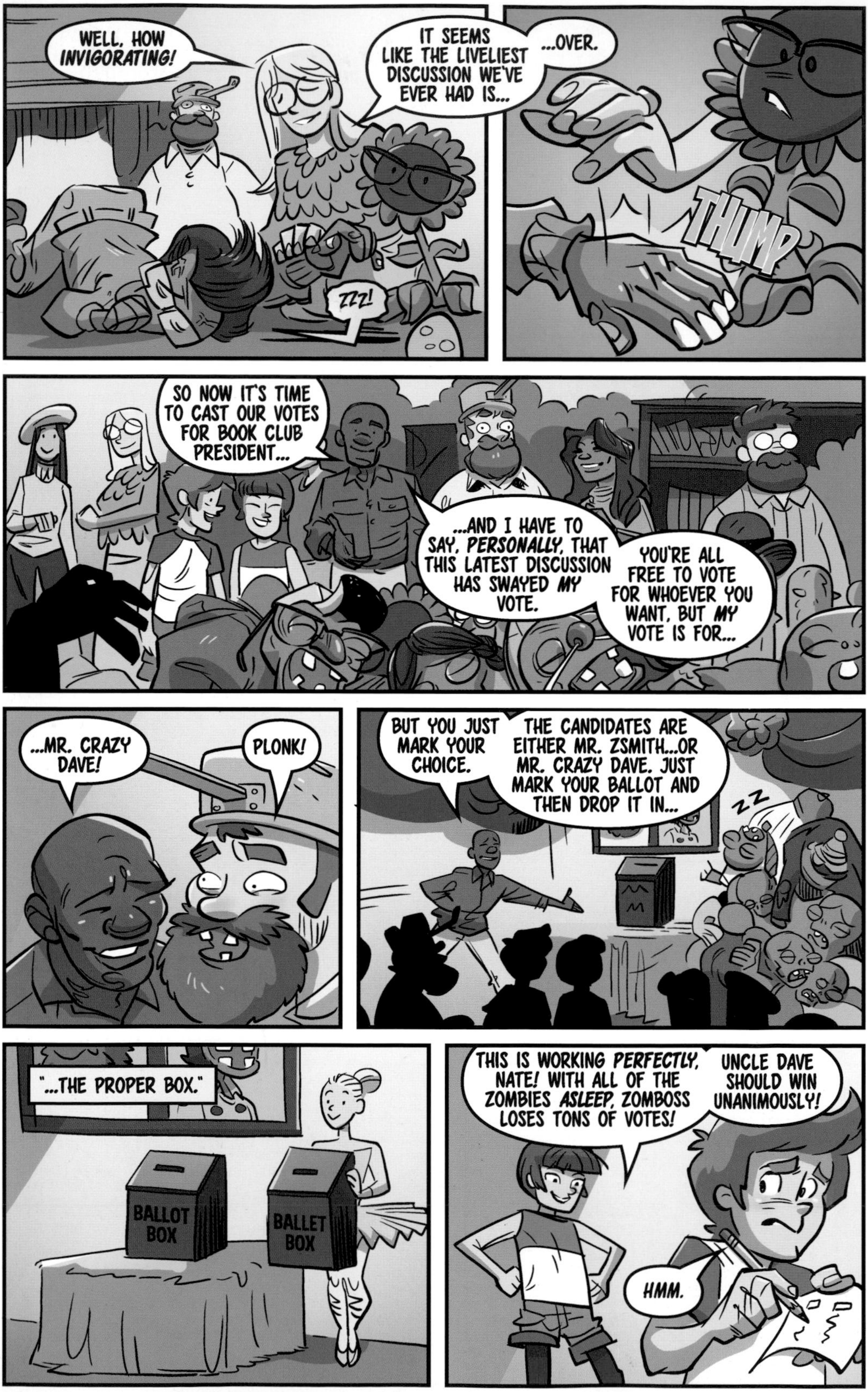
WELL, HOW INVIGORATING!
IT SEEMS LIKE THE LIVELIEST DISCUSSION WE'VE EVER HAD IS...
...OVER.
ZZZ!
THUMP
SO NOW IT'S TIME TO CAST OUR VOTES FOR BOOK CLUB PRESIDENT...
...AND I HAVE TO SAY, PERSONALLY, THAT THIS LATEST DISCUSSION HAS SWAYED MY VOTE.
YOU'RE ALL FREE TO VOTE FOR WHOEVER YOU WANT, BUT MY VOTE IS FOR...
...MR. CRAZY DAVE!
PLONK!
BUT YOU JUST MARK YOUR CHOICE.
THE CANDIDATES ARE EITHER MR. ZSMITH...OR MR. CRAZY DAVE. JUST MARK YOUR BALLOT AND THEN DROP IT IN...
ZZ
"...THE PROPER BOX."
BALLOT BOX
BALLET BOX
THIS IS WORKING PERFECTLY, NATE! WITH ALL OF THE ZOMBIES ASLEEP, ZOMBOSS LOSES TONS OF VOTES!
UNCLE DAVE SHOULD WIN UNANIMOUSLY!
HMM.

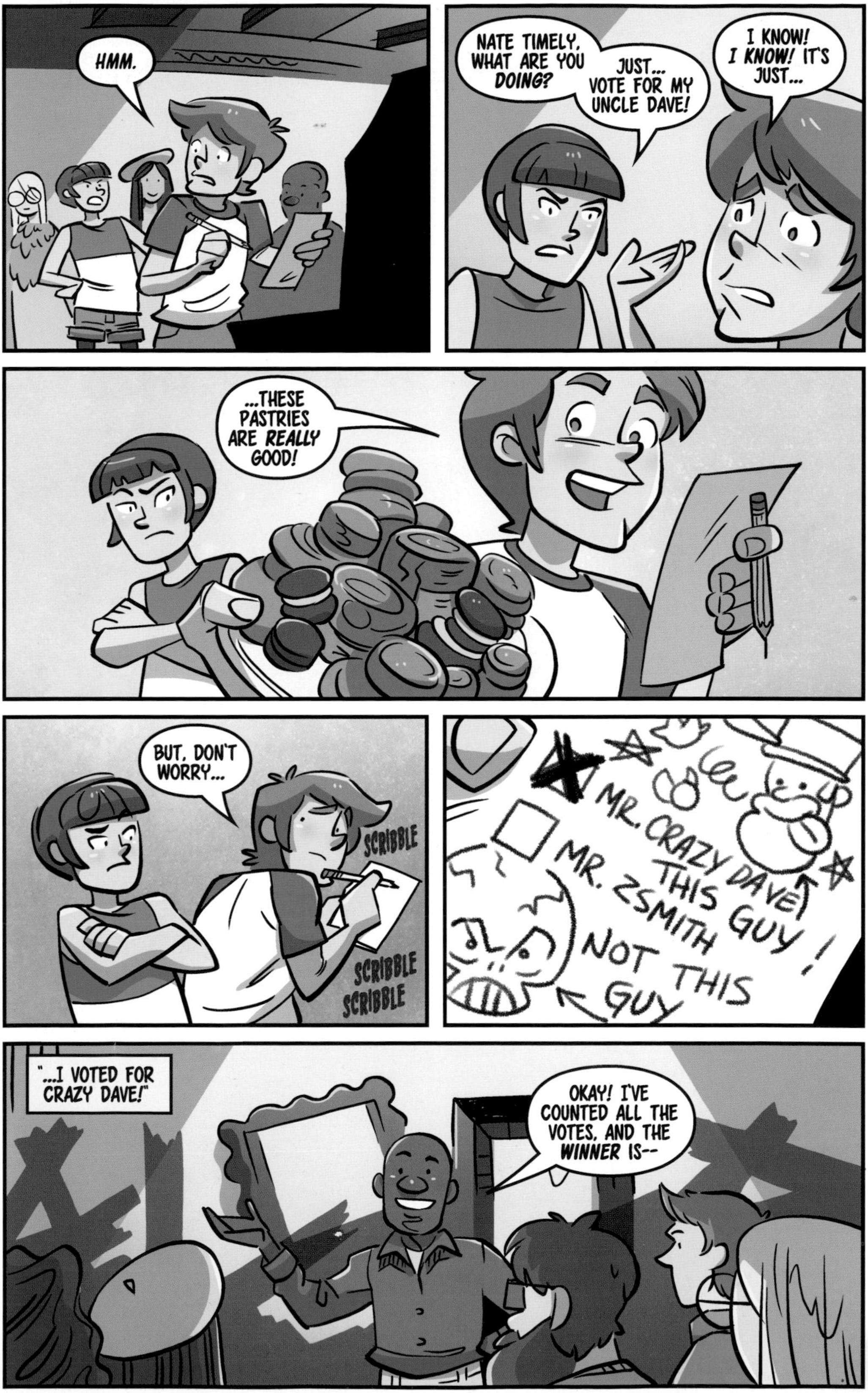
HMM.
NATE TIMELY, WHAT ARE YOU DOING?
JUST... VOTE FOR MY UNCLE DAVE!
I KNOW! I KNOW! IT'S JUST...
...THESE PASTRIES ARE REALLY GOOD!
BUT, DON'T WORRY...
SCRIBBLE
SCRIBBLE
SCRIBBLE
MR. CRAZY DAVE
THIS GUY!
MR. ZSMITH
NOT THIS GUY
"...I VOTED FOR CRAZY DAVE!"
OKAY! I'VE COUNTED ALL THE VOTES, AND THE WINNER IS--

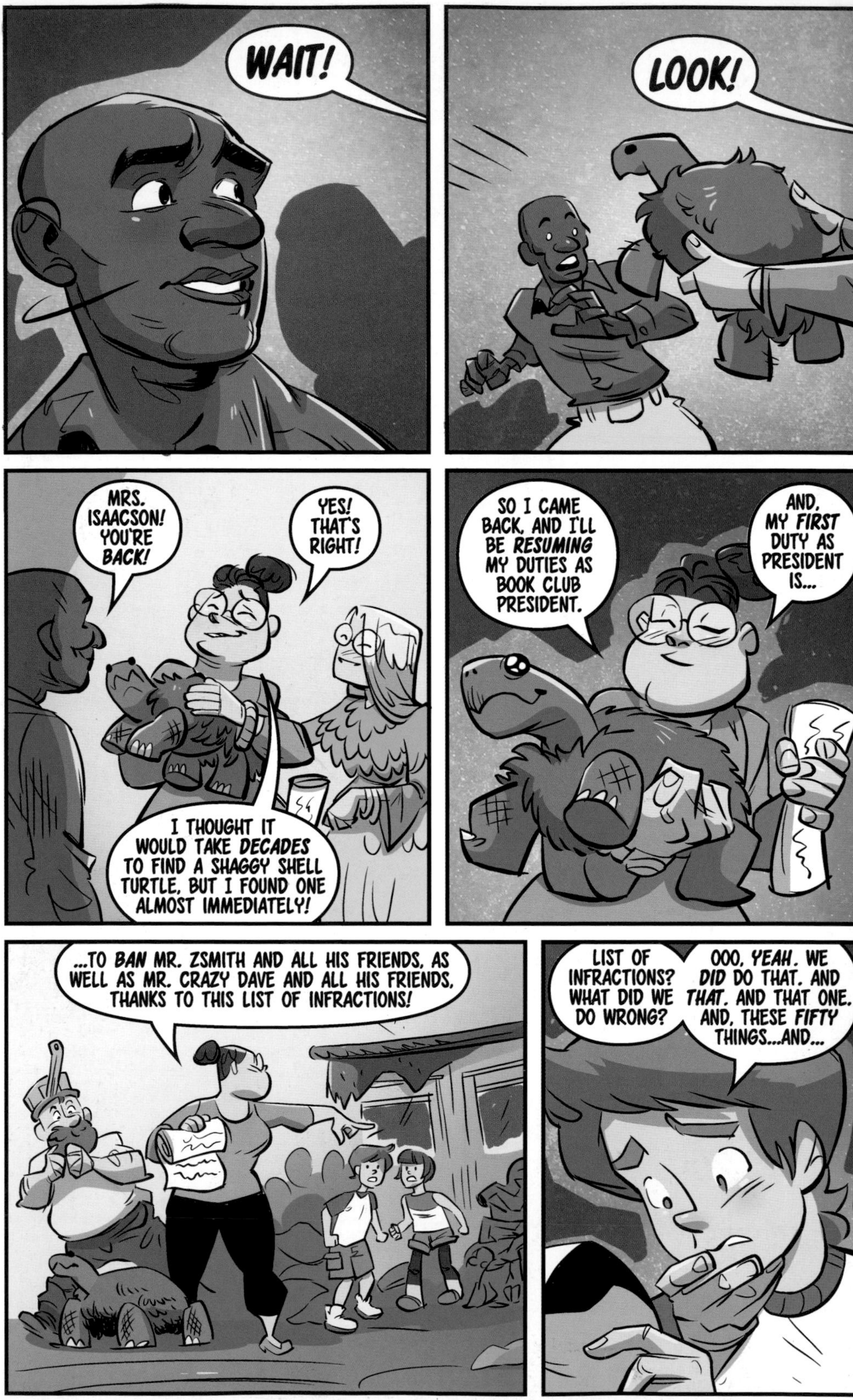
WAIT!
LOOK!
MRS. ISAACSON! YOU'RE BACK!
YES! THAT'S RIGHT!
I THOUGHT IT WOULD TAKE *DECADES* TO FIND A SHAGGY SHELL TURTLE, BUT I FOUND ONE ALMOST IMMEDIATELY!
SO I CAME BACK, AND I'LL BE *RESUMING* MY DUTIES AS BOOK CLUB PRESIDENT.
AND, MY *FIRST* DUTY AS PRESIDENT IS...
...TO *BAN* MR. ZSMITH AND ALL HIS FRIENDS, AS WELL AS MR. CRAZY DAVE AND ALL HIS FRIENDS, THANKS TO THIS LIST OF INFRACTIONS!
LIST OF INFRACTIONS? WHAT DID WE DO WRONG?
OOO, *YEAH*. WE *DID* DO THAT. AND *THAT*. AND THAT ONE. AND, THESE *FIFTY* THINGS...AND...

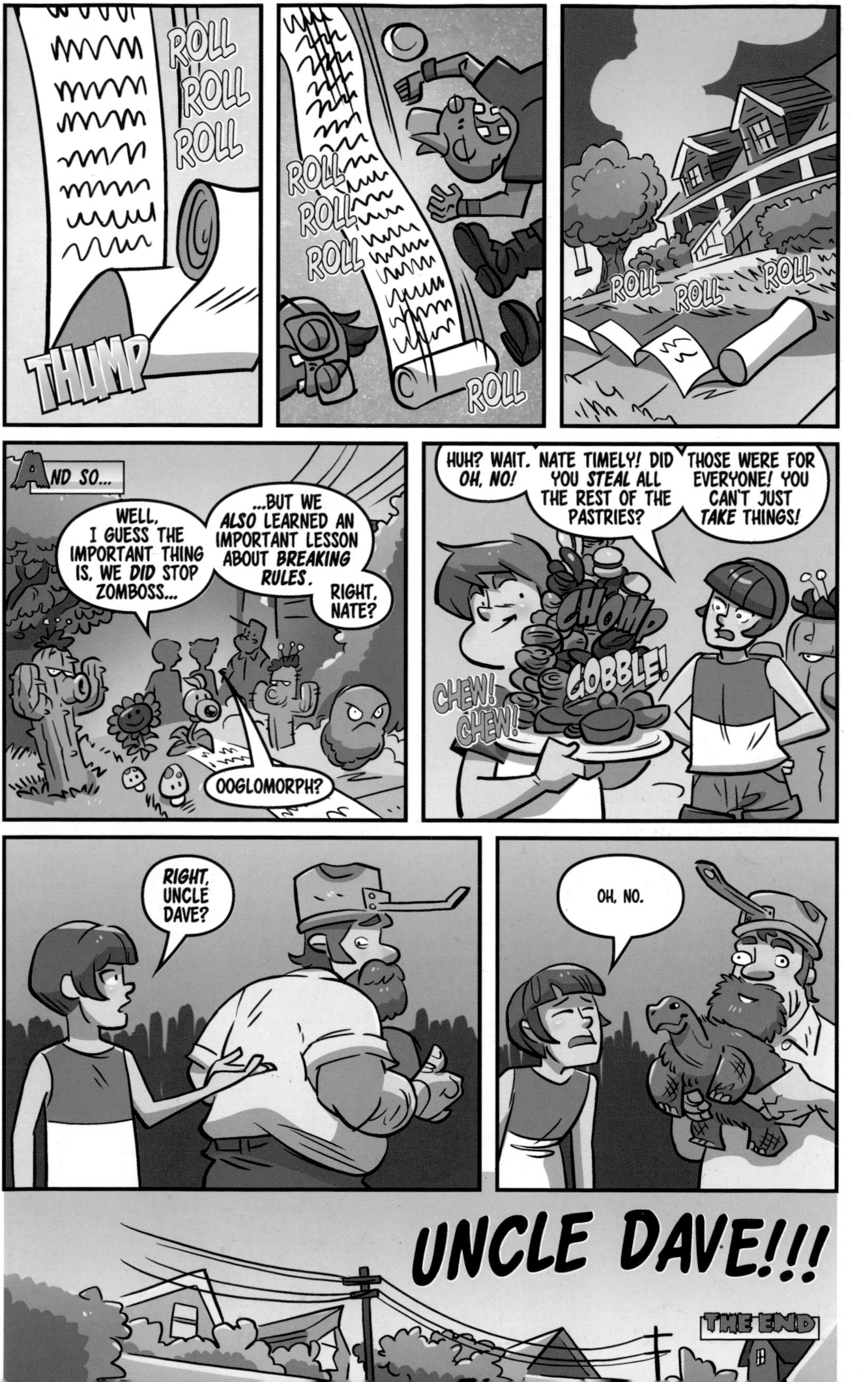
ROLL
ROLL
ROLL
THUMP
ROLL
ROLL
ROLL
ROLL
ROLL
ROLL
ROLL
AND SO...
WELL, I GUESS THE IMPORTANT THING IS, WE DID STOP ZOMBOSS...
...BUT WE ALSO LEARNED AN IMPORTANT LESSON ABOUT BREAKING RULES.
RIGHT, NATE?
OOGLOMORPH?
HUH? WAIT. OH, NO!
NATE TIMELY! DID YOU STEAL ALL THE REST OF THE PASTRIES?
THOSE WERE FOR EVERYONE! YOU CAN'T JUST TAKE THINGS!
CHOMP
GOBBLE!
CHEW! CHEW!
RIGHT, UNCLE DAVE?
OH, NO.
UNCLE DAVE!!!
THE END

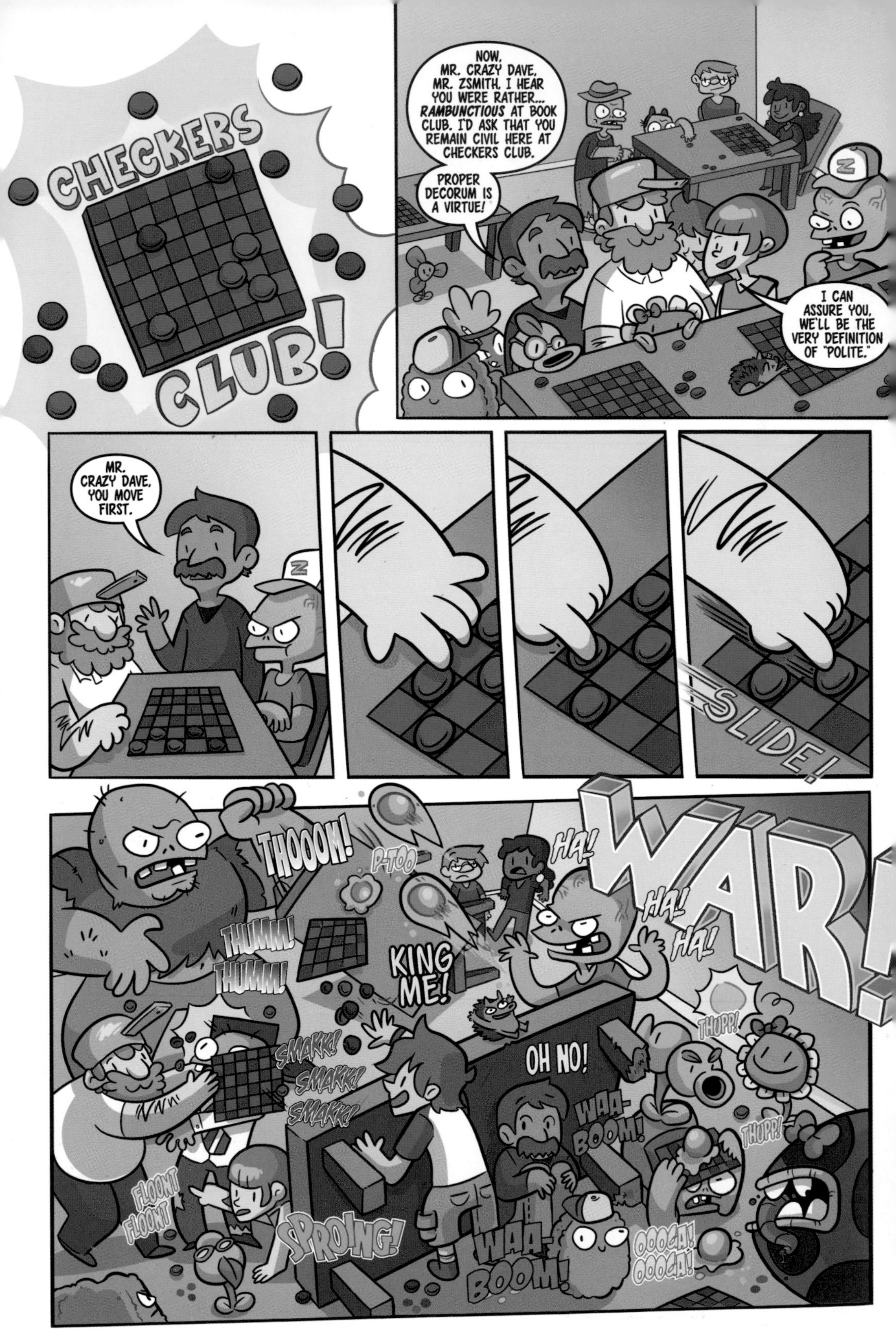
CHECKERS CLUB!
NOW, MR. CRAZY DAVE, MR. ZSMITH, I HEAR YOU WERE RATHER... RAMBUNCTIOUS AT BOOK CLUB. I'D ASK THAT YOU REMAIN CIVIL HERE AT CHECKERS CLUB.
PROPER DECORUM IS A VIRTUE!
I CAN ASSURE YOU, WE'LL BE THE VERY DEFINITION OF "POLITE."
MR. CRAZY DAVE, YOU MOVE FIRST.
SLIDE!
WAR!
THOOOM!
P-TOO
HA!
HA!
HA!
THUMM! THUMM!
KING ME!
SMAKK! SMAKK! SMAKK!
OH NO!
THUPP!
WAA-BOOM!
THUPP!
FLOONT FLOONT
SPROING!
WAA-BOOM!
OOOGA! OOOGA!

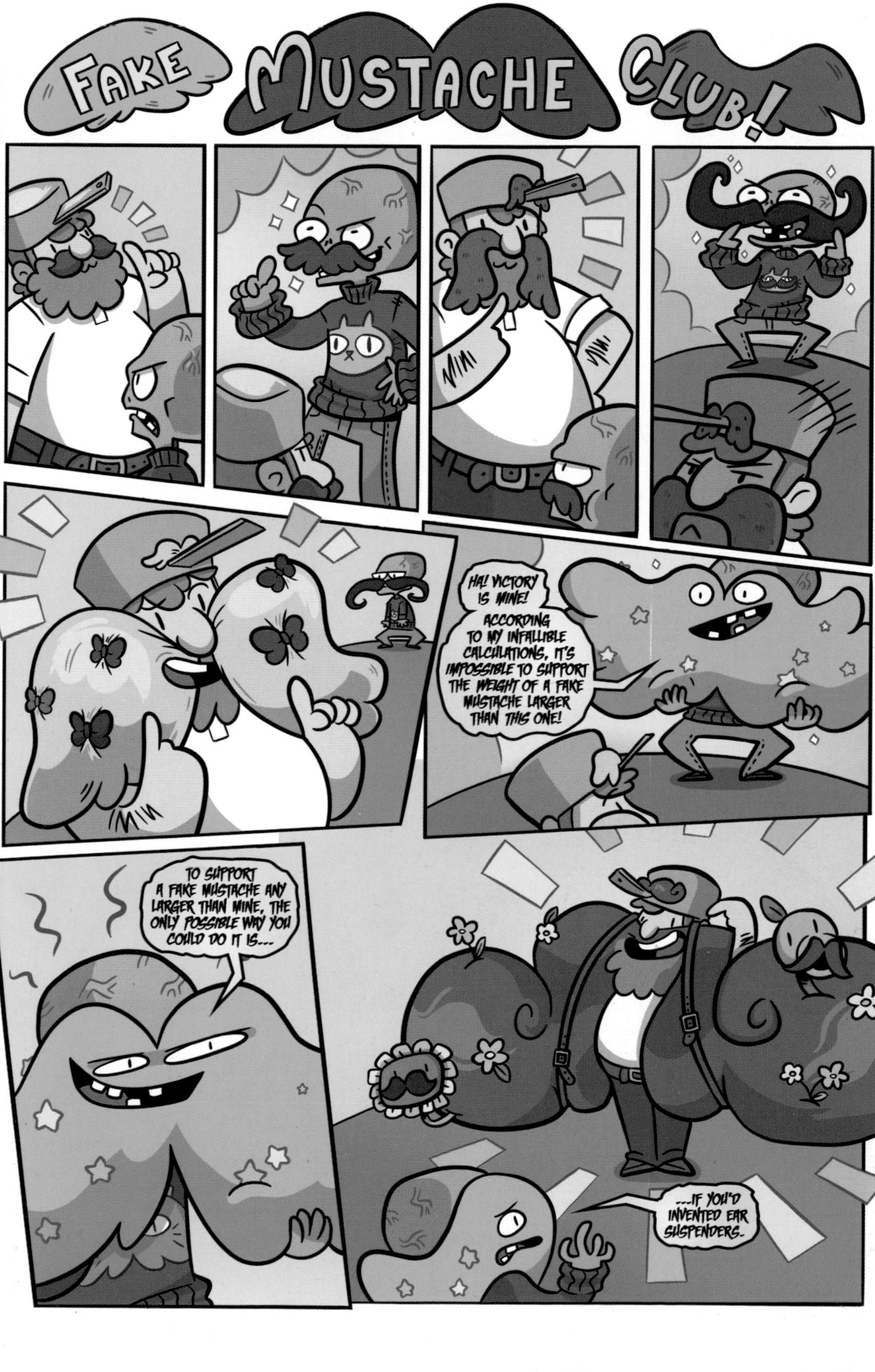
FAKE MUSTACHE CLUB!
HA! VICTORY IS MINE!
ACCORDING TO MY INFALLIBLE CALCULATIONS, IT'S IMPOSSIBLE TO SUPPORT THE WEIGHT OF A FAKE MUSTACHE LARGER THAN THIS ONE!
TO SUPPORT A FAKE MUSTACHE ANY LARGER THAN MINE, THE ONLY POSSIBLE WAY YOU COULD DO IT IS...
...IF YOU'D INVENTED EAR SUSPENDERS.

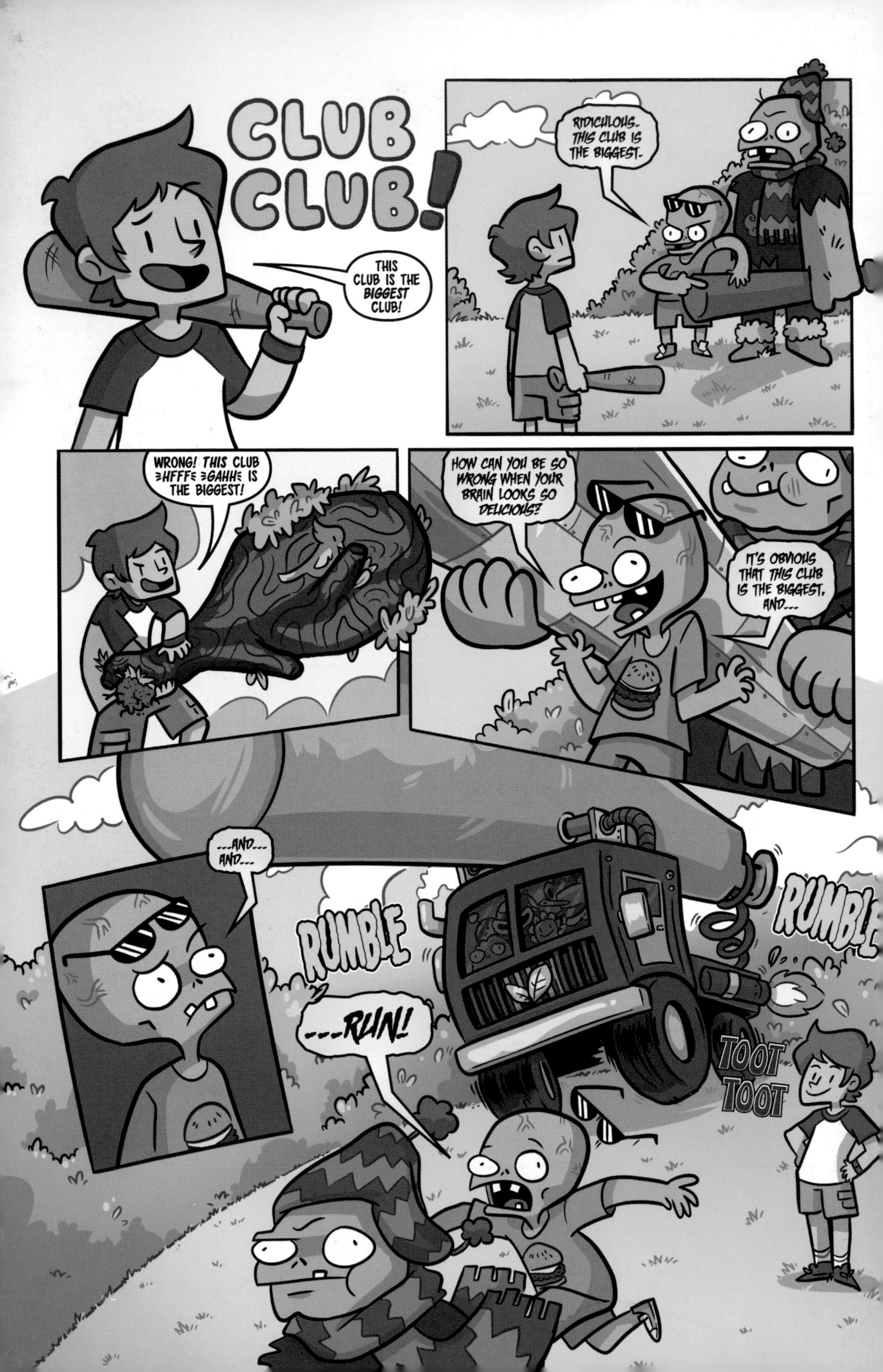

CLUB CLUB!
THIS CLUB IS THE BIGGEST CLUB!
RIDICULOUS. THIS CLUB IS THE BIGGEST.
WRONG! THIS CLUB HFFF GAHH IS THE BIGGEST!
HOW CAN YOU BE SO WRONG WHEN YOUR BRAIN LOOKS SO DELICIOUS?
IT'S OBVIOUS THAT THIS CLUB IS THE BIGGEST, AND...
...AND... AND...
RUMBLE
RUMBLE
...RUN!
TOOT TOOT

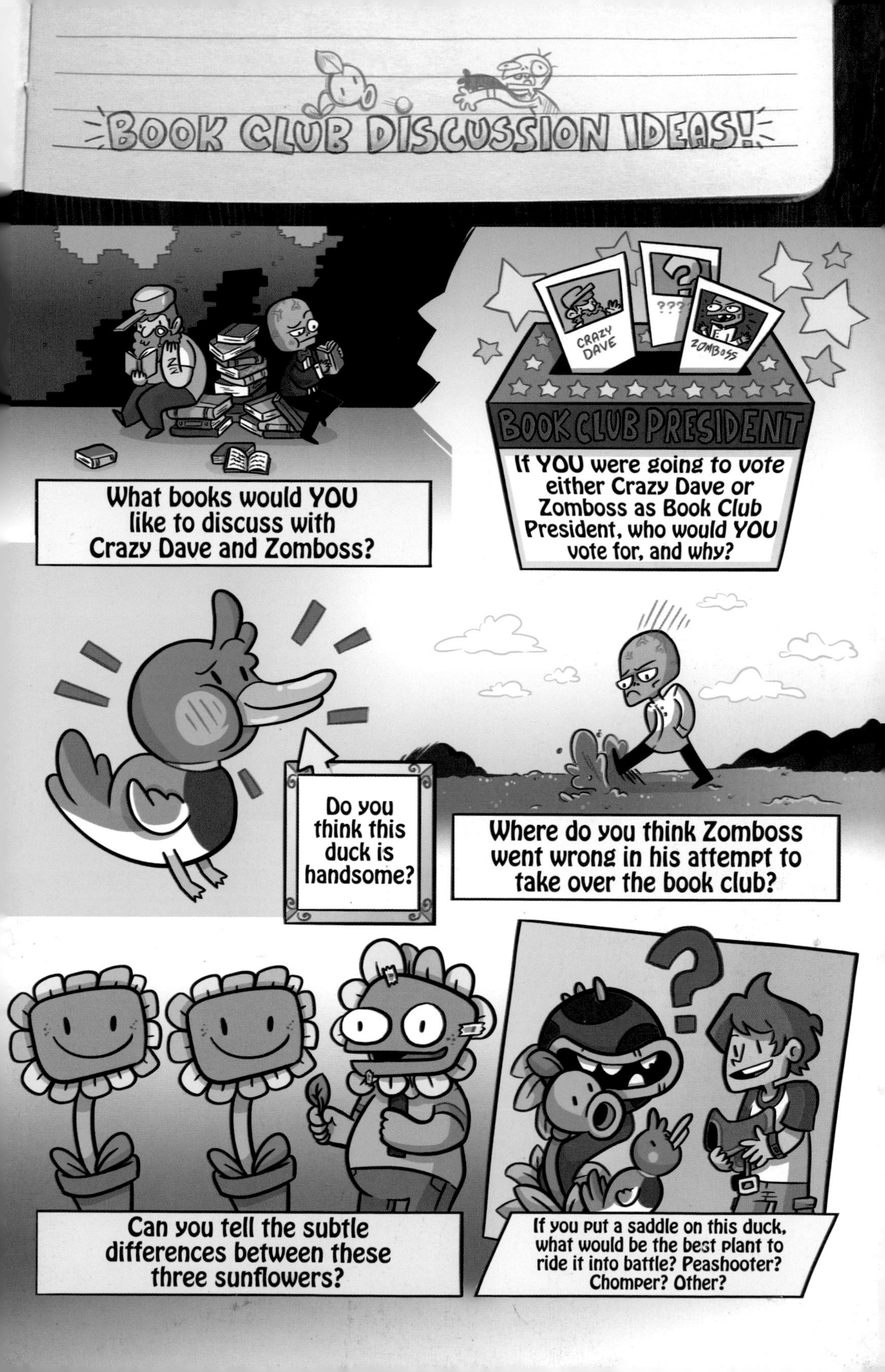
BOOK CLUB DISCUSSION IDEAS!
CRAZY DAVE
???
ZOMBOSS
BOOK CLUB PRESIDENT
What books would YOU like to discuss with Crazy Dave and Zomboss?
If YOU were going to vote either Crazy Dave or Zomboss as Book Club President, who would YOU vote for, and why?
Do you think this duck is handsome?
Where do you think Zomboss went wrong in his attempt to take over the book club?
Can you tell the subtle differences between these three sunflowers?
If you put a saddle on this duck, what would be the best plant to ride it into battle? Peashooter? Chomper? Other?

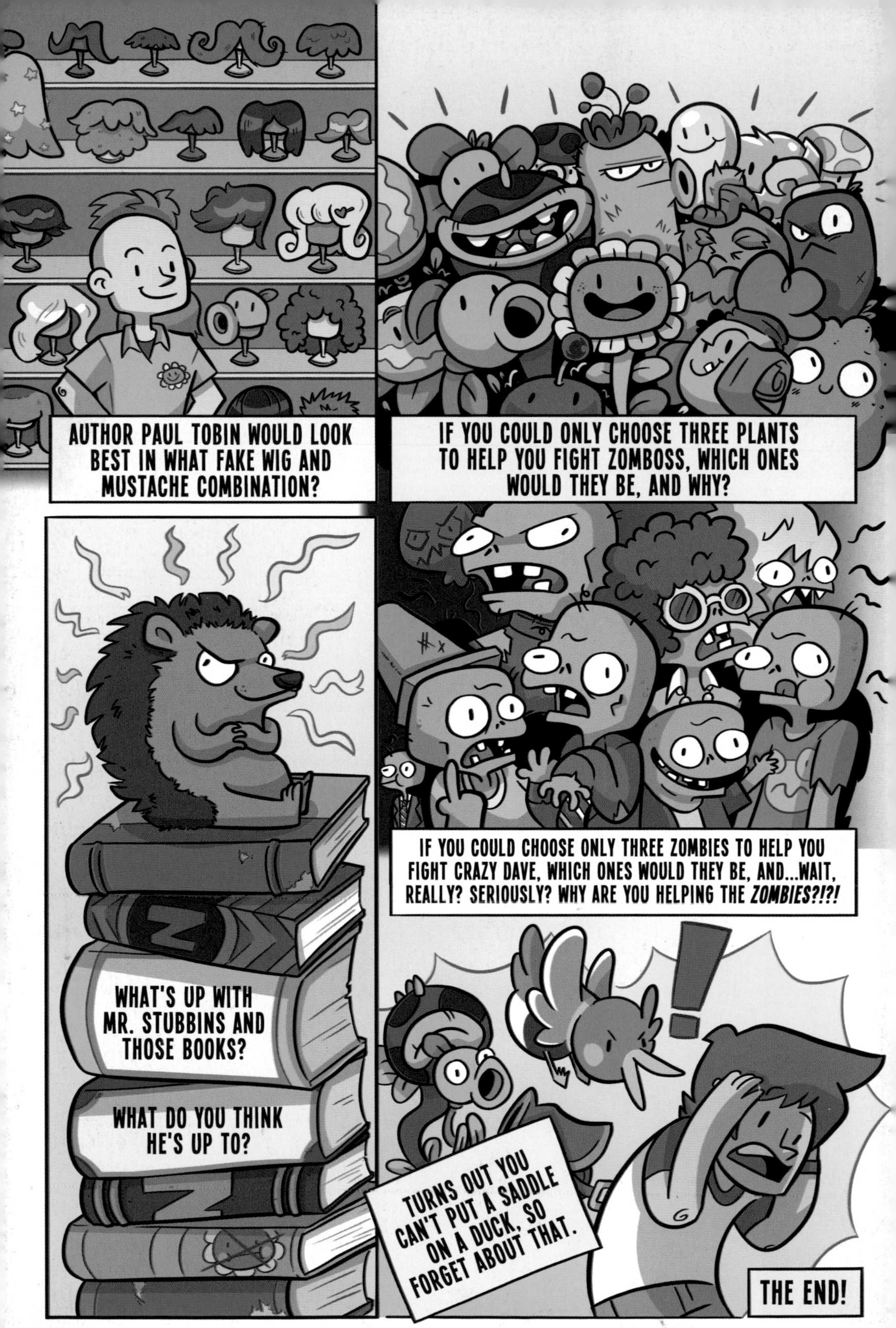
AUTHOR PAUL TOBIN WOULD LOOK BEST IN WHAT FAKE WIG AND MUSTACHE COMBINATION?
IF YOU COULD ONLY CHOOSE THREE PLANTS TO HELP YOU FIGHT ZOMBOSS, WHICH ONES WOULD THEY BE, AND WHY?
WHAT'S UP WITH MR. STUBBINS AND THOSE BOOKS?
WHAT DO YOU THINK HE'S UP TO?
IF YOU COULD CHOOSE ONLY THREE ZOMBIES TO HELP YOU FIGHT CRAZY DAVE, WHICH ONES WOULD THEY BE, AND...WAIT, REALLY? SERIOUSLY? WHY ARE YOU HELPING THE *ZOMBIES?!?!*
!
TURNS OUT YOU CAN'T PUT A SADDLE ON A DUCK, SO FORGET ABOUT THAT.
THE END!

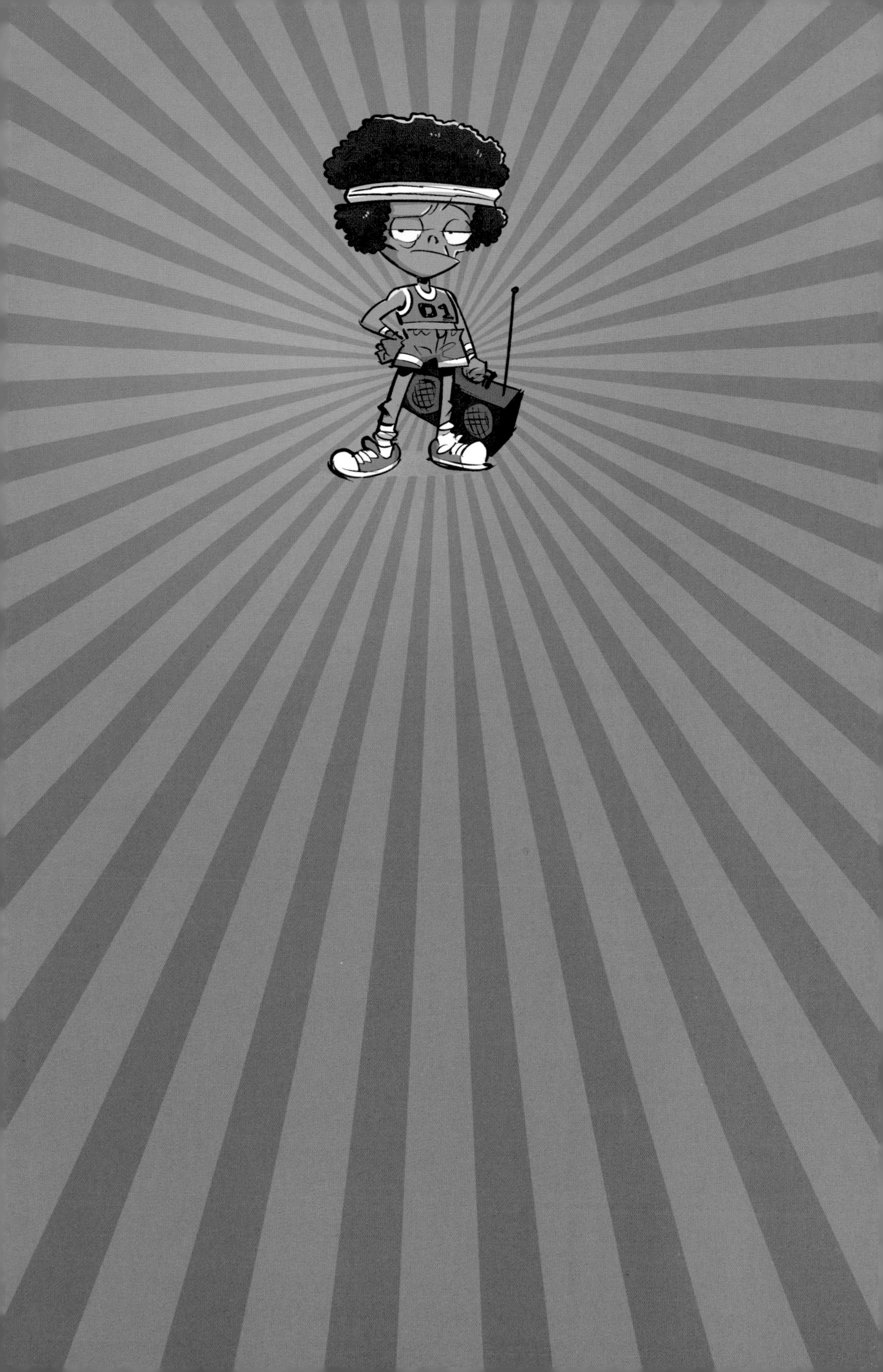

PLANTS VS. ZOMBIES: WAR AND PEAS

cover pencils by Ron Chan

PLANTS VS. ZOMBIES: WAR AND PEAS

cover inks by Ron Chan

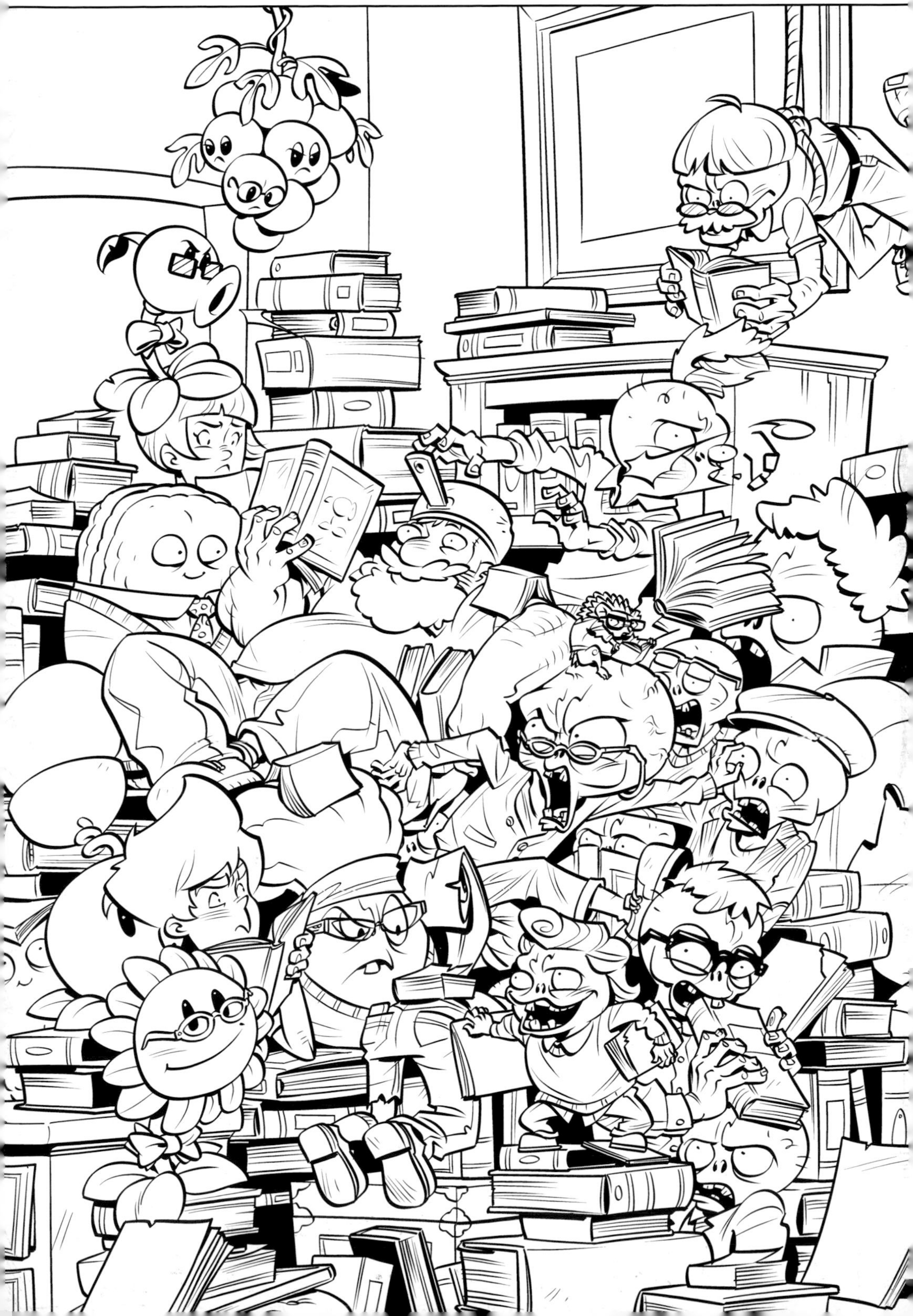

PENCIL ART FROM *WAR AND PEAS* PAGES 42–44 BY ARTIST BRIAN CHURILLA!

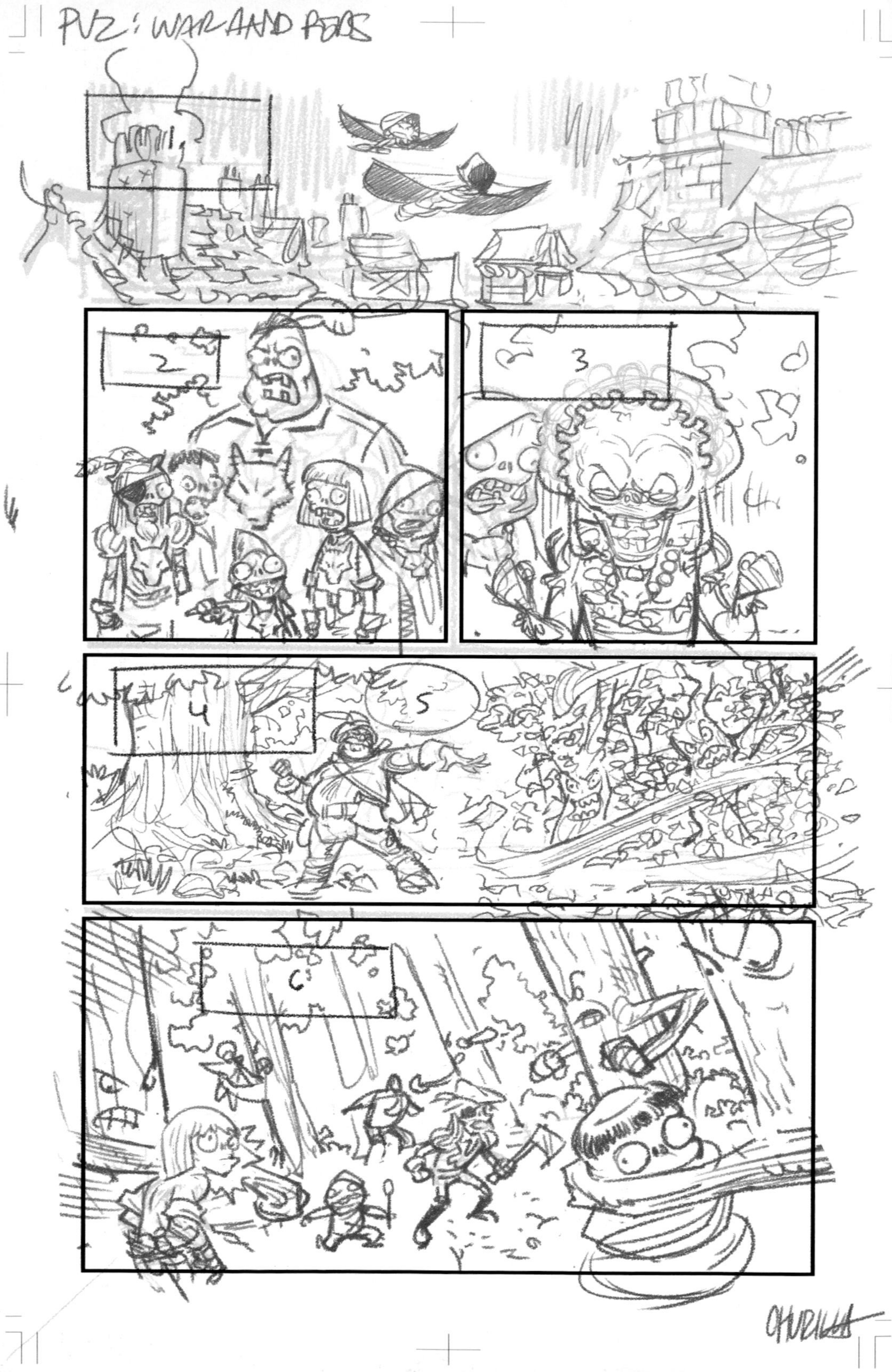

PVZ: WAR AND PEAS
2
3
4
5
6
CHURILLA

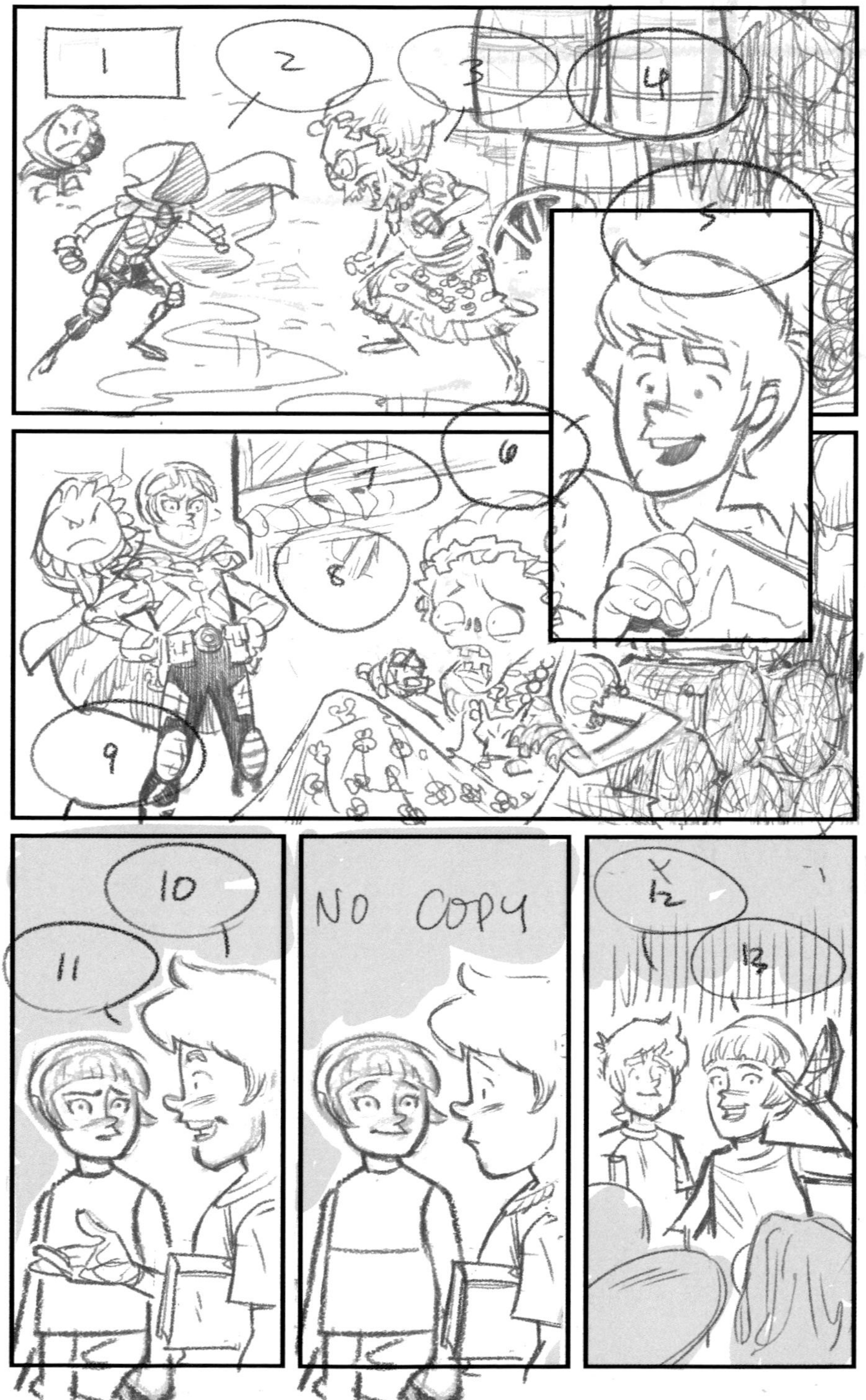
1
2
3
4
5
6
7
8
9
10
11
NO COPY
12
13

CHURILLA

PvZ! WAR+PEAS

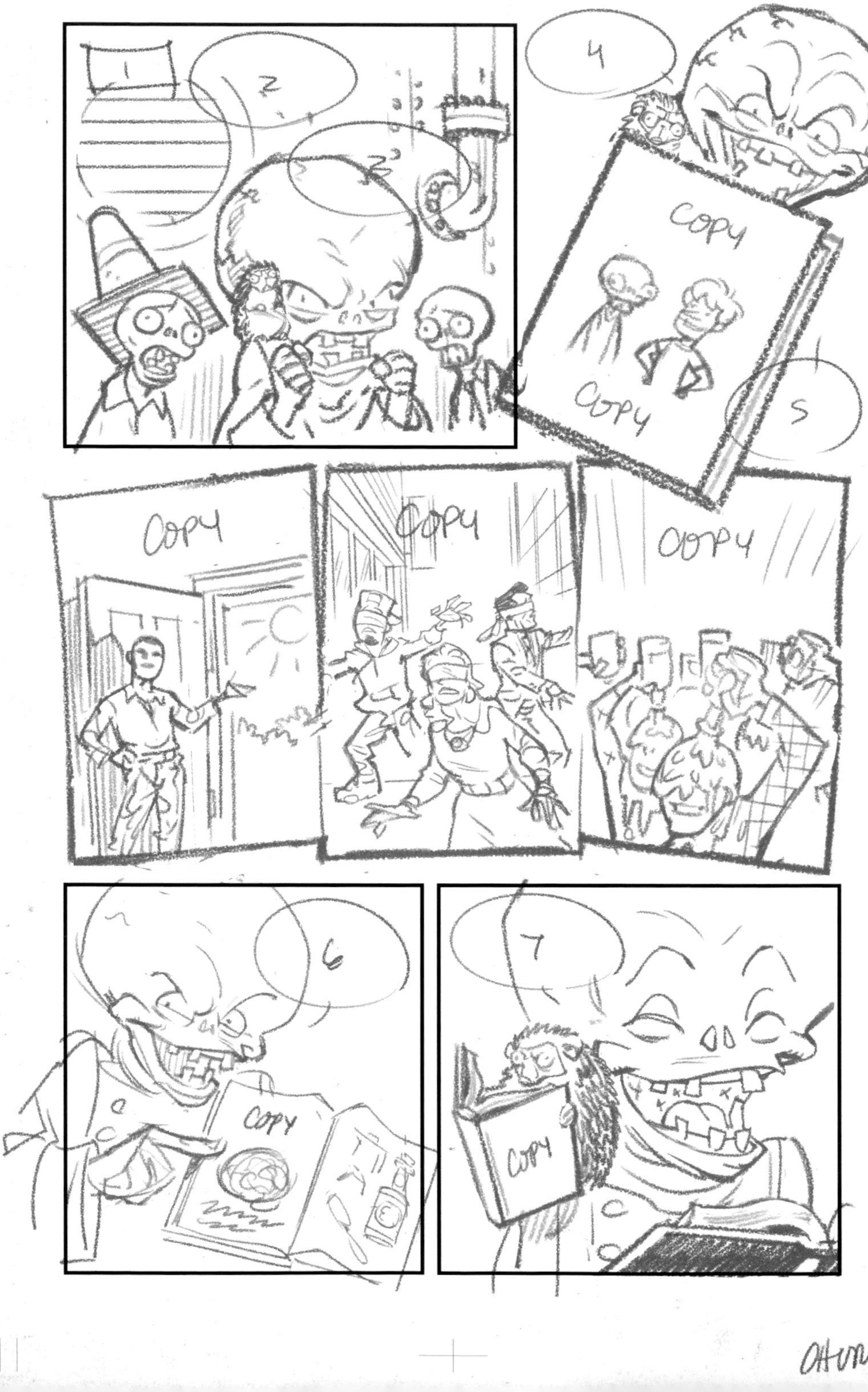

1
2
3
4
COPY
COPY
5
COPY
COPY
COPY
6
COPY
7
COPY

A SPECIAL NOTE ABOUT THIS GRAPHIC NOVEL!

Dark Horse Comics and PopCap Games ran a fun contest last year through one of our special mailing lists to librarians, and the following real-life librarians won cameo spots in this graphic novel! Special thanks to everyone who entered the contest—and congratulations to everyone who won a spot in this book. (Can you find them all??) These real-world librarians appear in *Plants vs. Zombies: War and Peas* . . . Maria Aghazarian (Swathmore, Pennsylvania), Katie Carter (Springfield, Missouri), Sandy Moltz (Swampscott, Massachusetts), Daniel Patton (Canton, Michigan), and Martha Tomeo (Healy, Alaska)!

CREATOR BIOS

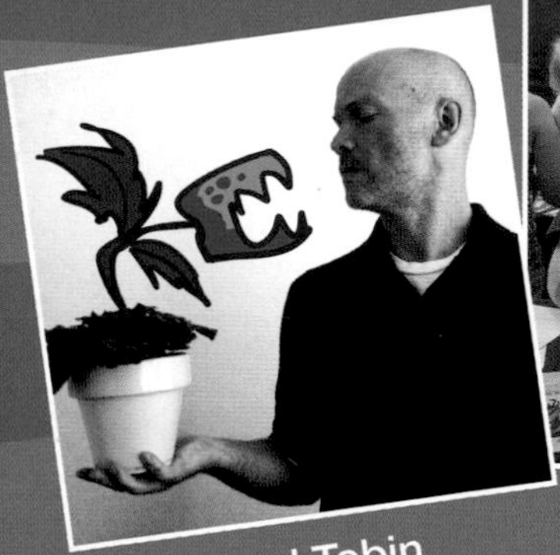

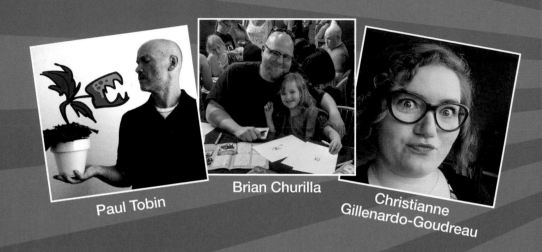

Paul Tobin

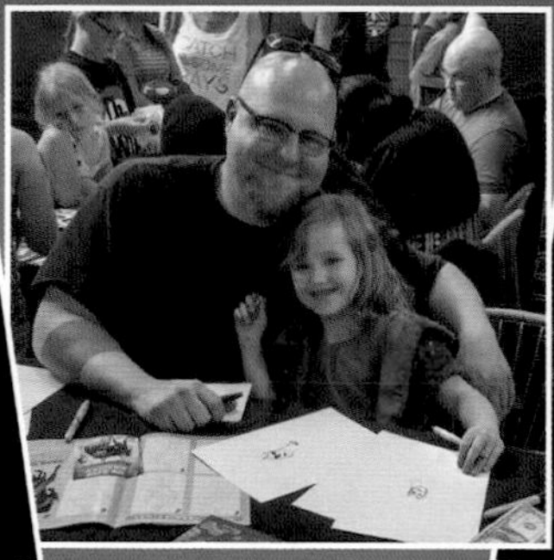

Brian Churilla

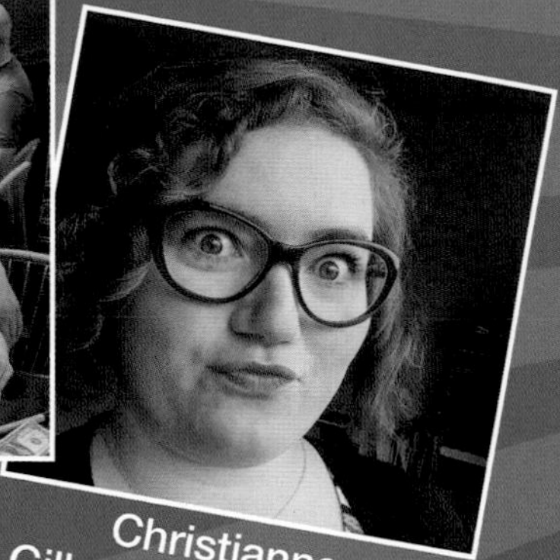

Christianne Gillenardo-Goudreau

PAUL TOBIN has written hundreds of stories for Marvel, DC, Dark Horse, and many others, including such creator-owned titles as *Colder and Bandette*, as well as *Prepare to Die!*—his debut novel. His *Genius Factor* series of novels about a fifth-grade genius and his war against the Red Death Tea Society debuted in March 2016 and continues with Paul's third book, *How to Tame a Human Tornado*. Paul has won some Very Important Awards for his writing but so far none for his karaoke skills.

BRIAN CHURILLA's *Plants vs. Zombies* bonus stories appeared in *PvZ* comic book #6, which was collected in *Plants vs. Zombies: Grown Sweet Home*. In addition to working for Dark Horse Comics, Brian (pictured with his daughter Maya) has been published by Boom! Studios, IDW Publishing, Oni Press, and Marvel Comics.

CHRISTIANNE GILLENARDO-GOUDREAU is a comic artist and illustrator who lives in Portland, Oregon with her wife Donna and their cat Hot Dog. She is the co-creator and artist of the webcomic *Full Circle*, and her work is featured in volume 1 of *Beyond: The Queer Sci-Fi & Fantasy Anthology*.

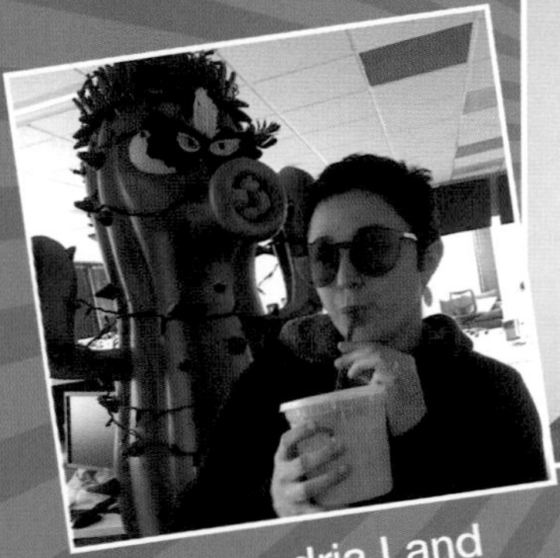

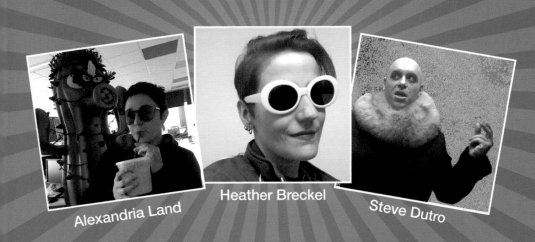

Alexandria Land

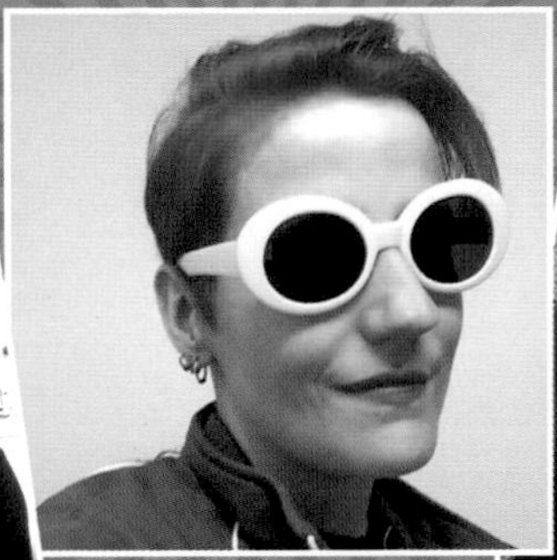

Heather Breckel

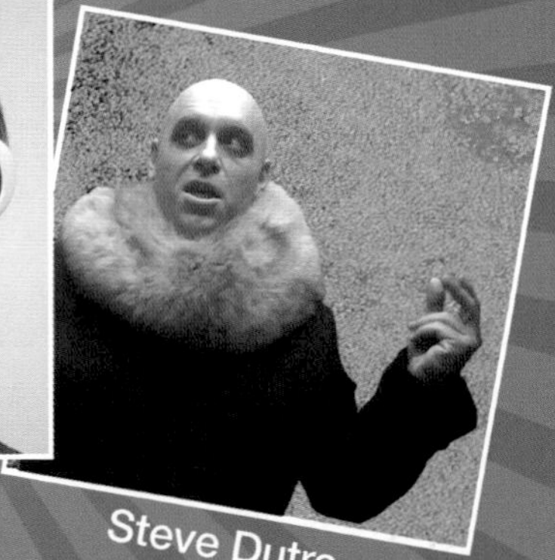

Steve Dutro

ALEXANDRIA LAND is an illustrator, comic and novel enthusiast, gamer, crafter, gardener, pet owner, and Dungeon Master based out of Seattle, Washington. Armed with a strong desire to constantly be doing something creative, she finds her time consumed by projects big and small that utilize her sweet skillz. She also currently works on the *Plants vs Zombies* games over at PopCap! Her favorite color is spring-leaves-green, she loves corgis (and has an adorably nutty corgi named Cosmo), and was awarded the "cutest zombie drawing" award by co-workers.

HEATHER BRECKEL went to the Columbus College of Art and Design for animation. She decided animation wasn't for her so she switched to comics. She's been working as a colorist for nearly ten years and has worked for nearly every major comics publisher out there. When she's not burning the midnight oil on a deadline crunch, she's either dying a bunch in videogames or telling her cats to stop running around at two in the morning.

STEVE DUTRO is an Eisner Award-nominated comic-book letterer from Redding, California, who can also drive a tractor. He graduated from the Kubert School and has been lettering comics since the days when foil-embossed covers were cool, working for Dark Horse (*The Fifth Beatle*, *I Am a Hero*, *Planet of the Apes*, *Star Wars*), Viz, Marvel, and DC. He has submitted a request to the Department of Homeland Security that in the event of a zombie apocalypse he be put in charge of all digital freeway signs so citizens can be alerted to avoid nearby brain-eatings and the like. He finds the *Plants vs. Zombies* game to be a real stress-fest, but highly recommends the *Plants vs. Zombies* table on *Pinball FX2* for game-room hipsters.

ALSO AVAILABLE FROM DARK HORSE!

THE HIT VIDEO GAME CONTINUES ITS COMIC BOOK INVASION!

PLANTS VS. ZOMBIES: LAWNMAGEDDON
Crazy Dave—the babbling-yet-brilliant inventor and top-notch neighborhood defender—helps young adventurer Nate fend off a zombie invasion that threatens to overrun the peaceful town of Neighborville in *Plants vs. Zombies: Lawnmageddon*! Their only hope is a brave army of chomping, squashing, and pea-shooting plants! A wacky adventure for zombie zappers young and old!
ISBN 978-1-61655-192-6 | $9.99

THE ART OF PLANTS VS. ZOMBIES
Part zombie memoir, part celebration of zombie triumphs, and part anti-plant screed, *The Art of Plants vs. Zombies* is a treasure trove of never-before-seen concept art, character sketches, and surprises from PopCap's popular *Plants vs. Zombies* games!
ISBN 978-1-61655-331-9 | $9.99

PLANTS VS. ZOMBIES: TIMEPOCALYPSE
Crazy Dave helps Patrice and Nate Timely fend off Zomboss' latest attack in *Plants vs. Zombies: Timepocalypse*! This new standalone tale will tickle your funny bones and thrill your brains through any timeline!
ISBN 978-1-61655-621-1 | $9.99

PLANTS VS. ZOMBIES: BULLY FOR YOU
Patrice and Nate are ready to investigate a strange college campus to keep the streets safe from zombies!
ISBN 978-1-61655-889-5 | $9.99

PLANTS VS. ZOMBIES: GARDEN WARFARE
Based on the hit video game, this comic tells the story leading up to the events in *Plants vs. Zombies: Garden Warfare 2*!
ISBN 978-1-61655-946-5 | $9.99

PLANTS VS. ZOMBIES: GROWN SWEET HOME
With newfound knowledge of humanity, Dr. Zomboss strikes at the heart of Neighborville . . . sparking a series of plant-versus-zombie brawls!
ISBN 978-1-61655-971-7 | $9.99

PLANTS VS. ZOMBIES: PETAL TO THE METAL
Crazy Dave takes on the tough *Don't Blink* video game—and challenges Dr. Zomboss to a race to determine the future of Neighborville!
ISBN 978-1-61655-999-1 | $9.99

PLANTS VS. ZOMBIES: BOOM BOOM MUSHROOM
The gang discover Zomboss' secret plan for swallowing the city of Neighborville whole! A rare mushroom must be found in order to save the humans aboveground!
ISBN 978-1-50670-037-3 | $9.99

PLANTS VS. ZOMBIES: BATTLE EXTRAVAGONZO
Zomboss is back, hoping to buy the same factory that Crazy Dave is eyeing! Will Crazy Dave and his intelligent plants beat Zomboss and his zombie army to the punch?
ISBN 978-1-50670-189-9 | $9.99

PLANTS VS. ZOMBIES: LAWN OF DOOM
With Zomboss filling everyone's yards with traps and special soldiers, will he and his zombie army turn Halloween into their zanier Lawn of Doom celebration?!
ISBN 978-1-50670-204-9 | $9.99

PLANTS VS. ZOMBIES: THE GREATEST SHOW UNEARTHED
Dr. Zomboss believes that all humans hold a secret desire to run away and join the circus, so he aims to use his "Big Z's Adequately Amazing Flytrap Circus" to lure Neighborville's citizens to their doom!
ISBN 978-1-50670-298-8 | $9.99

PLANTS VS. ZOMBIES: RUMBLE AT LAKE GUMBO
The battle for clean water begins! Nate, Patrice, and Crazy Dave spot trouble and grab all the Tangle Kelp and Party Crabs they can to quell another zombie attack!
ISBN 978-1-50670-497-5 | $9.99

PLANTS VS. ZOMBIES: WAR AND PEAS
When Dr. Zomboss and Crazy Dave find themselves members of the same book club, a literary war is inevitable! The position of leader of the book club opens up and Zomboss and Crazy Dave compete for the top spot in a scholarly scuffle for the ages!
ISBN 978-1-50670-677-1 | $9.99

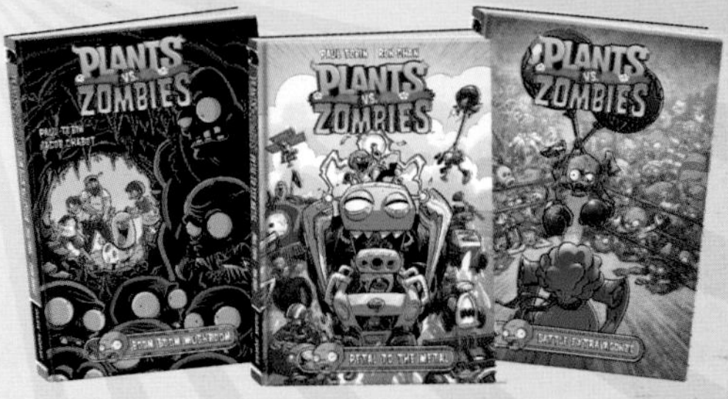

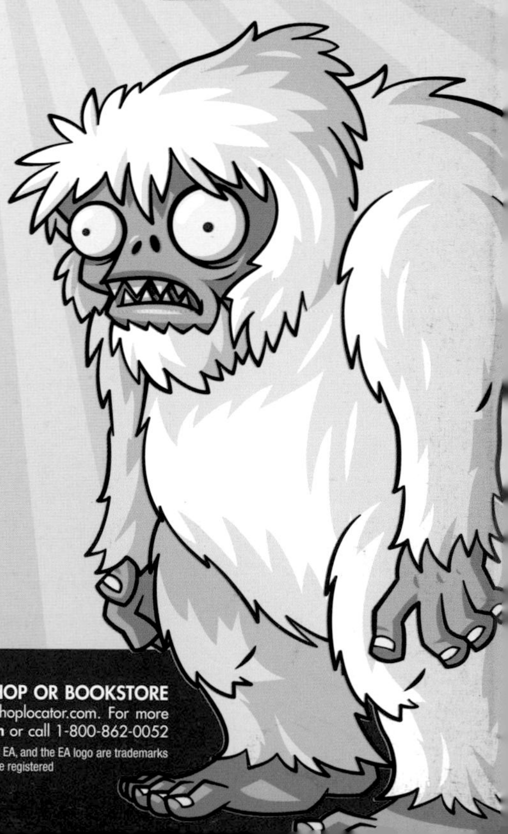

DARK HORSE BOOKS

PopCap

AVAILABLE AT YOUR LOCAL COMICS SHOP OR BOOKSTORE
To find a comics shop in your area, visit comicshoplocator.com. For more information or to order direct visit **DarkHorse.com** or call 1-800-862-0052

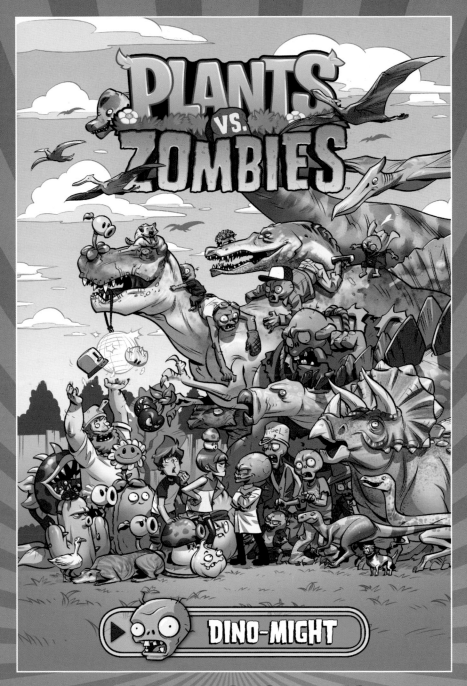

DINO-MIGHT

PLANTS VS. ZOMBIES: DINO-MIGHT—CHOMPING IN FEBRUARY 2019!

Dr. Zomboss is back with another set of nefarious plans to defeat the pesky plants and Neighborville's resident adventurers Nate and Patrice! When Zomboss sets his sights on destroying the yards in town and rendering the plants homeless without anywhere to grow, it's up to the daring duo, along with Crazy Dave and his band of plants, to thwart his plans and claim victory once again! However, it turns out that those plans include dogs, cats, rabbits, hammock sloths, and even more pets—plus dinosaurs—making things a lot zanier!

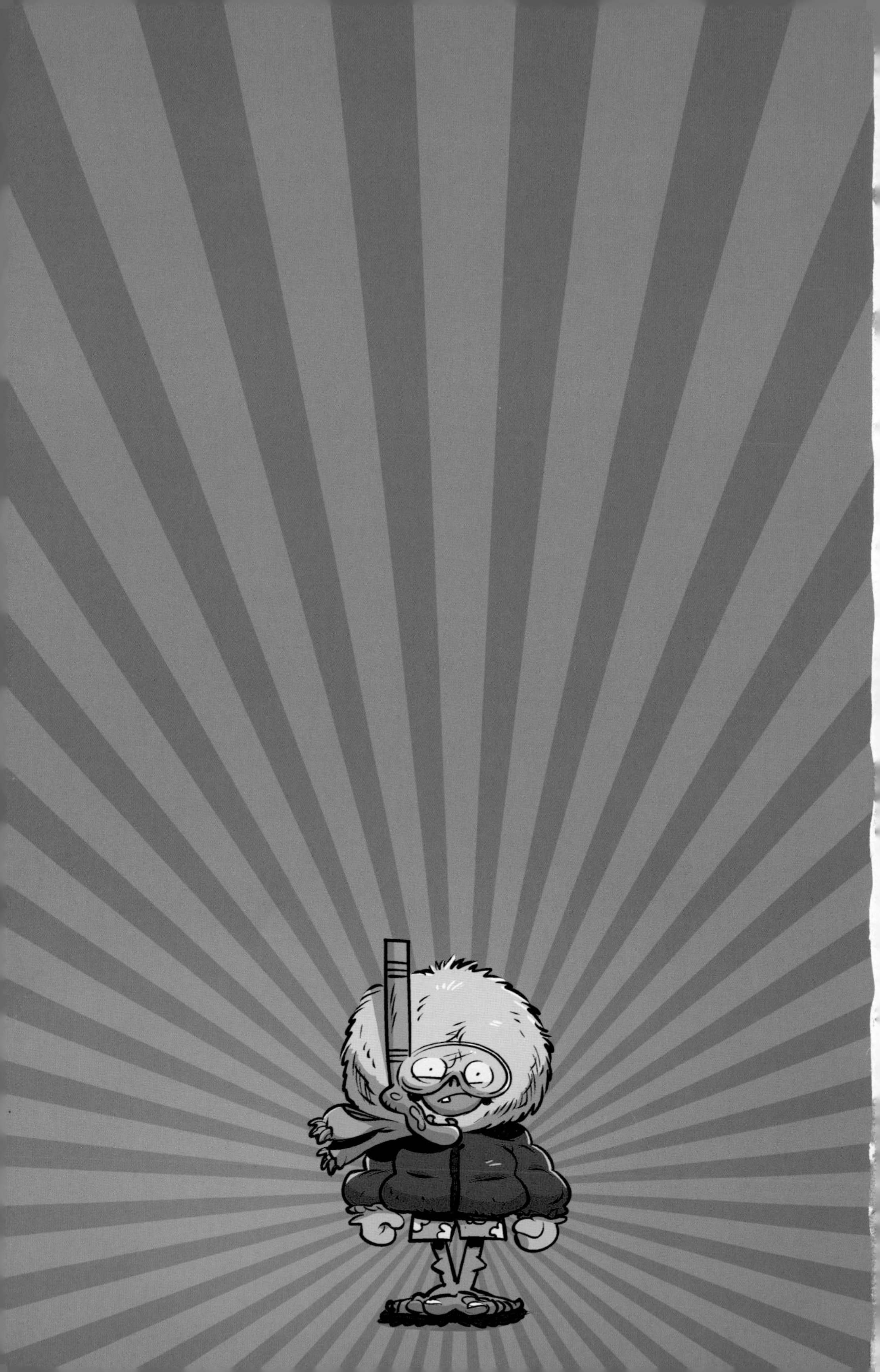